Dirty Laundry

Printed in Australia

First Printing: April 2022

Shawline Publishing Group Pty Ltd
www.shawlinepublishing.com.au

Paperback ISBN- 9781922701503

Ebook ISBN- 9781922701527

A catalogue record for this
book is available from the
National Library of Australia

Dirty Laundry

LA CHICHITA

I dedicate this book to my mother who is looking at me from heaven and my family, especially my sister and daughter, who have helped me with the editing of the book and who were my first fans.

Acknowledgements

I acknowledge the patience and care of my husband during the long hours that took me to finish this book.

Chapter 1

WHERE IT ALL BEGAN

'The greatest wealth is to live content with little.'
(Plato)

Part 1 - La Macaca

This is the first part of my life story, Emanuel, my loving brainy great grandchild!

I know it will be difficult for you to understand some parts of the text, because you are still a child. Are you eight now and still bored to death? I believe you will need more years of life to appreciate what I and others went through. But hopefully, the occasion will come when you are able to gather all the stories. Then, you will be able to make sense of it all.

I have split the first text in two sections to make it easier to read and consider. I could not possibly have been able to write in English. Therefore, I wrote it in Spanish and for the record I had asked my eldest daughter Carmela to translate it into English for you; here it is!

———————

I was the last of 12 brothers and sisters and my large family loved me so much. Or so I thought... I had grown to be quite tall and skinny, and I was certainly quite fair, and my skin was pale white, but I was never hairy. So, I could never understand why everybody called me

1

with affection *La Macaca*, the Spanish word for the 'the monkey'. Perhaps the nickname originated from my early age obsession with green bananas, which I used to steal from our large pantry. Or as a sarcastic yet affectionate way of describing my skin colour, which was extremely pale.

When I was playing with dolls my sister Carmela made for me with discarded rugs, my older brothers and sisters already had a juicy story to tell. My brothers were busily working with my father in the Fruit and Vegetable/ Delicatessen business he owned in the near 'open markets'. My brothers all had very busy social lives, going out almost every night. Some of them were already married or chased by dubious women for their affection and pesos.

My elder sisters had all been married off to much older, respectable men, introduced to them by my father's spinster sisters. Yes, we were living in the early 20th Century Argentina, in a respectable and prosperous Italian family. Then, "decent females" were born to be under the eye of the father and under the thumb of older brothers until they married, then be to the absolute service of their husbands.

To confirm, when barely old enough, these "decent females" would become the property of acceptable suitors by legal marriage. These suitors were commonly three or four times the age of their brides having come from the same respectable Italian village as the bride's parents.

My sister Carmela, by the way the name of my first daughter, lived with us and at 18, already had a history of repeated abortions with her elderly husband, but she was cunning enough to hide her last pregnancy until it was too late to terminate.

The impossibility of terminating that pregnancy would cost her dearly; her health and her relationship with her husband, who took to the habit of visiting other 'more obedient women', as he used to say. But it gave my sister Carmela the joy of a child, who we affectionately always called *La Nena*, which means 'the young girl' in Spanish.

'Francisco… Now you come at last! These are not hours to come! Disgraziato… Where were you when La Nena was so sick? I needed some money for food and medicines!' my sister Carmela complained frantically, only to bury herself in her own tears.

'It is none of your business where I was! Where is my dinner now? This is cold! Ah, and I need my grey suit and white shirt with the gold cufflinks for tonight's party.'

'It is ready, darling!' Carmela would say.

'No, this will not do, bloody hell! I want it ironed again. I do not want any creases from it being hanged in the wardrobe, you dirty bitch!' grumbled Francisco, her elderly husband.

This was a far too common scene for me in my household and I did not know anything different; so, I was not going to pay much attention to it anymore.

Therefore, I remained happy. My father loved me so much that he allowed me to go to bed without eating the forever-dreaded lentils my mother prepared for dinner every second night. In secret, my father would give me my favourite pecorino cheese and hot salami slices with a piece of bread, a piece of my favourite chocolate and a green banana I would devour in my bedroom before falling sleep.

My father would roar like a tiger to everybody, even to my poor mother to get what he wanted, except to me. I was 'the apple of his eye', his 'princess', the dear 'object of his affection', as he continually claimed.

So, when I asked him to go to school, he bought me a school apron and black shoes and sent me to the local school with some white paper from his shop and a pencil case with a pencil, crayons, and a ruler inside. For my Saint-Day[1], he also bought me an abacus to use in Maths.

I was the only female who had ever gone to school, and I was so proud of it. School was my secret love, not because of my friends, but because I loved learning. I was the first to arrive, as I left home at the crack of the day when my father and elder brothers left for work. This was even before the church bells rang to wake up the kids in the neighbourhood! I was so proud to be already sitting at the school front door, attempting to read anything I could get my hands on.

I absolutely loved my teacher, and nothing was difficult for me to understand. Although I had started school late, soon I was able to read and write correctly. I was the best student in the class for maths and science and I was also good at writing stories.

Then one dark and fatal day, I overheard a conversation between my mother and my brothers with my father.

'La Macaca is not pulling her weight. I am too tired with so many men to attend to. Now that Martirio got married and left us, it is only just me to do everything in the house. My life starts at four in the morning and does not stop till late at night, only when you are all finally sleeping. I need help in the kitchen, in the laundry and with household chores', my mother said without any interruption in broken Spanish.

'Yes, it is true,' some brother responded, 'mum is too tired to serve all nine of us. Remember four brothers are still at school. It is essential for them to have an education to join in the business later... but La Macaca...'

'Let's be fair...', another brother finished his sentence, 'La Macaca does not need to go to school, right?'

'She is just a girl; girls are born to get married and serve their husbands and children. They do not have to worry about bringing the dough home, right?'

'But she loves school, and she has been praised by her teachers,' said my father.

'No and no, there is nothing that will convince me', said my mother, 'she is a female; her place should be here with me to learn to be a woman and a good housewife.'

'That's right,' said another brother, 'mum has been too pale lately, God forbids, we do not want her to get sick. This situation cannot go on any longer! La Macaca needs to be with mum all day as from tomorrow.'

My whole world started to collapse. My body was shaking, when my father agreed saying to my mother, 'Yes, my love, Macaquita will help you starting tomorrow. She is a fast learner. Soon, she will take over your responsibilities, I am sure...'

I felt destroyed; I was only nine years old and had only attended a few years of primary education when I would have to abandon my beloved school forever.

My mother went on to have yet another four children who were all stillborn. She became thinner and thinner and paler and paler with an increasingly huge belly, even when she was not pregnant. She could no longer walk unassisted, nor could she move from her commode, where she was able to instruct me along with a hired maid on the art of housekeeping.

As my father predicted, I was indeed a fast learner. My house was large to accommodate us all with ten bedrooms, four bathrooms, the kitchen, the laundry with a boiler, tub and washing board, two big lounges with lots of sofas and poufs and a huge dining room with an oversized solid timber table and brown velvet upholstered chairs. There was also a huge basement where all the business merchandise was stored: cured hams and salami hanged from the ceiling, all sorts of cheeses, legumes and nuts, fresh vegetables, and fruit.

I learnt how to knead dough to make bread ready for breakfast as well as cook the most delicious Italian homemade meals, like all sort of Italian pasta dishes, stuffed meats and vegetables, risottos, legume stews, pickles and even delicious cannoli, panettones, gelatos, and cassatas.

I also knew how to wash the dishes efficiently, wash and iron the never-ending pile of clothes, scrub floors, clean toilets, make beds and dust furniture. I tendered to the large fruit trees, vegetable and flower gardens and kept the basement spotlessly clean under the instructions of my mother first, and then left entirely to my organisation and creativity.

I cannot comprehend now how the hours of the day were enough for me to do everything I needed to do so nobody complained. I even had time in those days at night to play with my dolls.

Despite it all, we all adored my mother as if she was a saint, even though everybody could see that at 52, she was becoming aloof and enjoying her extending siestas more than worrying about domestic responsibilities.

My father, who was of the same age as my mum, on the other hand, looked robust despite his frequent and severe attacks of blood pressure and gout. I remember once to my horror the doctor had to be called to 'drain his blood' with leeches to 'stabilise his blood pressure'. Despite these sporadic troubles with his health, my father absolutely continued to lead with an iron hand.

Sadly, I recalled that one day, we had the first scandal in our family. My eldest brother, Pino had a big fight with my father about some sort of business transactions. I remember Pino completely out of character, was swearing loudly, then he gathered some clothes in a bag and left the house. My brothers tried to reach him, but he was nowhere to be found or seen in Buenos Aires.

Many years later, Pino was found far away on a slum in some province operating a rundown grocery business and living with an older woman and a few children.

Nobody could ascertain whether he would have married this woman or not, but it was well known that she was always drunk early in the morning, and their children, although it was never confirmed whether they were my brother's, were walking in the streets begging, riddled with sores and lice.

Pino still refused to have anything to do with our family.

Regrettably, years later, we found out Pino had suffered a massive heart attack that tragically killed him instantly. I have no idea what had happened to those close to him or his business in his provincial village.

When Pino left, my father had just turned 53. He was first disheartened and felt deeply dishonoured about my brother's behaviour. It was understandable; he was the first born, and, as in all Italian wealthy families, Pino would have been entitled to inherit his fortune as well as the care and control of the rest of the family after (and sometimes even before) the patriarch died.

My father was never the same after Pino left. He became extremely withdrawn, prone to rages of bad temper and violence towards all of us. Even towards my ever so frail mother.

But nothing would prepare us for our next scandal. My sister

Santa at 15 had married my uncle Rocco fifty years her senior. At 16 she had just had her first baby named Angelina only four months ago. Tired of her responsibilities, she had eloped with her lover, a young, handsome man leaving her baby behind.

Rocco was shocked and angry. He left the baby with us to take care of. The fact was, although I enjoyed looking after the baby, this increased my already overloaded list of responsibilities. I was just 14 when Angelina replaced my beloved dolls. I loved feeding her and putting her to sleep, but she also left piles and piles of dirty clothes and nappies that had to be washed and whitened separately. Besides, everybody took me for granted. Nobody thanked me for anything.

My father became like a monster, shouting and swearing when things were found out of order, or dinner was a bit late.

My brothers were given the task of looking for Santa and I did not want to even imagine what could have happened to her if they ever found her. Luckily, she was never found, at least not whilst my parents were still alive.

Then we started to notice another brother, Santino, was using my sisters' make up and other items from their wardrobe when he went out at night. Rumours were rampant in the neighbourhood that he was queer.

I do not want to remember the night my father confronted him, and he confessed he was gay. Poor Dad, he was red as a tomato and his eyes were about to pop out of his sockets. I wished then my father's cries would be heard in heaven and an acceptable solution could be found.

I hoped I had just been dreaming of this horrible scene. And for a minute I thought 'God has heard my prayers', because suddenly all was calm, as my father's heavy body fell to the floor. He had suffered a massive stroke and died instantly. The family doctor told us nothing could have saved him this time, not even the leeches.

I lived the next four months in the clouds, not knowing exactly who I was. I was grieving the death of my father, still overloaded with household responsibilities. I was also experiencing excruciating pain in my mouth from 'gumboils', as my sister Carmela called the pain.

Many years later, I learnt from a dentist the most common cause of 'gumboils' was teeth abscesses. Teeth abscess usually form because of advanced tooth cavities so bacteria ferments gum tissue and continues to invade the inner ligaments and jawbones, over the diseased root. Gumboils occur simply, from lack of dental care and basic hygiene. Eventually, the rotten teeth causing the gumboils, should be extracted by a dentist to completely relieve the pain. Sadly, nobody in my family even knew what a dentist was because nobody in my family had ever visited one.

My sister Carmela would visit us and offered me sips of hot water and salt to rinse my mouth. This would alleviate my pain for a little while. As you could appreciate, I hardly had any time to see my mum who remained like a ghost, remarkably unobtrusive and obedient to her destiny. Her corner armchair doubled as commode.

On top of that, after binging on grapes, I was rushed to hospital with a peritonitis attack. The surgeon, who operated on me offered me my appendix full of grape seeds to keep in a container with alcohol and gave me the news; my mother had died, a couple of doors away in the same hospital.

Nobody explained to me why my mother had died. Rumours had it that it was a malignant tumour in her uterus, yet others said she had yet another stillborn child. I always thought she had died from loneliness after my father's sudden death four months before.

I was only 14 years old and unexpectedly an orphan. I could never have anticipated what my destiny would be. As for little sweet Angelina, she had been swiftly delivered to her old father's relatives when I was in hospital. I would never be able to hold her again.

---

[1] The custom originated with the Christian Calendar of Saints: believers named after that saint would celebrate that saint's feast day.

Part 2 - 'La Macaca'

When I finally realized my parents were not coming back to the life of the living, I discovered my older brothers had sold our family home, its contents and anything that looked like value and shared their proceeds among themselves. Whatever was left, pots and pans, mops and brooms, broken memorabilia, old tea towels, and the chickens, were contended fiercely and finally taken by my sisters and other relatives whom I did not even know, as if they had always been their possessions. My sister Carmela secretly rescued and gave me my mother's wedding ring and my old rag dolls.

My youngest brother Pepe and I, being minors, had nothing to say in the deal and weren't given any trust money from the inheritance. We were lucky enough to be sent to live with two older siblings and their families to be their servants.

My luck took me to my older sister Constanza married to elderly Romeo. At the time, they had six children, all boys, alive, as some other infants had mercifully died of different diseases.

For me, their six children were plenty as I had to look after them day and night although some were just a bit older than me.

Constanza was pregnant again but still glued to her sewing machine from the sound of the cock in the morning, until she collapsed into her marital bed late at night.

I did not know exactly what Romeo did during the day. All I knew was he loved the children, including me. When he was around, he would play with us *Guardie e ladri,* which was the Italian for 'cops and robbers' and gave us candy if we won.

Despite his age, Romeo looked elegant and smelled sweet whenever he went out at night. Years later, when he was violently killed, I learnt he used to meet his *compadre* and other *compagnos* and was involved in dubious businesses and heavy gambling.

I admired this family though. We had plenty to eat and we were always singing, playing, and laughing. I was as naughty as the boys and just as rough. As I seemed to be the one in charge, I thought I had to mature a bit and impose my authority.

However, I was always getting into trouble. The worst occasion was when one of the children was thrown for fun by us and landed straight into the brazier amongst our cracked laughs. Luckily, he survived the bad burns, but his backside had to be exposed to the air and the sun for weeks and he could not go to school. Romeo thought the sight of him out in the open was enough punishment for him. As for me, he just smiled and asked me to be more vigilant next time.

Playing with the children and having fun did not relieve me of my duties. Besides taking care of the children, my job was to wash, iron, cook three meals a day and keep the house clean and tidy, which I did when the children were at school.

The happy arrival of baby Dino did not make things easier for me, as then I had to take care of yet another soul. I did not have much experience with baby boys, but somehow, I managed to keep him growing healthy, clean, and content.

By then, I had also made good friends with a girl a bit older than me who lived next door. Rosa lived with her parents and two brothers. She and her brothers were all born in Argentina, although her parents were originally from Spain.

Rosa had also been to school for a few years and loved reading and listening to the radio. She lent me *Señoritas*—a young lady's trendy magazine—to read. I was surprised I had not forgotten how to read and how much I still enjoyed it. I also discovered I liked listening to the radio, to different music like tangos, rumba, and jazz; and on Sundays when I finished all my duties, I enjoyed listening to comedy, drama, opera, and musical shows on the radio.

My sister Carmela continued to be my second mum. She used to come frequently to keep an eye on me, and bring me clothes, including underwear, which she used to sew for me. She also brought other personal female necessities like towel pads she made herself and leaves of 'ruda' and 'cedron' to make infusions for stomach and period pain and for my Saint Day she gave me a radio, just for myself!

Then, one day we had the visit of two of my aunties; they had found me a suitor.

'His name is Pasquale, and he has a lot of money.'

'How old is he?' I asked shyly.

'I believe he is almost 60, but he does not look it, my dear. He will be able to provide for you well.' With that, I was dismissed swiftly.

Not long after, Pasquale visited the family. This was to be the first of many subsequent visits. He would always bring lots of my favourite candy and presents for me: a gold necklace, gold earrings, gold bracelets and finally an engagement ring with a real diamond, which he put on my finger. At the time, I almost believed life could only improve for me from then on!

Not long after, I went to answer the front door, and there was this elegant lady with three young children. She said she wanted to talk to me. 'Why?' I asked.

'These children are Pasquale's, dear,' she said. She had been seeing him for 15 years.

'You cannot marry him. I love him', she continued. Then, she could say no more. I slammed the door and run to my bedroom to cry, holding my rag dolls and maybe for the first time, truly attempting to call on to God for help.

My dream world had collapsed without any warning again. In his last visit, Pasquale insisted he wanted to see me and explain, but all I could do was to throw all his presents, including the engagement ring at his face.

Years later, I felt grateful I did not have to go through an arranged marriage at such a tender age! Truly, after my first shock, I was happy to be relieved of being sacrificed to this old man.

I heard a lot about Pasquale in years to come, including his wedding to another young Italian girl, but I thanked God profusely that I never saw him again after his last visit.

My sister Carmela, as always, came to cheer me up and then offered to take me to serve another of our sisters, Yolanda. My life might just turn to be easier.

Yolanda was also married to an older man, Inocente, but they only had two children who were much older than me and they would not need as much attention as baby Dino.

The family did not live far, and I would be able to move in straight away, taking my few things in the old suitcase by foot. I decided immediately to move in with them, as I really needed a change and perhaps, I could have a bit more time to myself. I was going to miss Rosa and her friendship though...

I also felt so guilty. I could still see the children in my mind many days after, all very sad and fretting as I was leaving and Constanza chaotically trying to calm them down with hot chocolate milk and churros.

It was not easy to settle down in my new house. The house was small with only one big bedroom for the whole family, a kitchen/dining room, a toilet with laundry attached in the back yard and an ever so tiny room with some chairs which they called living-room. Outside there was a small run-down veggie garden with a sick lemon tree.

Inocente brought a single old mattress, which he placed on the floor for me in a tiny corner in the only bedroom, next to the door entrance. I kept my clothes in my old suitcase because I did not have a wardrobe for myself. Inocente found an old and broken stool, which he fixed with a few screws so I could sit at the table with them to have my meals.

Yolanda, like Constanza, also worked sewing for a clothes factory and I believed Inocente was retired because he looked too frail to work.

Their son Rocco and daughter Monalisa had finished school already and had found jobs, thanks to a connection they had in the police department.

My days disappeared one after the other because I still had a lot to do. I needed to think strategically to keep the family happy. I had to do the shopping but the few coins I was given to pay for it were many times not enough to buy food for all five of us. So, my mind was always thinking how to make ends meet and keep them all satisfied. Many times, I pretended I was not hungry, so there was enough food to go around. I also found discarded seeds to plant in the garden, so we could have some more green vegetables and tomatoes in winter. I also fed the lemon tree with discarded vegetable scraps.

I must have been in my new house for about 8 months when late on a Saturday night, I was on my mattress in the dark, listening to a play with my radio next to my ear. I did not make any noise or disturb anybody, when I heard something moving.

The rest of the family was fast asleep in the bedroom, or so I thought. Then I heard the noise of someone close and a heavy smell of alcohol. I saw Inocente getting into my makeshift bed, his hands clamped on my breasts.

My first impulse was to shout out.

'Shush,' he said swiftly, 'you will wake up Yolanda!' I took the radio and slapped it on his head, my whole body pushing him out as much as my strength would allow me. I heard a sound of the sheets where Yolanda seemed to be sleeping. As luck would have it, Inocente got up grotesquely, tumbled a few times until he finally found his bed. I heard him loudly burp a few times and then there was silence. At the same time, and inconveniently, the throbbing pain from my gumboils was unbearable.

Still in the dark, I organised my suitcase and waited for the morning when Yolanda got up to say goodbye before going to work. I said I was sorry, but I missed Constanza's children too much. I had decided to return to Constanza's family, and although her gloomy and teary eyes told me otherwise, I sincerely hoped she believed me.

Everyone welcomed me with open arms at Constanza's. The boys had grown up and the older ones were starting to shave. Even little Dino was running around and making noise, playing with some pot lids. Constanza was pregnant again, hoping this time it would be a girl, but the pregnancy had not been good, and she had been exhausted with all her charges. Sadly, the baby, who was at last a girl, was born prematurely and did not survive.

My routine with the boys, however, became the same as before except we were all growing up and we played less and less rough games. Some of the boys seemed to do things behind closed doors in the bathroom that I was not allowed to look at. They confessed to me they liked this girl because she had a good backside, or they liked that other girl because she had big boobs. I thought it was hilarious! I also wondered what they thought of me, as I was starting to develop, and my body was beginning to take the shape of a woman...

Soon the boys would be allowed to go out to the dance in the local club and they would bring home their friends who would, at first, stare at me as if I was from another planet.

Eventually, they all discovered I had a radio and that I loved listening to music. I felt accepted by the boys!

Not long after, they asked me if I knew how to dance, and when I said I did not, they offered to teach me. Soon, the house became a dance training place. They all wanted to have a go and practice the latest step with me, so they could show up their talents at the club dance on Saturday nights!

It was unthinkable of me even to ask if I could go out to dance on Saturdays. I had to stay home, like any decent girl, whilst my 'protégées' and their male friends of the same age as me, went out to have a good time.

I always accepted my destiny with grace and joy, and because I was still allowed to participate in their excitement and conversations. I did my duties without complaining; the shirts had to be spotless, the shoes needed shining, and their dancing clothes, often nice trousers, or a suit had to be ironed to perfection.

Many years later, my nephews brought a new friend to the house, Paquito, from the neighbourhood to practice 'tangos and milongas'. I soon noticed not only that Paquito danced very well but he was also very handsome. He was a bit taller than me with dark skin, black hair and with the weirdest green eyes. Those eyes reminded me of the shine of cat's eyes in the dark.

Every time he looked at me, he smiled, as if he wanted to say something, but would not dare. I wished he would say he liked me! I thought Paquito was very attractive!

Soon Paquito also became my favourite dancing partner as we became more used to each other and practiced so many steps. We did *el ocho* and *la sentadita*, the slow tango and the faster milonga and in the end, all his other friends were asking us to demonstrate this or that step so they could learn from us to be able to dance better on Saturdays.

Paquito was giving me his full attention and he started to talk to me more and more. I learnt he was an only son, he had four sisters and his parents had come from Spain, eloping from their families. I thought that was daring, but very romantic. Later, his mother told me many stories about the plagues and diseases in Europe before they migrated to Argentina and how many of her relatives had perished in those days. Unfortunately, I could never find out why they fled from Spain so suddenly.

Paquito also said because he was an only son, his family was hoping one day he would have sons to bear his surname, otherwise his surname would stop with him. This was important because apparently his father's family once had a title in Spain and his surname matched the House of the Royal family of Austria in Spain. Wow! That was amazing!

Paquito told me he had finished an apprenticeship and he was now working as a qualified artisan upholsterer for a progressive company. Paquito's father, Rafael, was also an artisan and was strict at home. His rules had to be obeyed without question. Rafael was also shrewd with his money and Paquito had to give most of his wages to him to complement the family budget.

Like me, Paquito loved to read. He brought me lots of magazines that he and his sisters had already read: *LEOPLAN, Radiolandia, El Grafico, Billiken* and even the comics of *Patoruzu*. I enjoyed them all, often reading them more than once in the light of a candle to save power at night once everyone was sleeping.

One day, Paquito told me he liked me very much and another day he asked me if I wanted to be his girlfriend. I flatly told him I was only prepared to be just his friend, for the time being.

Then something extraordinary happened, he brought me some money he had saved from his allowance, for me to see a dentist and fix my teeth, so I would not suffer anymore with the gumboils. His generosity won me over, as I knew how little his allowance was!

Then Paquito asked my brother-in-law if he could take me to the Saturday dance as my boyfriend and surprisingly my brother-in-law accepted it, provided I kept under the close watch of his sons. I could not wait for the next Saturday to come when I would see Paquito again.

Paquito and I became inseparable during the weekdays, and the best dancing partners on Saturday nights. He would come to see me now every day after work and on Saturdays, we would meet on the dancing floor, and we would dance until there was no more music to dance to.

For *Carnaval*, we won the Tango competition at the club and were given 50 pesos as a prize. The next Monday, Paquito brought me an engagement ring with four small diamonds on it. I was in heaven and in love! I would be the first and only female in my family allowed to choose whom to marry and marry for love!

The 50 pesos we won in the competition became the first portion of many little savings we collected in a discarded tin container for our future together. Within the first three years, Paquito managed to save enough to purchase outright a bit of land with a timber, dilapidated one bedroom/kitchen and bathroom house in the outskirts of Buenos Aires.

During the time of courtship, I soon learnt Paquito and I not only shared our passion for dancing and reading, but we both enjoyed listening to music and playing cards. We both dreamt of having a family, going on holidays, and travelling within Argentina and the world. He promised me one day he would take me to Spain.

Paquito took me to meet his family. They lived in a nice tidy house, not far from Constanza's. His father was an artisan carpenter who made fine furniture and his mother was a housewife, who lived to look after the family and cook delicious Spanish meals. I loved them all instantly and they also seemed to love me to death. I soon also became close to two of his sisters who were married with children and lived in the same neighbourhood. Another sister was engaged to be married like us and his youngest sister was still at school.

Paquito worked long hours trying to save money for our wedding and to make our future house more comfortable. Saving was difficult and slow, because Paquito still had to give his wages to his family's upkeep account and was only allowed to keep a pittance. In the end, we decided to bring our wedding forward anyway.

My sister Carmela sewed my trousseau and my wedding dress, and as wedding presents. Constanza gave us a clock, my other brothers and sisters all gave us household items for the house: cups and saucers, plates, pots and pans, cutlery. Paquito's eldest sister Emilia and her husband gave us four towels; his other sister Luisa and her husband gave us bed sheets and one blanket. Rosita gave us a water jar with glasses and his youngest sister Pepita gave us two metal brand new buckets with all the money she had saved from her pocket money. Paquito's father Rafael made our bedroom suite and table and chairs for our kitchen.

We looked so elegant in our professional wedding photo our friends gifted us! We had a family party at Paquito's family backyard to celebrate the start of our new life together. Paquito had managed to save a bit of money for our honeymoon, and we went to the mountains in Cordoba straight after the party finished. I felt like exploding into happiness and thanked God for all the blessings!

I had never been outside my neighborhood, so going to Cordoba was for me like going to the moon. We travelled by train all through the night and in our tourist class cabin we kissed more than we slept, at last free from my nephews' watchful eyes.

On arrival, we had to walk to the hotel carrying our heavy suitcases which we had borrowed from some relatives. The suitcases were awkward to close and open because the locks were damaged. It looked like we were about to lose our clothes at any minute on the way to the hotel.

We finally arrived at the hotel past midnight, and the owner of the hotel settled us in our small room. We were so tired that within a few minutes we were both fast asleep on the bed, still with our clothes on.

However, once we rested, Paquito was still tired, in fact, he was always sleeping or eating whatever he could manage. To my horror, I also discovered he was pale and had developed somehow bad cramps and stomach pains. He had brought with him five bottles of coconut milk and a big bag of pumpkin seeds, which a friend had recommended for his malaise. But whenever he drank the coconut milk and ate the seeds, his pain got worse. I was getting worried. He confessed to me, rather embarrassed, he thought he had la lombriz solitaria—Taenia solium as it is scientifically known—or the dreaded pork tapeworm in humans.

I did not know anything about that disease, so he explained to me that sometimes this worm measured up to 10 meters and attacked the digestive system. His fears were confirmed when he started to defecate parts of the worm eggs and after much coconut milk and a good dose of pumpkin seeds, he finally expelled the worm's body and then its head.

During the whole week we were there, we had hardly gone out of our room except to have our meals, when Paquito devoured anything offered at the table. The other guests looked as if they understood our behavior as normal, after all we were just newly married, but in fact, Paquito spent all his time fast asleep when in our room. When he was awake, he said he was exhausted, and a bit sick, which I understood. After all, he had been working up to 16 hours a day to save some money for us.

In the end, after he had recovered a bit from the worm, he had yet another secret for me, he said he was a virgin and inexperienced with women and alas... he believed the worm had made him impotent, but hopefully temporarily.

I was terrified because although Paquito always made me feel excited when we kissed, I never had a boyfriend before Paquito. We had never petted heavily or seen each other without any clothes on, or even in our underwear for that matter...

We decided it might be better if we had a good time and enjoyed the good rest for the time being. We both agreed to leave the subject of sex alone and, if given the chance, we could enjoy the neighborhood as tourists.

As it turned out, the holiday included a tour to the jagged mountain range on horseback. I had brought a pair of culottes for the occasion and Paquito looked stunning in his brand-new overalls. However, neither of us had been on a horse before. After taking a photo of us, the hotel let us have a young boy, Tito, who came with us on another horse and acted as a guide!

We decided to take the tour early in the morning on the last day of our honeymoon. It took us hours to finally settle on the saddles and stirrups and get the old horses going. It really looked as if the old horses wanted to have a rest rather than doing any work, let alone taking us, two silly inexperienced beings, around the difficult terrain.

In the end, Tito had to use the whip and then the horses started trotting and then galloping. I guessed we were on our way to the mountains.

'Wait,' I shouted. 'Get me out of here. I am going to fall!' I became petrified of tumbling over and besides my horse was too wide for my body, so my bottom was getting sorer and sorer. Paquito was not better off than me, his body now curled around the horse, and he was losing his balance. Luckily, Tito shouted and did something turned the horses around and the horses knew where to go. In a few minutes, we were back where we came from and safely on the ground again.

We packed our clothes, tied the suitcases with a bit of old rope the owner of the hotel kindly provided, and we headed for the station to take the train that would take us back to Buenos Aires. We were sure we would feel more comfortable back home and finally arriving at our beloved, although still rundown home.

Once in Buenos Aires, we had to change trains and our house was seven long blocks to walk from the nearest station. Our relatives had organized all our wedding presents inside the house. They had even found an old mattress to put in our new bed. We felt grateful to have some furniture and the bare necessities to commence our new life as husband and wife.

Unfortunately, when we arrived at our new suburb, it was raining, the roads were muddy, the streets smelly, our house smelled of mold, the electricity had been cut off somehow and our tin roof was leaking. Paquito cheered me up, got the buckets we were gifted under the roof leaks and asked me to forget about the world outside.

He took me to bed, our very own bed, at last. He took my wet clothes off and, in the shadows, we made sweet, sweet love for the first time and again and again throughout the night, discovering each other deeply in body and soul. I was certain our first child was conceived during that long, dark, and wet night, because Carmela junior was born nine months exactly after.

Chapter 2

GROWING UP IN BUENOS AIRES...

'It is during our darkest moments that we must focus to see the light'.
(Aristotle)

Part 1 - Carmela Junior

Emanuel has been pestering mother and me to write my life story for 'his book'. Oh dear, he can be a real pain in the neck, this grandson!

I still feel a bit uncomfortable to share my secrets with him, big blue eyes, super smart Emanuel, and I would have preferred to have taken them to my tomb.

But in any case, I love this grandson to bits, and I cannot deny him anything!

Bingo then, here it is Emanuel, the first parts of my life narrative.

My mother's witch doctor predicted I was going to be born by Christmas, but despite the most advanced labor potions, extraneous exercises, and invasive poking, I did not want to face the world yet.

The family legend revealed my aunty Carmela saved me from sure death when she took my mother to her house and took care of her for another month. I was born on 26th January on my Aunty Carmela's bed. The delivery was assisted by the local quack midwife and everyone who was handy. My father was relieved and over the moon with the safe arrival of a little girl.

My father had hoped for a boy, and heir. As the only live son in his family, his surname would disappear if he did not produce a male.

My aunty Carmela was rewarded for her wise actions. She was to be my Godmother and I would bear her name, Carmela.

I do not remember much from my childhood. I remember once slipping down from the highchair after being allowed to have a bit more than a sip of wine for dinner. It does not seem unusual to me, because in my family all children were allowed to drink wine, usually watered down with soda water, with their meals.

Another time, I still remember the shocked face of my parents when I interrupted their love game. I stepped into their bedroom when they were having a siesta and caught them playing body fighting or so I thought, because they were wriggling violently with almost no clothes on.

I remember being jealous of my Aunty Carmela, my Godmother, and other members of my mother's side of the family, though I barely remember their names. Mother gave them her full attention and care.

Aunty Carmela was the only one who used to visit us and help my mum with cooking, especially when I had fallen very sick. I recall laying on a mat in the patio for days on end, feeling terrible; dizzy and feverish. The doctor examined me and gave me medicines, I was then left totally to myself, day and night. I can still hear as in a dream, my mother talking for hours to her favorite sister Carmela about the different illnesses affecting their family.

I also remember visiting her brother Domingo and his wife Felisa and Minguito, my cousin. I hated these visits because my aunty Felisa had whiskers that hurt me when I was forced to give her a kiss. Besides, she had horrible bad breath that exuded and all the cookies she offered were stale and smelt like her.

I heard their first son Carlitos had died from meningitis, or rather, from severe neglect. According to what I overheard from my mother, they did not want to see a doctor because they were stingy, and when they did so, it was too late for poor Carlitos.

Minguito was my age and we used to play in the backyard,

throwing each other dirt from the garden. He got polio when still very young, and mother spent hours away from home visiting him, as I was told he was in hospital in an iron lung.

I overheard the neighbors warning my mother that polio was very contagious and that she might bring it home to me. But my mother kept on going every day until Minguito died, and for the mercy of God, I guess I did not get the polio. I searched my mind to remember where the hell my mother left me when she went to visit the hospital as I was still so young, but regrettably, I could not remember. I suspect I was left on my own.

Tío Domingo and Tía Felisa went on to have another Carlitos, but I believe he was neglected as well, and he acquired some mental illnesses. Carlitos used to become really possessed when he did not take his medicine, and he was taken many times in a straight-jacket to the mad-house. One day, I heard he was roaming the streets saying he was the 'savior of the world' and later, he threw himself in front of a fast-oncoming train.

I was lucky I guess, because I must have won my father over even if I was not his wanted son. My dad seemed to love me as much as I loved him. He tried to please me whenever he could and within his means.

Dad brought me a white puppy that I named Carolo. Carolo was good with all of us, except my father. Carolo even let me dress him with old clothes and ribbons, but the small puppy grew up to be a big, handsome dog.

My father had had an aversion to dogs because of bad experiences in his childhood and whenever the dog was near him, Carolo showed its teeth and growled, ready to attack him. I think Carolo must have felt my father's fear and in the end, Carolo was confined to our terrace upstairs and one day he suddenly disappeared, possibly left roaming the streets in some slum far from our neighbourhood.

Father also brought me a small monkey that I named Titi. Titi was cute, but naughty. He used to go up our climbing wisteria and visited and terrorized our neighbors, stealing the hens' eggs and throwing them. He also appeared in our neighbors' bedrooms frightening the ladies.

I believe Titi eventually fell in love with my mother when he grew up. He tried to show her disgusting sexual acts like masturbating and one day Titi also disappeared. I overheard my mother had gifted him to our rubbish collector who lived in a big farm somewhere in the country.

To be fair to my mother, I believe I was always clean and tidy, and I felt cherished until my two sisters came along, Edith and especially my younger sister Florinda, who demanded my mother's full attention all the time. Golly! How much would I have done to get my mother to see what I was doing in those early days! I moaned and moaned, but my laments always fell on deaf ears. A real tragedy would have to happen to finally get my parents' attention fully.

After my sister Florinda, we affectionally called her Flor, was born, I clearly remember visiting my Aunty Emilia's house for her annual big party on New Year's Eve.

I must have been just over nine years old. My mum dressed me with a beautiful, new white organza dress and had made ringlets in my black hair, adorned with white organza flowers. I really felt like a princess.

I cannot remember much about the food at my Tia Emilita's house, although it most probably was party canapes, finger crustless sandwiches, a variety of small cakes and also lots of nuts, turrones, and yummy chocolate bonbons.

I remember clearly though how I was for the first time, allowed to play with the older boys, my cousins, with detonating rockets and homemade fireworks.

I had many male cousins, but Amadeo was my favorite. He was only a few years older than me; we liked the same games and were always together playing or holding hands.

I remember as it was only yesterday, when playing hide and seek, I hid behind the stairs. The place was dark, and I was not afraid. Suddenly I saw my uncle Arturo approaching me with a big smile, then I smelt the stench of heavy tobacco and alcohol on his teeth as he kissed my mouth and his big rough hands were trying to get inside my lovely dress and panties. I screamed and screamed, and he let go and disappeared.

I remember crying, running to my father to tell him, but the words did not come out. I was so distressed that my parents had to cut the party short and returned home. When I calmed down, I told them what had happened. I thought they did not believe me as I was always complaining about this thing or the other at home, and they always dismissed me as a drama queen.

However, this time, my mother examined me all over and she said I was all right. I cried myself to sleep that night and many other nights after! I heard my dad had visited my Aunty Emilia's family, but Uncle Arturo denied he ever touched me, the dirty liar! Nevertheless, I guess my parents must have believed me somehow because we never visited my Aunty Emilia again for New Year's Eve, or if we did visit occasionally, I had to sit tight beside my parents.

Not long after, I started to sleepwalk and talking aloud in my sleep. Not that I remember much, as I was asleep!

I was told fruit disappeared from the fruit bowl at night, only to be found in the patio in the morning, money from my father's wallet disappeared also to be found among my piano books, and once, next to the toilet bowl. Screams were heard now and again when I woke up suddenly in the dark after stepping accidently on the odd cockroach running on the floor.

My parents tried every possible 'cure' and well-meant suggestions for my sleepwalking: they gave me different purges and potions, they left me without dinner for days and they even sent me away with some Spanish neighbors to the countryside to see if the fresh air and a different environment would do the trick and stop my somnambulism, but all attempts were to no avail.

My parents also followed me in my errands for a while, but they got tired of being woken up at night, and they knew I would eventually return to my bed. Consequently, what they did was to hide the key to the outside patio and street door locks to make sure I did not wander outside or in the streets during the night.

I was told years later, my Aunty Emilia also suffered from the same syndrome. She also talked in her sleep and sleepwalked around her home. I also heard she also ate fruit during the night or pretended to have visitors at the dining table. One day, she also got hold of some cash money during her nocturnal strolls. She must have cut the bills into pieces and put them all except a few pieces down the toilet bowl, then flushed the toilet. When discovered, I believe she was severely punished for this with a good beating by her husband, my uncle Arturo! Poor Aunty Emilita, she was like a bird, so lean, fragile, and vulnerable, even a strong wind would have toppled her over.

My Aunty Carmela, my Godmother, visited us often, especially when someone in the family was sick with a cold or other ailment. I can't remember much about her looks; except she also demanded my mother's attention unconditionally. She was forever gossiping about somebody being sick or recovering from sickness but on the other hand, she also made the yummiest Spanish potato omelets or *tortillas* I have ever tasted.

I would have liked to have a better relationship with my Aunty Carmela, especially because we shared the same name, but unfortunately, neither of us could find anything meaningful or exciting to talk about except exchange lots of kisses and hugs.

It was not until many years later that my mother told me Aunty Carmela used to see and interact with ghosts and dead people. Their dead mother and father visited her often, usually at night to advise her on routine things in life. But the most interesting visitors were those that would tell my Aunty Carmela something about her or somebody else's fate in the world of the living.

For example, many times she would know what numbers would come up in the quinella, somebody getting seriously sick or even dying soon or wicked affairs people would only do behind doors.

Because of her skills, she was popular with young, nosy girls who wanted to know where their prince charming would come from, the scandalmongers who loved to spread the poor soul's dirty laundry around the neighborhood and even the funeral directors, who were eager to know who their next customers would be to get their businesses better organized.

My mother was worried about her because she thought Aunty Carmela was losing some of her marbles, as some of her findings were becoming outrageous and unbecoming. My mum sought counsel from our family doctor who recommended a psychiatrist.

There was no way Aunty Carmela would go and see a therapist. Hence, my mother organized to bring the psychiatrist at home, a Dr Filipo, on a day when Aunty Carmela was expected to visit. The idea was for Dr. Filipo to tease her out for details and information on her experiences.

I still remember this elegantly dressed and friendly man smoking his pipe and waiting for Aunty Carmela to come. My mum introduced Dr. Filipo as one of Dad's bosses who was waiting for my dear father to give him some orders.

But Aunty Carmela was too smart for all of us! As soon as Dr Filipo opened his mouth to ask her a question ('How are you today?'); she responded amusingly with another question.

'What is this shrink doing here? Please get him to go quickly, or he will charge you an arm and a leg, Macaca.' She added 'You do not believe me, but I am the sanest of you all here!' With that remark, she dismissed Dr Filipo, got up and started to make our cakes and prepare the table for coffee and afternoon snacks.

I was fascinated and wanted to ask Aunty Carmela more questions about her supernatural experiences. After all, she was my Godmother, but Aunty Carmela and mother just did not want to discuss any dirty laundry with me. They told me I was too young to comprehend her, and such matters were only for adults!

In those days I was not ashamed to pretend I was sick, often because I wanted to visit our family doctor and pediatrician, a Dr. Sabiondo. Dr Sabiondo had moved into the neighborhood after his graduation not long ago. He was young and handsome and was very good at his job. He not only tried to heal your body when ill, but he also gave people counselling about daily routine practices and modern activities designed to improve their overall lives, and especially those of their children.

Dr Sabiondo was married to another doctor, although his wife did not practice medicine because she was always pregnant or looking after her latest babies. At the last count, she had about nine children.

Some of these children were about my age but unfortunately, I did not have much access to them because they lived in a boarding school, and they only came to the neighborhood during school holidays.

Dr Sabiondo's popularity and wisdom were spreading fast and soon he was so busy we needed to ask for an appointment in advance to see him.

However, something happened that would change his destiny forever. Dr Sabiondo had instructed Doña Rosa, our next-door neighbor, to give her husband, Don Chucho, an 'enema' whenever he was badly constipated. One day, we heard Don Chucho shouting and swearing as if the very devil was killing him. There was a commotion next door with many people coming to see what the matter was.

Dr Sabiondo came with his bag of instruments, but nothing could be done for Don Chucho and I learnt later, he had passed away. It was rumored Doña Rosa had given Don Chucho the prescribed enema, but as she was so old and could not see properly, she had tried to push it somewhat in the wrong place, thus Don Chucho had bled to death!

Don Chucho's causes of demise spread exponentially amongst Dr Sabiondo's many patients, and many even considered him a murderer.

As the news spread, Dr Sabiondo's patients started to dwindle until there were not many visiting his practice. Our family continued to visit him for advice on our bodies, minds, and souls. My mother used to visit him to seek wisdom, even when she had to take personal decisions, like purchasing a new dining suite without my father's ready consent.

I was devastated when Dr Sabiondo and his family eventually moved out of the neighborhood, as I had admired him for his progressing thoughts, insight, and knowledge. I was sure he was responsible for many of my parents' advanced ideas on education and child rearing, for which I eventually benefited greatly.

To be fair to this story though, I was always disappointed with my life at home. My younger sisters were too young, and the world of adults was not accessible for me. I was truly unhappy at school because I was very bored, and I could not make any friendships. The other children teased me and bullied me. They said I was weird because I did everything the teachers asked me to do super quickly and 'perfectly' and because my hair was bluish black, therefore they were sure my mother tinted it at home, which was silly and not true.

I became withdrawn and decided to learn by myself whatever I was able, or somebody could show me. I especially loved to be with my grandma Luisa, my father's mum. My dear grandma, who was living with us after grandpa Rafael died suddenly, taught me to sew, knit (including crochet), embroider and above all, she taught me to sing and dance Spanish songs. She also instructed me about God and his Holy Book, the Bible.

If I was not with my grandma, I was always moaning, but my mother had little time for my complaints, especially when my youngest sister Flor was born, because she was very demanding and wanted to always eat. Besides feeding me, I felt I was practically abandoned to my own devices by my family.

But soon, my predicament was going to change. I remember well when my father taught me to read and write the newspapers, long before I started school and he also bought me, on the advice of Dr Sabiondo, a collection of an encyclopedia called *El tesoro de la juventud*. They were amazing books and a great source of general knowledge. I believed these books or rather the content of these books changed my dull life for the better at such an early age!

My father had really nailed it; these books replaced the attention I was sorely seeking from my mother. They brought new facets to my senseless life. I was no longer bored to tears, and any minute I had to spare I would spend reading and chewing over what I read on their pages. Some of the best sections included: 'Things we should know' (Science); The book about Latin America and famous people (History); The Book of our Life (Philosophy), History of the Planet Earth (Geography/Astrology), Countries and Customs (Geography/ History) and Loose Ends (Miscellaneous). I loved it all, especially the miscellaneous section, where I read about Aesop and other Fables, Homer and classics like Antoine Marie Jean-Baptiste, Roger de Saint- Exupéry, Alexandre Dumas, Jane Austen, Edmundo de Amicis, Cervantes, Shakespeare, The Holy Scriptures, and many others.

I was eager to learn about life and the world and these books supplied me with food aplenty. I started to question the meaning of life as I read and meditated on famous people's phrases and opinions that would stick with me and inspire me for the rest of my life.

One of these phrases by Hebbel especially encouraged me to move forward when things were rough. It would become my motto later in life: 'If you are drawn by a small light, follow it. That it takes you inside a pool of stagnant water, you should be able to get out of it. But if you do not follow it, you might be miserable all your life with the thought that perhaps it was your Star.' Wow! It still inspires me to move forward even today!

My mother, desperate to keep me busy and out of her wits, enrolled me in piano and classical and Spanish dancing lessons. Then, thanks to the advice of Dr Sabiondo, who advised to my parents an education was not complete without learning foreign languages, my parents paid for me to have private lessons to learn English and French. My teachers were not that good, but with the help of books and dictionaries, I was to become fluent in both languages.

Now, I could read books not only in Spanish but in other languages too. I was bored no longer and within some months, at last, not just my mother but everyone was taking notice of me! They were saying I was a child prodigy.

Later, my father also bought me another collection of 24 books written by classical authors from different countries and throughout time. These books were badly produced and sometimes I needed to tear their still bound together pages to keep reading, but I did not care. I was only interested in their rich content, and I was busy comparing the written styles through different generations.

At school, they could no longer keep me in kindergarten as I was a burden to the teachers. So, they agreed to do something very silly that would have effects on the rest of my life. They believed they could solve the problem enrolling me in grade two, two years ahead of my cohort, without thinking too much about the consequences.

I loved the conversations I had with my teachers, but the bullying from my public-school mates worsened and became intolerable.

One day, my mother must have been in a hurry and could not take me home to change into my ballet gear after attending my classes. Therefore, she dressed me with my mesh ballet suit underneath my clothes and apron. I needed to pee at recess but could not maneuver my clothes and remove my one-piece ballet suit underneath my school uniform and apron. Ick! When we were back in class and in a middle of a lesson, I could not hold my pee any longer and I did it in my pants. I can still feel today the warm liquid travelling down my legs and into my school shoes, and along with my warm salty tears dropping down my face.

My teacher asked one of the other students to fetch the school secretary, who took me away and finally took my wet mesh ballet suit off. Instead, she fitted me with underpants, too large for my body. Luckily, it was time to go home soon so I did not have to go back to class.

After that episode, the teasing from the school children increased and I became more and more withdrawn and teary at school. I started to resent going to school and found any excuse to stay home, usually pretending I was sick or having 'accidents' that would badly stain my white apron.

That was when my parents decided to 'invest' in me, as they said, and changed me to a private Catholic school, Escuela San Cayetano. It was not far from home, but far enough to take the bus or get a lift in a car to get there.

This new school did not solve my problems entirely. I loved that it was only a school for girls, my new school uniform and the nuns and teachers who appeared indeed very caring. However, although the discipline was better, I was still two years ahead of my cohort, and I could not identify with any of my new school mates.

The problem grew worse as we aged. The girls were forever talking about and flirting with boys. I did not have the slightest interest in them! I longed to have a best friend but outside the school, I wore different clothes to them, we had different bodies and interests, and we had nothing in common to talk about or socialize.

Besides, this was the time when I fully discovered God and His Grace. I started reading an old Bible that my grandma long ago had given to me, and soon I could identify with and befriend some young nun trainees at school and talk about spiritual things

I asked my dad to be taken to school early to be able to attend mass before school and talk to my new friends. In those days, the mass was in Latin. To be able to understand it better, I studied Latin on my own and with the help of an old book my grandma had given me. I found Latin fascinating. I was then able to read the Bible in Latin as well as many more historical classics written in Latin.

The school continued to be rather boring, as knowledge appeared to be delivered in little chunks and I wanted to know 'everything'. In those days, I did not always have the means available to do more research.

However, by the time I was about 11, I had questioned the meaning of life and was devouring the Bible and its different interpretations. I felt some parts of the Bible stood out and talked to me directly and made my soul alive.

One day, in the quiet of the night, I heard Jesus calling me 'Carmela… Carmela… Come to me! Take your cross and follow me.' It was a profound experience, and I would never forget it. I felt the awakening of my spiritual side to God and a great peace within my soul. I understood what Jesus has done for me and felt a great peace. By the age of 12, I was convinced I should become a nun and dedicate my life to Him, helping my community as a teacher or perhaps better still, as a medical doctor. For the first time in my life, I felt I had a purpose.

Sorry to say, I should not have shared my sentiments and plans readily with my parents. My plans did not appeal to them, and they swiftly changed me to another private, non-religious, mixed school where I could study the commerce stream rather than teaching. My parents alleged education was not a good career for me. Teachers in those days were not paid well, if paid at all. I could not dismiss their concerns as this sad fact on teachers were true.

The school change was somehow softened by friends I made in the neighborhood. Around this time, I met with three girls who lived near me, mainly through Gabriela, a girl I travelled with to the city for my English classes. I thanked God for them. They were all different, but I cherished their unbiased friendship, our bicycle rides, our chats, our little dancing parties at home where we were allowed to invite some boys from the neighborhood. My parents gradually promoted our friendship, my father: by taking us to Parque Saavedra on his bus to ride our bikes; my mother: by accompanying us always to different dancing venues where our virginity and reputation were cautiously guarded.

Many years later, even after I was firmly settled in Australia, I would visit Argentina and my dear friends would always make me feel as if I had never left Buenos Aires. It was such a strong connection!

When one of them died from a brain tumor and another one got dementia and did not recognize anyone, Gabriela continued to be my friend. We shared unforgettable and treasured times together in each other's homes in Sydney, Argentina, even travelling together in Europe.

Returning to my childhood, I prayed to the Lord that my commitment to Him would not waiver overtime. How wrong I was. It was at this new school where I finally discovered boys and their tricky, maniacal ways.

I was at last starting to develop physically, but I still looked like a child compared with my female schoolmates, who were already talking about their own or their friends' sexual pleasures and fantasies.

Nevertheless, at this new school my schoolmates seemed to love me a bit more—or rather use me, which I did not mind. I felt especially appreciated when my new-found friends discovered I was able to do or explain the most complicated exercises in mathematics, chemistry and physics and I could help them with their English homework. At last, I could have real friends, even if I discerned, they only wanted me near to exploit me to their advantage.

I noticed one of the boys, in my class, Dario, stared and smiled at me a lot from a distance. He was a bit short, but when close, he had the most beautiful green eyes, although his skin was rather dark! He was always well groomed and seemed calm and polite.

Dario approached me after school one day and asked me where I lived. Unfortunately, we lived in different train directions, but the next day he asked me if I wanted to have an ice-cream with him before boarding our trains and I reluctantly accepted. He offered to pay for it, luckily, because I had no money in my pockets.

We continued to find opportunities to talk to each other. We talked about our families, our hobbies, and our passions. I told him about my Tesoro de la Juventud and book collection, and he told me about his family 's passion for collecting guns. His father was a serious collector of weapons.

Dario shared with me a deep love for music, especially classical and South American and we both played the piano. Soon, we were excellent mates. We started to visit each other's houses, played the piano to each other, and had meals together in our homes.

Dario belonged to an exclusive Italian shooters' club in Buenos Aires, and he wanted me to go with him there during our spare time. But unfortunately, I had not the connections nor the means to belong to such a club. Miraculously, his dad applied and paid for me to join and paid for my ongoing membership. What a dream! Now I had ready access to other social stratum, full of educated and friendly young people! I felt as if a new world had been created for me!

I learnt how to play tennis and I often played against Dario. We also played bowls, and attended classes to learn and practice horse riding, polo, and judo, for which I reached a green belt. When it rained, we played canasta, chess, bridge, and other card games with my many new friends at the club.

My parents seemed to be happy that finally I had a friend to spend time with. Dario seemed to be tidy, polite, peaceful and above all he had a normal family.

At each other's homes, Dario and I usually spent hours talking about school or activities in the club or just playing new songs on the piano and singing. Dario and I both graduated from High School at the same time, although I was only just 15 and Dario was 18. I got a score of a perfect 10, with the corresponding accolades, including an article in the newspapers with my family, when Dario, despite my constant coaching, barely passed with the minimum score of 7.

My silent accomplishments were so much more: I got a gold medal from the school for my performance in all my subjects. The same year, I also graduated with honors in my piano course and in my Classical and Spanish dancing courses. I also completed my Oxford English course. My teachers all predicted I would have a great and prosperous future! My parents never made a fuss about any of my achievements. Occasionally, my father would tell me quietly that he felt proud of me.

I asked my parents whether I would be allowed to go to university to study medicine, which I sensed it was my true calling—imagining my future just like the medical programs I had seen on TV, like Dr. Kildare and Ben Casey. Watching these programs fascinated me! I dreamt of operating on brains or hearts or helping people to recover from rare diseases and incurable ailments or doing some serious research to make new vaccines to help indigenous people out of disease and poverty.

Unfortunately, my parents again had other plans for me. Mother told me they needed to educate my two sisters and they could not afford to pay for any more education for me.

'We have invested enough for now,' my mother grumbled. I felt quite disappointed, but not yet beaten.

A hope was rising in my heart: I should go to work, and I should pay for my education myself. But I was still a minor, I was not able to get a job, as the legal age for full time work in Argentina was then 18.

My cousin Amadeo who was already working in marketing for a large publishing company advised me there was a vacancy for a junior where he worked and he would fill in the forms for me to apply, although he would have to state I was a lot older. He must had put in a good word for me because I got the job. The pay was not much but it was a start, and at that stage, I could not be too picky!

My mother could not believe when I got the job, but my father especially was secretly delighted his daughter was, 'moving on in the world' despite being a female.

As for myself, I loved to be able to travel to the city, although the work itself was extremely boring: I had to forever fill envelopes with paper advertisements to purchase books and records by mail; then get the packages ready to post. The best part of the job was lunch, which we had in a local canteen with Amadeo and his friends.

Lunch in Argentina is the main meal of the day and we had one full hour for it. We usually went to a 'taberna' nearby and we had steak or chicken with chips and salad, home-made milanesas (schnitzels), fish and veggies, or pasta with meatballs, followed by a *'flan con crema'*, my favorite dessert, or fruit salad and ice-cream.

I had been in this dreary job for only one month when, in desperation, I sought the general manager to beg him to give me another task.

I told him I was bored to death and that I might be able to help him with English or accounting. He looked a bit surprised by my boldness, but he dismissed me with a smile.

I never knew what happened but the very next day when I arrived at work, I was sent to another section where they did account reconciliations. The work was still quite boring, but the conversations among my female colleagues were entertaining and at 15 they made my imagination fly. They talked constantly about their sexual lives, real or fantasized, giving details of what they did, or did not do, in bed with their husbands, partners, or lovers.

I was grateful to my parents who allowed me to keep my salary which paid for my transport and lunches, and I could save the rest, which was not much, although it kept growing slowly. In those days, I did not have any idea on how to open a bank account, plus I was too young to open one without my parents' consent. Therefore, I kept my small savings in an envelope.

I could not enroll at the University yet, but I had enough money saved and I was able to enroll in an Advanced ABC Bilingual English-Spanish Shorthand course, which I thought would allow me to get a better job.

At the ABC school, I met many young English-speaking women and men much older than me who were fully bilingual and whose manners and ambitions I instantly admired. They dressed elegantly, and spoke with slow and melodious voices, and were all looking for brilliant careers. It was hard at first.

'What is this child doing here?'

'Wow! Looking at her clothes, they are not designer clothes! She might be from the province or from another poor country in South America.'

'But her skin is quite fair, and she seems educated'

'I am bored. Let's try... I am going to talk to her and see...', I overheard.

I was treated like a curious item in an antique shop, ready to be discovered and exhibited in the elegant cafes they attended first, and then in their sophisticated mansions. I did not even know these houses existed in Buenos Aires!

I quickly became their friend and confidante. I was impressed and amazed. They dressed tastefully, they drank high tea with scones and jam in elegant buildings, they had amazing houses with maids and above all, they daily read and commented on the *Buenos Aires Herald* bilingual newspaper!

They were all looking for bilingual well-paid positions, jobs that would take them overseas, in high government posts or in the diplomatic service. One day, maybe I too could get a job like that and maybe I could become well off and refined like them. After all, I was learning the ABC shorthand much faster and better than them! Maybe one day even my family could get out, once and for all, of the poor suburbs and purchase an elegant apartment in the northern quarters of Buenos Aires.

When I told Dario about my dreams and ambitions, he was not as excited as me! He wanted a simple easy life, maybe getting married one day, having a family, a job at his father's company and to keep visiting the Sporting Club. He was not a dreamer, he told me. His family was already well off and he did not need to fantasize like me. I felt belittled and disturbed, as if a sharp sword now kept us apart.

For the first time, I was deeply disappointed to be Dario's girlfriend and, in any case again, I felt this moment was the beginning of my new journey for my life, not at all the end of it.

Part 2 - Carmela Junior

The *Buenos Aires Herald* became my constant companion on the train travelling to my city job. Through this English publication I had access to life in other countries, different perspectives on government issues, births, deaths, engagement, marriages, and other events involving people with distinguished surnames, some of them those of my already newly found friends at the ABC Shorthand course. But above all, this newspaper kept on publishing bilingual, interesting and lucrative jobs I could aspire to and every single day this newspaper kept on giving me new high hopes.

I had not finished my ABC course yet, when I was ringing employers communicating only in English and offering my services. Negotiating jobs was a lot easier now because I already had my Employment Work Code I.D. and Social Security Number even though I was still underage for employment.

Not long after starting my search for a better job from the *Buenos Aires Herald*, I got myself a job as secretary to a middle manager in a Printing Export/Import Company. This job was much more interesting than my previous one and my salary had now more than doubled. I was using my English language, travelling to other parts of the city, dressing better, but above all, I was using my brain and making new friends.

One of these friends was my colleague, German secretary Cecilia. Cecilia was young, yet she had a long history of secret and complicated ventures. Her father was a weird and evasive man. He always seemed to hide behind the thick curtains when I visited Cecilia. Although Cecilia never told me outright, I suspected her father was an ex-Nazi general sought by the international authorities, hiding in our overpopulated city suburbs.

Many years later, I met Cecilia in Australia. She had to flee Argentina, but she never disclosed to me the reason. She had recently married her second husband in Germany and had migrated to Sydney.

Cecilia had a creepy story to tell me about her first husband. He had been introduced by her father to her and apparently, he had locked her in a trunk for months, only allowing her out to eat and make love to him. The reason for her atrocious confinement was the fact he thought she had been unfaithful to him. Eventually, I guess she must have managed to come out and travel in secret to Germany.

Cecilia's second husband was no better than the first, poor Cecilia. I believe she was bashed by him because she had met me for coffee for a few hours, against his wishes. Due to these circumstances, I lost contact with my dear Cecilia again, forever this time.

But coming back to my story and my younger years. I still wanted to enroll at university. But although I proposed to pay for it, my parents were still not happy with me to do any higher studies just yet, because 'I was still a minor and travelling at night to attend a public university was not safe.' It was certainly not in their plans for me. It was true Buenos Aires city was in a constant state of chaos, uncertainty, and violence. The Government run universities were then going through a sinister period.

Some communist aggressive student groups had taken control of some of the government run universities and the police were usually on horseback, deploying tear gas and color paint spray to identify the offenders or whoever was in their path, to later arrest them. During the day my parents instructed me to get out of their way and seek refuge in any of the subway stations to avoid arrest or even worse, the chance to disappear or be killed. The city was not a safe place to wander around or enjoy, in those days.

Besides the riots in the city, one of my friends, Gabriela's boyfriend, was arrested at home in our neighborhood on suspicion of plotting against the government. Nobody knew where he was taken, and he disappeared never to be found again. Everyone was in a state of alert and shock. I could not blame my parents for their concerns and restrictions when it came to my desire to study further.

Dario was also arrested, and his parents' home and garage were raided and searched for political propaganda by a special government squad, but they found nothing compromising. Dario's father talked to high-ranking officials and luckily Dario was released with a warning not to get involved in dirty politics ever again. Dario never told me if he was politically involved with any organization or not, and I found the whole operation very strange.

I was fortunate. I never had any incidents travelling to work in the city. I managed to convince my parents I could perhaps go to a private, safer university to study away from the city buzz and violence.

I was still allowed to work and keep my salary; therefore, I had enough money to enroll at University of Belgrano. I decided to study economics, which was the only stream available after work for me.

Some of my subjects were marketing, economics, political science, accounting and tax laws. I loved it all and read and studied more than was asked, because I was thirsty for knowledge and experience. My motivation was always to socially climb, get out of poverty and improve myself as a person.

My university teachers soon noticed my talents and ambitions, and I was soon rewarded with distinguished marks in my assessments and year end results.

Despite being so young, I was invited by the university staff to participate in political and economic debates and forums after class, which by some miracle, my parents allowed me to attend.

I continued to enjoy my now frequent conversations with interesting people. Mostly intelligent and highly ambitious men I had met in my course. One of these men was Manuel, who also worked with me in the printing company as a Sales Manager. He was 18 years older than me, handsome, with a kind spirit, and single.

Manuel and I became the best of friends, and he took me to meet his family, whom I loved. I brought him to meet my family and I introduced him to my boyfriend Dario.

Manuel wanted to learn English, so I offered my services to teach him, for a fee. At that stage, I was already teaching English to other students from the neighborhood in my spare time to supplement my income.

I was soon able to save a substantial amount of money in Argentinian pesos. However, our currency, with rampant inflation, was constantly devaluing. Nevertheless, I quickly learnt how to preserve its value. As soon as I had the equivalent of one thousand

American dollars in Argentinian pesos, I would change it into U.S currency at the best daily rate. I kept these American Dollars in cash at home, in a cardboard box.

Manuel continued to attend lessons at my house on Saturdays. Apart from being gorgeous, he was also smart, witty, and very quick to learn. I taught him English from my old books, from short stories and from contemporary songs like the Beatles.

After my lessons, we talked about his activities in his spare time. He played rugby and he also went out at night to clubs and trendy discotheques, which for me, still underage, were forbidden. I would have given anything to be able to join him in one of these places, although I could do nothing but wait to grow up.

One day Manuel confessed to me he wanted to purchase an apartment, but he was just short of some money. Without any hesitation I offered him my savings in US dollars. He rejected it at first, but a few days later, he came back and accepted my offer.

Manuel promised he would give me the money back in US dollars as soon as he could save it himself. He did as he had promised, and he also brought me a huge bunch of red roses and a card in which he promised he would always be my friend.

My parents were curious, because I did not disclose my money lending activities to them, but I felt I could not tell them the truth and I had to lie to them to keep the peace. I told them Manuel had a promotion because of his improved English skills, and he felt he wanted to share some of his extra money with me as he was grateful to me for my English lessons. Luckily, my parents swallowed the lie without any further investigation.

I started to admire Manuel more and more and wanted to know more about him, but I was shy with men, and I did not know how to make my emerging feelings known to him. Besides, I already had a boyfriend.

I would have loved to become romantically involved with Manuel, and sometimes, I day-dreamt about it. However, and disappointedly, he never gave me a hint he even liked me as a partner, not even a bit. I guess my life would have been very different with him...

Years later, when I was no longer in Argentina, he confessed to my mother he had been in love with me all along, but he thought he had to wait a while, until I had matured more. He also said he was waiting for me to come back to Argentina to hopefully start a romantic relationship with me, perhaps even marry me.

By that time, I had moved on and our romance never happened. Manuel eventually married an air hostess and had a child, but his marriage did not last. We remained friends for life, and I visited him every time I travelled to Argentina, but I lost contact when he left the company he worked for and could not trace him anywhere when I became elderly. For a while, I suspected he might have died, as he had been erased from the face of the digital world.

However, Manuel had been alive, and he had learnt of my efforts. We reconnected again, many years later. We were able to see each other again in one of my last visits to Argentina. He lived in an expensive suburb in Buenos Aires and owned a huge apartment overlooking the River Plate. He had been romantically involved with a lady from Germany for many years. He seemed happy indeed! Returning to my Argentinian university days... I continued to attend evening classes as part of my economics course. But unfortunately, my optimism about finishing my degree would not last for long. My lectures were in the evening after work and unfortunately in those days the many disturbances and violent riots in Buenos Aires became worse and even horribly gory, even in the quieter suburb of Belgrano.

As expressed before, the best way to avoid any involvement between the rebels, and government horse-mounted police, which could result in serious injuries or even death, was to run to any building or the subway underground and stay there until the demonstrations, uprisings, and sometimes the shootings, ceased. I always followed the instructions whenever disturbances arose, so I was able to survive these chaotic times without a scratch.

But my parents' concerns for me were renewed yet again. They feared for my safety as I travelled the streets so late at night. Without further explanation or discussion, they forbade me to continue my studies at night and I had to agree that for my protection and security, they were right.

It was around this time I got more students at home interested in learning English. As I had my evenings free then, I could now give lessons during the week after work as well as on Saturdays. My students were kids from the neighborhood whose parents dreamt of them doing better at school so they could one day and miraculously get them out of poverty. I also started to attract adult students who wanted to travel.

My parents offered me a small room in the attic which had not been used for a long time to use as a classroom. I cleaned it, furnished it with a table and a few chairs I had found in the trinket room, and I painted the walls white. My father also built a bookshelf for my books and stationery.

This place provided an ideal place for my students, away from the noises and activities of the household and the students provided some extra cash for me. The small room also became a sanctuary for me; it was there where I could have some privacy: read, meditate, and evaluate the happenings of the day. I could also plan for the next day and especially plan for my future.

Soon, I was able to save serious money, which was immediately changed into US dollars and kept in the cardboard box hidden now in my 'teaching room'.

Although disappointed Dario could not measure up to some of my other friends, like Manuel for example, my relationship with him continued to blossom because soon we were adding interesting tasks to our routine activities.

We started to cuddle, kiss, and touch each other, at his home first, discovering, carrying on and much enjoying the pleasure of our sexualities. Our behavior changed from our friendly nature of our relationship to a more serious one and we started to get jealous and more demanding of each other.

He wanted to know where I was and with whom when I was not with him, which he resented when I truly told him. He also wanted to know my timetable and why I suddenly had these weird ambitions about career and social climbing.

We had massive and crude fights, although we always finished up making up and forgiving each other. It was during one of these fights that he proposed to me to go all the way with sex. I was still not mature enough and naïve to make a wise decision. I had no idea of what the physical and emotional consequences might be. I felt nauseous thinking about it!

I brushed aside his advances, but he continued to put pressure on me, impairing our friendship by warning me to either give in to his sexual demands or finish our relationship altogether. He also warned me there were plenty of girls who were more than willing to experience the joys of sex, especially the Jewish girls who frequented our sport Club.

I felt jealous and inadequate and wished I was a bit older, or I could talk to somebody like my mother or a girlfriend. At the end of the day, I did not want to lose him. I still valued his friendship. So, I gave in. We went to a cheap motel paid by the hour in Flores which we called 'El Su'.

I was terrorized because although I was curious, I could somehow foresee he would hurt me and it would not work in the end. Even then, I suspected my feelings for him were only a deep friendship.

Dario stated he was experienced, which made me even more jealous. I should have guessed his claims were not true… He tried to persuade me not to worry, but just feel the pleasure. It was going to be so exciting… However, my first sexual experience was neither pleasant, nor exciting. It left me sore, disappointed, and lonely because it was not something I could share with anybody, least of all, with my mother.

I think Dario must have liked the experience because he wanted to go to 'El Su' all the time and practice different positions and different types of sex. For me everything he suggested was revolting and a torture!

I liked Dario as a pal to hang around, but I hated his love making, his advances, and his sexual experiments. I tried to avoid any conversation that would lead to a possible engagement, as I was not sure I loved him enough to stay with him for the rest of my life.

Nevertheless, he gave me a gold ring with some precious stone one night and he told me with that ring he promised to be mine for the rest of his life. I was appalled, to say the least!

Besides, I could not help fantasizing what making love would have been like with someone else, like with Manuel, for example.

One day we were at his place alone and Dario wanted to have sex. I was dismayed; one of his parents could come in at any minute. But he insisted and insisted. He put a condom on, and he started to take my clothes off and kiss me. When he was finished, he went to the bathroom to wash but he must have failed to flush the toilet after dropping his condom in it.

His parents returned to their home not long after and his father must have found the condom in the toilet bowl, because he got serious and gave a lecture to us both. I felt belittled, ashamed, and cheap, as if I had committed a grave crime. From then on, my relationship with Dario's parents became cold and uncomfortable and I tried to avoid visiting them altogether.

I had tried and tried to enjoy our sexual encounters, at least a bit, but somehow, I always found an excuse not to give myself entirely to the task. It was always like a duty rather than enjoyment. I felt trapped, cornered, and irresponsible, with no ability to deal with the situation. I used to daydream Dario would disappear one day. And one day, miraculously, he did!

When Dario turned 20, he had to enroll for his compulsory military service. His parents had some connections; therefore, he was sure he was going to be given a cushy role close by, when he was recruited if he was ever recruited.

The day came when he had to present himself to the authorities at the military headquarters. His parents were teasing him and joking with him, just the day before, that he was going to be sent away to Bahia Blanca, or better still to Antarctica. His parents' connections had assured, Dario said to me, he was going to be stationed in Buenos Aires, probably in one of our national government ministries.

However, Dario was supposed to be enlisted one Monday and nobody heard from him anymore for a month. After many enquiries and pleas, his parents discovered he had been sent to Combunco in Patagonia, 1144 kilometers away from Buenos Aires.

My dream had come true! I felt as free as a dove and in heaven!

Dario was to do his full military training for three months and then he was to be transferred to one of the offices in the Combunco barracks.

After five months, I got a letter in the mail from him, but to my disappointment it had been typed and addressed to his parents. My letter was only a carbon copy of the original and it was almost unreadable.

After six months, Dario was allowed to visit his family just for the weekend, and I got an unexpected phone call from him inviting me to go to 'El Su', which I rejected absolutely. I told him we had very different priorities. If I was longing to see him, it was to tell him about my work successes and the new and many friendships and connections I had made during his absence.

Nevertheless, we still met briefly that weekend. It felt like being with a stranger, sad, and disappointed. Although my lips uttered that I was sad he was going so far away, my heart rejoiced that he was not going to be around for another six months.

Around this time, I became close to my cousin Amadeo. He had found another job closer to mine and we usually met for lunch, or we travelled back home together after work.

We both loved reminiscing, how we played when we were children, sometimes even sleeping in the same bed and sharing meals at his home or mine. Many times, I would go to his home and my Aunty Piruja would have bought my favorite Mar del Plata cheese with fresh bread for our 'merienda', then Amadeo would accompany me to my home which was about one and a half kilometers by foot.

We talked about anything and everything without reservations. 'What do you think about God? What are your plans for the future? What book are your reading? Arthur Miller? Leo Tolstoy? Henry Hemingway? John Steinbeck? The Talmud? The Koran? The Bible? Martin Fierro? Or Nietzsche? Hebbel? Do you like the ideas of Karl Max? John Kennedy? Juan Peron? Fidel Castro? El Che? Adolf Hitler? What songs do you like? What do you think of the Beatles? And Joan Baez? Elvis Presley? Nicolai Rimsky-Korsakov's Flight of the Bumblebee? Vivaldi? Albeniz? Georges Bizet? Manuel de Falla? And folk songs? ¿Los Fronterizos? ¿Tango? Carlos Gardel? What do you think of the Military Junta? What are your aspirations and desires? Would you like to travel overseas? See the world? What would life be away from Argentina?

We felt comfortable with each other, and we found out we could talk about anything and shared our inner thoughts without any reservations.

'Do you read the Buenos Aires Herald? Have you seen the jobs being offered at the United Nations?' Amadeo said.

'I am going to apply,' I replied, 'I think I have a chance'.

'There is this man called Silo', Amadeo said, 'I think he is a new philosopher talking about a new era in politics, society, psychology, and spirituality. He is going to give a speech in the Andes, do you want to come?'

'Hmm… Not sure my parents will approve. Hmm'

'…Come on… Let's go! It will be fun!'

Then there was this land my parents and his parents had bought in Mar de Ajo, on the Atlantic Coast. He wanted to go and see for himself how beautiful our seaside villages were in summer.

'Let's go by bus and take a tent and erect it on our land'.

'Yes, and we can take sleeping bags and lots of mosquito repellant'.

'And we can make a fire and we can cook our own meals, and bathe in the sea'.

'And go dancing at night.'

'And you got the most beautiful colour eyes I have ever seen, the colour of the sky when it is a sunny day.' 'And you are the nicest girl I have ever encountered, and I want to be with you forever'. 'And I love this song, *Hey Jude*, let's make it our song'. 'And… I love you! You are mi vida, mi amor, mi cielo… my soulmate.'

We were in love, and we could not keep our eyes looking at each other like children, nor could we get our hands and lips from each other. And yes, under the stars, below a makeshift tent planted in paradise, we made love, becoming one and swore to each other never to be away from each other. We never wanted these weeks to finish, ever!

But suddenly, we were back to reality! We both had work commitments and our families might be worried about us. So, we gathered our things and took the bus back to Buenos Aires. Again, even in public, we could not keep our eyes or hands from each other. We were so happy and in love and the next three months were the happiest days of my life.

Amadeo and I were inseparable every minute we were free from work. One day we were in the banks of the River Plate, sunbaking and looking into each other's eyes, when I heard a voice.

'Carmela, what are you doing here?' It was Dario's sister and her boyfriend. I introduced Amadeo as my cousin and felt very embarrassed as if someone had caught me robbing a bank. I had to come clean with Dario and fast!

That very night I wrote to Dario, telling him I wanted to break up our relationship because I was in love with someone else.

I never saw Dario or his family again. When he came back to Buenos Aires, he rang my mother to make sure I was not there. He wanted to exchange some things we still had, mainly music sheets, my fake engagement ring and other jewellery he had given to me over the years. I never saw him or heard from him again.

Amadeo gave me an amber antique brooch for St Valentine's Day and asked me to marry him, which I accepted without even thinking. I was in love, and I longed to be with him forever! We went to see some apartments to rent in the city, and I still remember today the joy I felt going up the stairs to inspect this tiny flat near Congreso. We were indeed on cloud nine and nothing mattered more than our love for each other and the sweet dreams we had for our future!

Amadeo told me that day, time and time again, that he loved me so much, he did not know how he was going to cope separating for a few hours during the day when we had to go to work once we were married. We spoke about perhaps travelling to another country to explore other horizons and possibilities. Finally, we also discussed informing our parents soon of our plans of being together and the joy of having our own children one day. We never thought about incest at that time. We already had blood cousins happily married to each other in our own family and with healthy children.

After that happy day, Amadeo suddenly disappeared. I was perplexed! I never heard from him for many months. I rang his home, but my Aunty did not know where he was. She told me he had been busy planning a trip to Brazil with his company.

I went to his work and waited hours for him to come out without success. I asked friends but nobody had seen or heard from him. I was dismayed and shattered. I visited his home many times and one day he was there, but he avoided me altogether and left abruptly.

Finally, I got an envelope in the mail from him. Inside there was a note with the words 'I do not want to see you ever again, please leave me alone'.

To top it all, my period was now considerably delayed. I had a look at a specialist doctor advertisement in the *Buenos Aires Herald*—a gynaecologist and I made an appointment. I was so sad, young, inexperienced, and scared… The doctor practised in a small apartment in the city. He examined me, put something cold and rough in my vagina and told me to go home to rest, without any explanation. That same night, I started to bleed as normal. I felt shattered. I was never to know whether the delay in my period was caused by my extreme misery and anxiety, or whether I had killed our baby. I should have asked the doctor many questions, but I had been unable to speak at all as I felt frightened and, in a daze, and I had to return home straight after the consultation.

The following Monday I received another letter, this time from the United Nations headquarters to ask me to go for an interview regarding the job I had applied for. The interview consisted of a series of psychometric and general knowledge tests in both English and Spanish, followed by a long interview in front of a panel of five bilingual men.

I was told at the interview I would get an offer if I was selected. A week later I got that offer to work as a bilingual officer for the United Nations in New York. I was to get free accommodation; a fantastic salary paid in US currency, excellent working conditions and free travel from the USA to Buenos Aires during my holidays once a year to visit my family. They would also pay for me to further my studies in a related field of my interest.

My heart was completely broken about my brief intense relationship with Amadeo and his sudden indifference, but the news about my future job was encouraging and exciting and indeed, it gave me some hope. It would also be the break I had been dreaming of. I could not wait to tell my parents.

To my shock, I was to learn my mother did not approve of my plans. She argued I was only just 18 and a good 'Catholic' girl, therefore, she would never let me go away from home unless I got married one day, as a good decent daughter deserved. I could not understand her; my parents had never gone to church except for the odd baptism or wedding and the work proposal I had was for a decent job… As it happened, I would not be able to get a passport without their consent to travel anyway until I turned 22, when you became an adult in Argentina! Therefore, feeling quite broken, I had to reject the offer.

I was destroyed but continued to work and concentrate in my job and my students, which were my sole consolation. I had not told any of my friends about my brief encounter with Amadeo, because at the time of the breakup we wanted to tell our families first, and I was also too upset to tell them about my job offer now which was unquestionably truncated.

Manuel noticed I was miserable and asked me what had happened to me, but I did not have the guts to confide in him either. He invited me to a rugby game where he was playing, to go out with his parents and to the movies to cheer me up.

He also told me he wished he could invite me to have a drink and a dance in one of the city nightclubs or discotheques where he used to go, but unfortunately at 18 I was still underage, therefore not allowed to enter any of these venues.

Not long after, I applied for another bilingual job at a very large American car company, and I was successful. This company was not situated in the city, but near the Autodromo of Buenos Aires, and luckily it involved a safer and more peaceful bus trip for me.

Therefore, my parents could not object to the change. My role was to be the executive and P.A. to the Financial Controller and the company executives Tax Consultant.

I was to train further for this job, which required strict confidentiality, lots of common sense, and impeccable manners including table etiquette, which I was to be trained for. My wardrobe was also to be changed to a smart casual style in the office and cocktail dresses and gowns with suitable accessories for formal occasions.

My salary was again to be raised exponentially and although so young, I was to get about four times the money my father was currently earning for the whole family. I was also to be enrolled in a local Tax Law course with the main purpose of learning how to legally avoid Argentinian taxes!

My new boss was African American who had moved to Buenos Aires with his family. He could not speak any Spanish but was very smart and efficient at his job and I started to admire him.

Soon, I had to organise and attend to appointments with him and on his behalf meet with businesspeople and bank executives in Argentina. I also had to organise dealings for other executives in the company including the General Manager and his secretary, Theresa.

Theresa was Irish, kind and about 55 years of age. She and the rest of the executives eventually became my only friends in the large company, as I was not allowed to mix with the rest of the staff. We all met at lunchtime at the company exclusive bistro, where we were served delicious, first-class foods, drinks and we also socialised amongst ourselves in English.

I soon learnt the occupational language of businessmen as well as the art of eating with the correct piece of cutlery. This art would include eating my fruit with knife and fork! Along with my new sophisticated clothes, I thought I was being transformed into a real lady and I just went along with it.

My father's work consisted of the re-upholstering of expensive cars with fine leather, but with the advent of car seat covers, his job was becoming obsolete and too expensive for his clients. His workload decreased dramatically, and his earnings were not enough to keep our family, therefore, he decided to purchase a private-school bus with the school route to supplement his earnings.

My father's bus business did well during the school year but there were three months of school holidays during summer, when there was no work. Therefore, he had no income. He tried to increase his income using the bus on short trips taking people to football matches on Sundays and any other private jobs he could find driving the bus. The bus was old and he and my Godfather 'El Padrino' were always repairing it. My father's efforts must have worked somehow, because we always had enough food at our table, but I suspected my parents were struggling to pay our other bills.

My father had extended our family home over the years and built two commercial spaces at the front of our house, which he rented out. His tenants had closed down and left due to the financial crisis in our country.

I overheard my parents discussing ways to pay the electricity bill, and even whether my mum would have a chance to find some work. I believed their beloved yearly holidays to the coast had to be cancelled as well. Our family was going through serious financial difficulties. I offered to give them some regular cash, but they refused.

Then I had an idea to solve the money difficulties in the family without hurting my parents' feelings and keep everybody happy. It would be good for me to start a new project, to occupy my mind and make my heart lighter from the profound pain I felt. It would also allow me to recover some self-confidence.

I presented two proposals to my dad; either he accepted some of my monthly salary, or with some of my savings I could help the family set up a general business in one of the empty shops at the front of the house. Reluctantly, my father chose the latter.

My vacation was coming up so I would have some free time for the project. Whatever I learnt from my short period at university helped with this. The family all got involved: my dad, my mum and my two sisters. We did the fit-out ourselves and personally negotiated the purchase of the merchandise directly from the wholesalers in the city.

We also rang or visited other suppliers and negotiated with them to leave their rather expensive merchandise with us: expensive toys, and children's games and equipment, on some sort of franchise scheme. The idea was that these expensive goods were only to be paid for once they were sold. This allowed us to have for sale such merchandise we had only dreamt of. Unsold items were to be returned, no questions asked.

We launched our business about a month before Christmas, New Year, and the Fiesta of the Three Kings on 6th January.

We also asked some of my neighbourhood friends if they were prepared to dress as Santa Claus and the Three Kings and they all were keen and amused. We decorated the patio at the back of the shop with themes of the season and placed my friends there. We invited our customers to visit our shop, and then go to see Santa and the Three Kings through the back door.

Every child who visited the site was given a lolly or a small balloon. As our mark-up had been reduced because there was no rent to be paid, we were able to offer competitive prices for our merchandise.

I was able to set up a simple accounting system for the business and my parents were more than happy with the results.

The whole exercise was a tremendous success for Christmas, New Year and for the Fiesta of the Three Kings! The shop was swamped with customers, and we had to employ extra people to be able to cope with the sales. My Aunties Rosita and Piruja came down to make sure people did not steal from the shelves. The whole suburb and other neighbouring suburbs were talking about our business. We even had an article of our success in the local papers with photos of our Santa Claus and the Three Kings in the back patio.

The business was a crucial achievement for me because it gave me much confidence for my future life. It also became the main source of our family income for many years to come.

After a few months, I did not have to contribute to the family coffers anymore, and I continued to save substantially. I was also able to financially help not just Manuel but other impoverished friends with different projects that really made a difference in their lives.

However, now I realized that with my generosity I could have lost a lot of money. I was young, very naïve and I did not see they could have easily tricked me. But in some way, I am glad I did trust them, especially Manuel, as my money-lending event cemented our friendship for the rest of our lives. As for the other friends I lent money to without any interest, they all returned what they had borrowed, some sooner, and others later.

Around that time, I saw an advertisement in the *Buenos Aires Herald* from the Australian Embassy asking for suitable people to migrate to one of the main cities, Sydney. I made some enquiries and found out I would qualify, so I applied and was successful. After a few medical checks, I got my permanent visa. This visa was attached to the condition I would get free travel and settlement support in exchange for remaining in Australia for at least two years.

In those days in Argentina, you became an adult at 22 years of age, but I was only 19 and the Australian visa would only be valid for one year. Again, my parents would not sign their consent for my passport so that I could travel. I thought I would have to again ditch this project too.

Then I learnt from one of my friends in the neighbourhood, Pietro, that both he and his brother, Giuseppe, had also been successful in obtaining a permanent visa to migrate to Australia.

I convinced my family to meet their family and talk about the brothers' travelling plans. It was a great opportunity for young people surely! I already knew Pietro.

Pietro was our friend along with other young men and women in the neighbourhood. However, all I knew about him was that he loved to come to our home parties, and he danced and danced like me. Neither any of my girlfriends nor I had ever heard of his youngest brother, Giuseppe, before though.

Giuseppe was blond with curly hair, different to dark Pietro. Giuseppe was a shy and sweet boy with a gentle nature. He was the youngest of five brothers who had migrated from Italy with his widowed mother and young uncle many years ago.

His uncle and eldest brother had an increasingly progressive plumbing business and all the other brothers worked for the family company. Giuseppe, being one of the youngest brothers, had been sent to high school and was well educated. He certainly seemed very mature, trustworthy, and much older than his 23 years.

After much coercing, my parents agreed to finally meet the brothers' whole family at home for an 'asado' (Argentinian BBQ). The family, especially his mother was happy for the younger brothers to migrate to Australia, because they recognised this might represent a brighter future for them. But my parents insisted I was too young to travel on my own, I was a decent female, she insisted, and I did not need a brighter future in Australia because I already had that in Argentina.

Then, quite by surprise, a miracle occurred: the coming-of-age law changed in Argentina from 22 to 21 years of age. I was already 20 by then and it would be only a matter of less than 12 months before I could finally decide my destiny without my parent's legal consent.

Under this pressure, my parents finally changed their mind, and reluctantly gave in and signed my passport application papers. I honestly believed that somehow Giuseppe, with his pleasant yet serious character had some positive influence in their decision. He promised my parents to keep an eye on me.

My boss tried to convince me not to leave the job. The company offered to promote me to the position of Chief Tax Officer in the company Latin America branch with a huge pay increase and the use of one of their luxury cars. There were other promotions in their sister company in Brazil on the cards too.

My boss, whose opinions I respected a lot, commented Australia would one day be taken over by China, either financially or by force. I thought it was odd, as Asian people were not allowed freely in Australia at the time because of the White Australia Policy.

All offers for me to stay in Argentina were coming too late. I had already made up my mind. I wanted to leave Argentina, maybe then I would finally forget about Amadeo and our brief encounter...

We had a huge farewell party where all our friends, my beloved Theresa, and some of my bosses, my whole extended family, Pietro and Giuseppe's family were invited. Amadeo's parents and sister came along with other relatives, but Amadeo, although invited, did not turn up.

I tried to see Amadeo one last time, to tell him I was going far away and for at least two years. I wanted to say my heart was broken because of him, I would never be able to love again, I wanted to be with him forever, I missed him so much that my eyes were tired of crying in the dark at night, he should tell me what had happened, or it would be too late, please, please, please…

But he was evasive, and when I finally caught him on the phone, he coldly said he was busy, he could not see me, and he certainly wished me good luck in Australia.

Chapter 3

MARRIAGE 1—AUSTRALIAN BEGINNINGS

'Life is really simple, but we insist on making it complicated.
(Confucius)

Part 1 - Giuseppe

I am writing this for Emanuel answering his request. I hope it is OK and clear enough for you, and if not, you could send it back to me, Emanuel, and I will try to amend it accordingly.

My life as I have been told and faintly remember, commenced when I was barely four years old, in a merchant ship, *The North King,* where we travelled from Genoa or Génova in Italy to Buenos Aires in Argentina with my mother Tonia, my uncle Antonino, my four brothers and myself. We had lived in Messina, Italy, where I was born. My uncle, although only 24 years old, had promised my father he would look after us should he not be around.

I vaguely remember that in Sicily, we lived in a large home in the country, but my father was not a peasant like everybody else in the community. My father was an important colonel in the army. We had a photo of him in his full uniform, in a silver frame, which I always admired. I thought he must have been brave fighting for the Axis Alliance against the Allied forces in World War II.

However, after Mussolini fell, I heard my father joined a group of

once the baby was born as my mother-in-law had agreed to take care of him or her.

The house was also progressing rapidly then under the shrewd supervision of Carmela. Then one Sunday, whilst we were watching TV, Carmela's feet and hands became remarkably swollen.

She had already experienced some negative remarks the last couple of times she had visited her gynaecologist: 'You have put on too much weight, your blood pressure is up, your urine test is worrying, I cannot find the baby's heartbeat easily…' Her doctor had said… Now for the first time, I realized I had never yet seen a belly so huge in a pregnant woman. Carmela was obviously distressed and asked us to be taken to the nearest hospital, which I did.

Her gynaecologist was called and after a thorough examination, she was discharged with an X-ray referral for the next day. Carmela had the X-Ray taken first thing in the morning and then insisted she was going to work, but I noticed she could barely sit behind the wheel even after adjusting the seats back to the maximum.

The X-Ray would be with her gynaecologist in the afternoon when she could ring for her results. I got the news from my mother-in-law when I returned from work: Carmela was hospitalised, she needed to have complete rest and be sedated to keep the babies as long as possible inside her, yes, babies in the plural, yes, we were having twins.

The news of my impending fatherhood added to my lack of confidence and whatever I had to do, threw me completely out of balance. There were too many problems at our building site to attend to, my customers started to become slack with their payments, I could not cope with the demands of study and work, some of my tools were stolen from my truck because I forgot to lock the toolbox, and now two babies were coming instead of one.

My world had collapsed without Carmela at hand and now I had the prospect of these babies, whom I had not really wished to have, complicating my life.

I guess the rest of my story is simple. From then on, all my dreams for a happy married life with Carmela collapsed drastically, forever.

---

[2] Translation: You are the most beautiful thing in my life, although I could not say it, although I could not say it. Tengo el Corazón Contento - Palito Ortega (1968)

[3] Translation: 'If you are not with me, I am not happy, I miss you at night, I miss you during the day'—[Corazon Contento—Palito Ortega (1968)]

[4] Translation: 'I would like you to know, that I never loved like this, that my life started when I first met you' [Corazon content- Palito Ortega (1968)]

[5] Translation: 'You are like the sun in the morning, that enters through by window, that enters through my window. You give joy to my life, you are my dreams at night, you are my light during the day' [Corazon Contento. Palito Ortega (1968)]

[6] 'My heart is happy, my heart is so happy from the moment you came into my life. I would like you to know, that I never loved like this, that my life started when I first met you' [Corazon Contento. Palito Ortega (1968)]

[7] 'I thank life and I ask God that you will always be with me, that I never loved like this, that my life starts when I first met you.' [Corazón Contento, Palito Ortega (1968)]

Chapter 4

THE FAMILY GROWING

'A woman is like a tea bag—you cannot tell how strong she is until you put her in hot water.'
(Eleanor Roosevelt)

'Humpty Dumpty sat on a wall,
Humpty Dumpty had a great fall;
All the king's horses and all the king's men
Couldn't put Humpty together again.'
(Mother Goose)

Part 1 - Carmela Junior

Here it is Emanuel, another phase of my story. Congratulations on your school accolades! I believe you are doing some advanced science course at Uni whilst still at school!

I have followed your instructions here and I resumed my story at the birth of my first twins. I have tried to be as honest as I could with my narrative. I realise now as you are growing up, you would be able to understand somehow more deeply the ins and outs of life.

I never quite liked playing with dolls when I was a child. However, I always secretly dreamt of having a family. Whenever I thought of children, my heart cringed at the thought of my deep love for Amadeo and our short-lived plans. However, at 28, I had enough of travelling and needed something more, I wanted a family. I had had enough trouble trying to fall pregnant, but after much temperature taking and experimental suggestions, like fully experimenting in several positions with semen discharged outside my vagina, it finally worked, and I was pregnant.

Now at last, I was so close to holding my baby. I felt sure this baby would fulfil my life completely. I had spent all my spare time preparing the baby's basket and sewing some newborn clothes. I did not know the sex of my baby, so I decided everything for him or her should be pale yellow.

My mother had promised she would take care of the baby whilst I was at work. I had also applied to be admitted to formal higher studies at last, and I had just been informed I had passed the English and admissions tests so, certainly, I would get a place this summer at the University of Sydney to study, not my beloved Medicine, but perhaps, my second choice would be viable, which was Economics.

However, I had not been feeling very well lately. My stomach was so big I could hardly sit or walk. I had felt the baby moving before, but lately it had hardly moved, and when it did, my whole belly would tremble with kicks everywhere. My doctor said I was too large for 33 weeks, and I had probably made a mistake with the dates.

He had also asked me to stop work and not to eat too much spaghetti as my weight was ballooning. I thought he did not believe me when I said to him that I only had one week to go at work before my holidays and I had not been eating much at all because I had no appetite and felt always bloated.

Again, my gynaecologist asked me to try to rest as much as possible and to avoid driving the car. If my feet would swell more, I was to go straight to the hospital and request for him to come immediately to give me a check-up.

On that Sunday, I had been resting in front of the TV feeling very miserable the whole weekend, when my mother noticed not only my feet had swollen but also my face, my arms, my hands, my legs! She asked Giuseppe to take me to the hospital for a check-up.

'Dr Hyde is not here today, but Dr. Simpson will see you as soon as he finishes his rounds', the nurse said.

We waited and waited, and finally Dr Simpson came. He had a listen to my tummy and said I had to have an X-Ray the following day, there was definitely something odd with my pregnancy, I had to go home now. He also advised me to ring Dr Hyde the following afternoon for the results of the X-Rays.

The next morning and still very swollen, when everybody in the family departed for work, I went to have my X-Rays done. As I was feeling a bit better, I decided to drive to work so I could advise my boss of my predicament. He was not amused with my news of leaving earlier as there was a lot of work to do, so I decided to stay for the day.

In the afternoon, I rang Dr Hyde for my results. He asked me to sit down and then gave me the news. I was carrying twins and I had to go immediately to the hospital for rest to avoid delivering them before their due time.

My boss, who had had experience with twins himself, convinced me I should resign. I only had three weeks holidays pending, and my mother would die if she had to look after two babies herself at her age.

I resigned from my beloved job there and then, and drove to the hospital, where I was admitted straight away.

All I remember about these times is I was prescribed Valium and I was constantly asleep or in a daze, only to be woken up and sat up for my meals, which I could not eat, despite the now insistence of the nurses 'to fatten up the babies'.

I do not know how many days I spent like this, but I do know the doctor did not want the babies to be born until at least Christmas.

However, early in the morning on the 6th of December I started having strong labour pains, so the nurses wheeled me to the delivery room. All I can remember is the ceiling full of bright lights. Although

I was half doped, I can still hear today the noise of the alarms ringing and dozens of young doctors and nurses galloping into the room. It must have been a good show to them, as in less than half an hour my first son, Christopher was born with hardly any assistance. Within seven more minutes, my only daughter Cassandra was also born, but this time, because she was a breech baby, the doctor in charge, I was informed, had to cut me open so he could take her out safely.

The babies were premature, but they were healthy and after a day or two in their humidicribs they were allowed to stay in the nursery like any other babies. Giuseppe came with a bunch of flowers, but he was shy and would not look at the babies much, let alone hold them.

My parents were thrilled and proud with the safe arrival of their first grandchildren. Many friends and even our neighbours came to have a look at the new twins and gave us lots of presents.

As for myself, I could not think straight. All I could think was I had to take care of them and learn how to breastfeed them both at once, which was quite a job.

However, when everybody went away and alone, I looked at them, I could not see any resemblance to Giuseppe or me, they were fair and seemed to have clear blue eyes. In those early days, I many times wondered whether they had swapped my babies with another mother's babies by mistake.

Christopher, Cassandra, and I left the hospital and went back home to my parents' flat. The house that was supposed to be finished by now was still an unfinished and complicated project. Giuseppe's tools had been stolen and he had not done much work. Therefore, we were extremely short of cash. Besides, without my help, his building course had become too much for him and he had dropped it, never to be picked up again.

Christopher cried all day and all night and sometimes he would wake up Cassandra. They both cried and cried and cried at night, waking everybody up... My parents and Giuseppe had to go to work but, they could not have a decent sleep in the tiny flat and it seemed to me they were counting the hours to go to work and have some peace.

I was left alone with these creatures, who then sucked my body alive all day. I wanted a baby to hold and to love, but I did not have arms to hold them both long enough to start loving them properly.

After a few weeks, I forgot whom I had fed, or changed nappies or tried to settle. I decided to start a book where I religiously wrote what I did to each of them during the day and night. However, and to tell the truth, I could not ascertain how accurate my notes were, especially when I felt half sleep all the time.

Giuseppe and my parents would come home from work and found me, madly ungroomed and still in my pyjamas. I had not prepared any dinner, nor had I cleaned any dishes or washed any clothes.

My doctor had suggested to me not to worry about the housework or cooking, but the dirty clothes were piling up, especially the terry cotton nappies and baby clothes. They needed to be routinely soaked in a big bucket, then washed, dried and folded. It was a dreadful task to accomplish every day.

Despite all my efforts to play the good mother, little Chris did not seem to have put any weight on and looked pale, he was always vomiting and kept whinging non-stop.

After another week, I took the two bundles of joy to the Baby Health Care Centre nearby who referred me to the children hospital.

We were all admitted to the babies' ward where Chris was weighed and examined. They asked me to feed him, but by then he was too weak to respond. He was then fed with a bottle, which was easier for him to suck, but as soon as he had taken some of the milk, it all came out flying out.

Chris' skin was now a greyish colour and he had lost so much weight, not that he had much to lose anyway. He had been the smallest of the twins since birth with 4.8 pounds... I did not need to be told he was dying.

The specialist told me he needed an operation urgently to save his life. A valve in his stomach was not functioning and the milk could not go through.

Before the operation, he needed to be hydrated though. His sister was fine and thriving, but she needed to be cared for. Before that day and when the operation was over, Chris would become the first premature baby to have microsurgery to correct pyloric stenosis in Sydney. He was only five weeks old and weighed less than two kilograms. I had only little Cassandra to cry with, and yes, I suddenly felt God with me again. I asked Him to save him, and I promised again I would follow Him all the days of my life.

The operation was a success and now both twins started to thrive, I finally settled into being a mother and my children became the special joy of my days. The babies still cried at night for no reason, until I discovered they wanted to be in the same cot together, cuddling each other.

My health started to deteriorate though, I was told I needed to visit a cardiologist as I had a heart murmur and I also had serious back pain, for which I got a medical body corset just made for me to wear and get on with my life.

I lived day by day without any time for myself, yet I was still happy if the babies were happy. Then I was asked to look after my youngest sister's baby, Martin, who was only a month younger than the twins. He was a hungry baby, so when he cried and his mother's expressed bottle had finished, I had no choice other than breastfeed him also.

Every afternoon, if the weather allowed it, I would pick the three babies up in my arms, go down the three flights of stairs to the ground floor and shuffle them in the twin pram stored under the stairs to take them to the nearby park where we spent the afternoon together playing.

The routine got more complicated when they started to be mobile, and I had to tie them up together in the pram. However, by then I was able to talk to them and they seemed to understand that I only wanted to keep them safe.

Although the house seemed to be forever untidy, I enjoyed this period of my life enormously.

I noted the twins' milestones in my book and compared them with those in the baby books. They always seemed to reach their milestones way before their due times in the literature as they were alert, tiny, but strong and wanted to be always entertained.

They were only six months when I got them walkers, and once they got the knack of it, they started walking first with the walkers but soon by themselves, holding onto anything they could grasp in my parents' unit.

I had tied down all the cabinet doors with elastic to keep the contents out of their reach. However, the twins with their cousin pal Martin would crawl to the kitchen and the boys would pull the elastic off the cabinets, whilst Cassandra would get into the cabinets to take all the pots and pans out. Once all the kitchen metal containers were out, they formed a music band, noisily tapping and hitting the pots and lids around the place.

By nine months the twins were walking unassisted and discovering what was inside all our other cabinets. They both also loved to be read books to and to be sang to, but Chris was interested in the sound of the letters and numbers which I showed them in flashcards, and he wanted me to read them repeatedly.

Soon, I also noticed that Chris talked enough to make himself and her sister understood. He was just over one year old when he started sound-reading big signs like *Coca Cola* or street signs like *STOP* and recognising street numbers.

Giuseppe continued to have problems getting paid for his plumbing services on time and our house's progress had been slow and problematic. Finally, by the twins' first birthday, we were ready to move in, but we were also in deep financial trouble. I had tried to do some work as an interpreter on the phone, but the calls were far between. I needed to get full time work and fast.

I had tried a child carer already when I got some temporary work through the local paper, but I was not happy with the arrangement because I could not fully trust her with my precious babies.

My youngest sister Flor and brother-in-law with young Martin were also having troubles paying their rent. The new house had a large self-contained flat downstairs with enough space to accommodate another family. I asked them whether they would like to move in with us, so that my sister could look after the young twins as well as their own son whilst I went back to work full time.

They accepted our offer straight away and I was lucky to find a job assisting the accountant of a large company in the city. The job and the pay were good, but my commute was one hour travelling by train and bus, so by the time I got home, it was already dark. The arrangement was I would do the cooking for us all, plus the babies' washing. This was fair. It was not easy for my sister to deal with three active toddlers and this arrangement allowed her to have a rest in the evening from the long day. But cooking dinner plus the daily washing, including soaking all the dirty cloth nappies, was exhausting, considering I had been working all day.

Besides, I still had to deal with Giuseppe's bad debtors and our bills, and by the time I could relax, I was drained, and I had no time for anything but to go to sleep.

My sister was great with the kids, considering her young age, but the toddlers were naughty and very active. They learnt to go up and down the stairs following each other and once they managed to lock Flor out on the upstairs balcony and she could not go back inside, getting more desperate by the minute, whilst the little ones had the run of the house until Giuseppe came back from work.

The arrangement lasted nine months and it was good for both families financially, because we were able to pay our credit cards and other debts and my sister, and her family had saved enough deposit to buy a small apartment. I had also been able to save a bit of money to purchase myself a small car to be able to move around easier.

Besides, once we settled and fixed all the building problems arising from Giuseppe's incompetence as a builder, the house was comfortable; except it had an atrocious access to the street because the driveway had not been approved by the Council yet. We basically had to climb a mountain to reach the car or any form of transport. This also made it difficult for any doctors or visitors to come to the house.

Unfortunately, since we moved into the new house, the twins were forever sick. The property was situated in the midst of a large national park, and I suspected the environment was not healthy for them. It took a bit of time and effort dragging the children to many visits and to different doctors until we were told the children were allergic to the native plants and the humidity of the area.

By then, I realized Giuseppe was not cut out to be a businessman and I suggested to him he should look for a permanent job, which he did with my help and my old friends at the airline company.

I also applied successfully to become an official freelance translator and interpreter. This gave me the opportunity to work from home on the phone or pick and choose the onsite jobs I could take; but that only happened when and if I was able to find a suitable carer for the twins.

I still desperately wanted to feel what it would be like to hold just the one baby, which I had always associated with real motherhood, and I had so many times visualised motherhood like this in dreams after my brief encounter with Amadeo. I pleaded with Giuseppe to retry our old methods to have another baby. He was a bit reluctant at first, but then he agreed.

We had already learnt what to do to make my pregnancy happen and with our renewed experimental strategies in the bedroom, in less than two months, I was pregnant again. At 5 weeks and thanks to ultrasound technology this time, I was informed I was having twins again.

The pregnancy was uncomplicated this time and Johny and Jack were born at full term healthy, but as soon as I got them home, they contracted infantile asthma, and again I was told it was from allergy to wattle and other native plants in the area.

Now I had four sick children, usually with bronchitis every second week. Many times, I thanked God for my little car that would transport me to the hospital in the middle of the night with one, two, three or four crying children burning with temperature.

As for our life as a couple, there was no time to think of love or socialising. I was still young and yearned to have some adult and meaningful conversation sometimes.

My birthday was coming up and I got enthusiastic about inviting some old friends for dinner. I had organised to cook the most delicious 'octopus in their own ink' and paella followed by my favourite flan con crema to celebrate the occasion.

I had invited two couples to share our dinner and listen to some music. It had been a lovely summer's day and I had hoped I could settle the children to sleep by the time our guests arrived.

Christopher had been unhappy and demanding but by the late afternoon, he started complaining of an earache. Hence, although we could not afford it, being the weekend, I started calling house doctors to check up on him. Finally, one accepted to climb down the hill to our house.

By the time our guests arrived, I was holding Christopher trying to soothe him. Not long after, the doctor arrived and gave Christopher a morphine injection for pain. He indicated he thought it was meningitis and I should go immediately to the hospital for further treatment.

I vaguely remember having the guests looking at us pathetically and departing swiftly, probably wondering where on earth their next meal would come from.

After exhausting tests, including a lumbar puncture, it was discovered Christopher did not have meningitis, but he had a bad ear infection, which would eventually burst and leave him exhausted and feeble.

Despite it all, I was slowly getting a good clientele in my small translating and interpreting business. I could not do much work, but it was steady enough to get us just out of trouble financially.

My days were overloaded, looking after four children aged under three years of age was demanding and I needed to be super organised to have some time to do my paid work.

Johny and Jack were a delight, always happy and amused with each other but I was worried about their heavy breathing, especially at night. Many times, I would bring them to our bed so we could all have some good quality sleep.

Christopher and Cassandra were not easy to deal with though. Christopher was always bored and wanted to be read to or be listened to when he read or solved hard puzzles or answered his never-ending questions. Cassandra was demanding too, she needed to be watched constantly as she climbed into anything, including the high kitchen cabinets.

One day in desperation, I gave Christopher an old, discarded watch and a set of small old tools. He spent hours pulling the watch to pieces and then assembling it again. To my surprise, the watch was then ticking after his 'operation', as he called it.

From then on, whenever Christopher was bored, I gave him anything old I could find in the house, like old lamps, their tricycles, and radios, then anything that needed actual repairs like our stereo, my exercise bike, the malfunctioning tape recorder and surely enough, he would repair them happily, effectively and without instructions; he even fixed our video and our old TV.

Cassandra would not leave him alone, and she would usually attempt to spoil whatever Christopher was working on, which he resented fiercely. She would win every fight arising from these confrontations if I did not intervene.

Luckily the other twins were easy to look after. They needed a good feed at the right time and a toy to be entertained with. They would have a good siesta in the afternoon, cuddling each other and at night, they would sleep all night, even when teething. They were the ideal children except for their heavy chest and wheezing noises despite their prescribed medication.

Around this time, I fully became aware my marriage was a joke. I dearly longed to go back to our old days, when Giuseppe and I could save a bit of money and travel to other countries or just go out somewhere. With four young children, I had no time to even think about anything but cooking, doing the huge washing including the never-ending nappy washing and folding, keeping the house reasonably clean, and attending to my children's needs.

Giuseppe would come from work and collapse in front of the TV. We had no conversation, let alone any intimacy. I was always nagging and grumpy when he was around and started to wonder what the reason was, that he was in my life. I needed to find a way out and fast!

Part 2 - Carmela Junior

What were my options? Perhaps life would have been easier in Argentina for us, I thought. Giuseppe had not seen his family for many years, so I suggested we could go and see them. Perhaps the change would bring about some spark in our lives.

We gathered our savings and bought the 6 airline tickets and travelled to Argentina. We stayed with Giuseppe's mother, and we visited her brothers and families and some of my aunties and cousins.

When I visited my Aunty Piruja hoping to see her son, to my dismay, Amadeo was not there. His mother told me he was in Spain on a work contract. She also said he had finished his training and he was getting a lot of interesting work in Argentina and overseas as a Graphic Designer. He had also tried married life with one of our old friends, but unfortunately it did not work out for him.

Giuseppe's mother accommodated us all in a shabby, discarded bedroom at the back of the house. Luckily, it was summer because I did not believe she had enough blankets for us all. We slept on a temporary bed and the kids were all on mats on the ill-repaired bedroom floor.

I observed that all my relatives and childhood friends, regardless of whether they could afford it or not, had home help: a maid, and/or a cook and a nanny. And they all had a good social life, be it going out for dinner, take outs or going to the movies or the theatre regularly.

However, I also noticed their standard of living was not as good as I would desire for my family: their electricity was restricted at certain times, they had constant blackouts, there was hardly any water in the pipes at different times of the day; you had to time your showers. The water issue also made my constant nappies and other washing a real nightmare as sometimes, in disgust, I had to use the same water several times.

But that was not all: the drains smelled, all their houses were badly maintained, essential appliances badly needed to be repaired, the streets were dirty and in bad condition, access to reasonable health professionals was very costly and to top it all, the schools and kinder gardens were shut because of rampant endemic infectious diseases such as hepatitis and lice.

I realized I could not live like that. I could not raise my children in those third world conditions. Besides, my relationship with Giuseppe, despite our socialising in Spanish, remained sour and meaningless. Therefore, I decided to return to Australia, to our old life, much earlier than expected.

When the older twins turned four, I realized they needed more contact with children of their own age, so I enrolled them at the local pre-school. I felt a bit uneasy because right up until then they had only communicated with us and our friends and family in Spanish. The recent trip to Argentina had cemented their Spanish speaking skills even more.

I realized the children did not know any English at all except for a few cartoons they watched on TV. The pre-school teacher ordered us to speak to them in English, which I strongly opposed.

I was right! Christopher and Cassandra did not seem to mind what language was to be used, they learnt English in no time and above all they were happy to play with other children at the local pre-school.

However, they continued to have respiratory tract and ear infections to the point that our family doctor recommended us to move out of the area. The area was beautiful with lots of native plants and native animals in the middle of the Royal National Park and by the Port Hacking River.

The children loved playing outside with the rocks and making friends with the small wallabies and blue lizards. However, although I now loved the house and its environment, we decided to sell it and get a house closer to my parents and away from the Australian bush.

It was around that time, when the younger twins were finally weaned from my breast, that my mind first and my body later started to wonder again what it would be like to have a normal marriage. A marriage where couples cuddled and in the privacy of their bedrooms had some intimacy where they could freely express their desires and fantasies.

The new house seemed to agree better with the children's health. However, the issue with Giuseppe was another matter...

By then Giuseppe had seen many doctors, specialists, psychiatrists, counsellors and even priests to solve his impotency problems. However, now he was seeing yet another Italian family doctor who had suggested to have some hormones and injections of testosterone and other male hormones. He was advised also to see a sexologist once a week. This new doctor also suggested I might also have sexual issues.

Suddenly, Giuseppe started to be more interested in sex. As for me, although I longed to be loved, I did not do much to reciprocate his advances. He was abrupt and wanted to penetrate me as soon as he had an erection, which would surely soon flop. Later, he would lock our bedroom door and demanded to be provided with his sex exercises given by his specialist, which actually repulsed me.

I was summoned to his sexologist who informed me that unless I cooperated, Giuseppe would have to find someone else for his therapy. I was shocked and although I tried to do some of the sex exercises, just the thought of going through with them, would make me nauseous.

The children might have picked up that I was not happy, as they started to have nightmares. Christopher would knock at our bedroom door and cry until we let him in our bed, which was a blessing for me, as the exercises had to stop.

Giuseppe became more unreliable in the house and with the children as well. He would not help at all with housekeeping and often he would forget to pick the children up from pre-school when I was doing the odd interpreting job.

I suddenly realized Giuseppe had changed from a sweet compliant husband into a hideous selfish monster. He started to threaten me with hiring a professional woman from the sexologist to do his revolting practices. The idea was abhorrent to me, so I decided if that was the case, he would have to leave the house, and our marriage was finished.

Giuseppe did not protest. He found a flat nearby, he prepared his suitcases with all his clothes and left without another word.

The older twins were at kindergarten attending the local Catholic primary school by then and we attended mass every Sunday. Therefore, after Giuseppe left, I went to speak to the local priest to seek advice about Christopher's nightmares.

Christopher had claimed he saw ghosts and shadows coming through the windows at night. It was disturbing and I thought maybe the priest could come to bless the house and scare the ghosts away. To my amazement and after I explained Giuseppe had left, the priest said to me I should find a way to get Giuseppe back. If I divorced my husband, I would not be able to take holy communion as I would be excommunicated from the church.

However, he would come to bless the house anyway, he promised. I waited and waited, but until I eventually left the house once it was sold many months later, no priest ever turned up to my house to bless it nor did I go back to mass ever again. I became cynical and disappointed with the Catholic church and its members.

As for Chris's ghosts, I discovered one day my brother-in-law Rolando was visiting my house without knocking at the door. Was he lingering outside, looking through the windows to see what I was doing? It could explain then Chris's sudden frights and his ghosts, and honestly, I was frightened too.

What should I do? I knew my younger sister had a good marriage and two young children after their rocky start. Should I warn her? Was her husband a peeping tom? I decided to firmly warn Rolando that I would certainly tell his wife next time he came around. He seemed to stop his nightly errands and after a while Christopher seemed to have stopped seeing his nightly visitors.

I had a few ladies who would look after the children occasionally, when I was offered a good interpreting job. I was gradually getting good and more clients from doctors, solicitors, the law courts, and many government departments.

One of these ladies was Viviana and her husband, Juan Jose, el Cuco for his friends and their two young children Adam and Eva. They were returning to Argentina because Viviana was too homesick and missed her family there.

However, Viviana told me el Cuco's mother, Sara had planned to come to Australia, and needed some translation and interpreting services to complete the purchase of some investment properties in Sydney.

I offered my services with generous discounts and, as I was on my own, I offered Sara accommodation for a small rent in my house until she had finished putting her affairs in order.

My parents had gone to Argentina again and Sara became a good friend and a substitute for my mother in those months leading up to my divorce from Giuseppe. I needed friendship because I was feeling vulnerable and guilty, as the sexologist had suggested I might be the real reason for our problems with sex and therefore, I had also contributed greatly to our marriage failure.

Sara reassured me it was not my fault at all, and she suggested I should find another relationship to forget my marriage and solve my doubts once and for all.

Giuseppe and I had to sell our family home, which had to be organised by me. We were to share equally the proceeds of the sale to purchase new, smaller homes in less expensive suburbs.

I soon realized with my 'casual interpreting jobs', I was not going to be able to work to sustain us all. Giuseppe was reluctant to offer any maintenance. Luckily, I found out there was a government allowance for mature age students who wished to improve their skills and go to university.

I had already done all the university entry tests in the past, before the first twins were born, so I applied to go to the University of NSW to do an Arts/Education Degree, which was the cheapest, and surprisingly I got accepted straight away.

I would have liked to enrol in Economics or my beloved Medicine, but the Bachelor of Arts Degree looked easier to do, especially as there were not many books that had to be purchased with my already stretched budget.

Around that time, I also started seeing Lucho, who was a mechanic and an old friend of el Cuco's. I met him when I was looking for a mechanic to fix my car. Lucho was a sweet talker and at that time I did not suspect that he must have talked to Sara about me, because he knew exactly where to push my buttons.

Lucho and I became intimate friends and with the help of Sara I was able to see him when the children had gone to bed. He proved to be a good lover and I thoroughly enjoyed his company. He also helped me to put my guilt of having any sexual problems to rest.

However, he was afraid of being seen together with me and he was always in a hurry to leave. And then, I discovered he was married. He told me his story, which I half believed—he had married only because he had to, to be able to get a permanent visa and stay in Australia. He also told me his marriage was arranged and he and his wife were not sleeping together and were waiting for the time required by the authorities to get a divorce. For the time being, I decided I would go along with his tale and lies.

Apart from the company and the help with looking after the children when I had interpreting jobs or wanted to go out, I learnt many things from Sara. She had been a successful real estate agent and auctioneer in Argentina and had an eye for purchasing the right property and making money. She would show me where good opportunities lay, and I would help her with the language to bring some of them to fruition for her benefit.

Sara also helped me in my relationship with Lucho so as not to feel as guilty about not being with the children some days or at night. She was very open minded, and she made me understand I should relax and enjoy my moments with him.

However, once I started to question Lucho more about his marital status and his 'other life', he started to visit or ask me out less and less, until finally he did not contact me anymore.

I helped Sara purchase a good town house in Sydney, which she also rented with my assistance. She also insisted she should sign a power of attorney for me to act on her behalf for any investments or business she may have in Australia when she returned to Argentina. I felt she was now a good friend, and I did not charge her for any of my services anymore.

Besides, she was looking after my four children for nothing if I was not able to get babysitting in time for unscheduled interpreting jobs, for which I was most grateful to her.

One day, Sara and I were watching a show on TV that showed an old lady living as a pauper alone in an old flat. When she died, her body was not discovered until many months after. When they cleaned her flat, they found lots of money from every possible currency: German, Swiss, English, Japanese, Chinese money, American dollars, and Australian dollars hidden under her bedroom floor. It was horrendous!

After the show, I noticed Sara was quietly crying and when I asked her what the matter was, she confessed the story of that lady could be her own story and she herself had money hidden in several houses in Argentina. I said to her that maybe God was showing her money was only good when we could enjoy it fully and with our loved ones. I noticed Sara kept quiet for many days, but I never knew if she intended to respond to my suggestion.

It took a few months to sell our marital home and a few more months for me to move to our new purchased home. Giuseppe had agreed to help me with a bit more money from the sale of our marital home to be able to go ahead with the transaction. Our new house was tiny and modest, but it was nicely wallpapered and laid out and although it was made of 'fibro', it had all the conveniences my children and I needed.

By then, Sara had to return to Argentina and to her other investments. The new home was much smaller than our previous home and with my income, I could not afford to send the children to private schools anymore. Thus, the older twins went to the local public school and the younger ones were driven by me to the university of NSW preschool, the *Winnie the Pooh childcare centre*. These children absolutely loved going there for the few hours when I had to attend my lectures.

Both Jack and Johny were placid, and content and I suspected the reason they looked forward to going to their preschool so much was they both loved food, and they were given plenty in the form of a hot lunches and accompanying sweets.

However, I realized later the preschool had a full teaching and social program and Johny and Jack were always keen to be with other children learning about new things and they seemed as smart as my older twins. As for their language, we only spoke Spanish at home, but it only took them only a few weeks at Winnie the Pooh to be fully bilingual.

Nevertheless, although my life went on after my divorce, I was always on the run, rushing to get to my lectures in time, then rushing to be at home to meet with Chris and Cassandra when they came back from school, staying up at night until all hours to have my assignments done in time or doing translation jobs to get extra income or also running and juggling babysitters to squeeze an on-site interpreting job here and there, which would give me more money to spare. Unfortunately, Giuseppe would not ever contribute to the family basket, unless forced by the authorities which I did not want to push.

Moreover, I also had to keep the house in order, cook and wash for us all and entertain the children. I did not have time to visit anybody, or receive many visitors, not even my parents.

Giuseppe would pick the children up occasionally and would bring them back a couple of hours later. I heard he had met this lady twice his age, who actively practised fortune telling and sexual therapies.

To be able to survive with so many things to do, I had to be organised. Fortunately, God has given me the right skills to thrive in crisis.

And in the middle of all this chaos, a few months after Sara had gone back to Argentina, I suddenly got a letter from El Cuco which threw me completely out of balance. Who on earth would guess at that point El Cuco was going to become my next husband for the next 21 years?

Chapter 5

SECOND MARRIAGE

A life without goals is like a ship without a rudder drifting where the winds and waves of chance direct you.
(Anonymous)

'If you're offered a seat on a rocket ship, don't ask what seat! Just get on.'
(Sheryl Sandberg)

Part 1 - El Cuco

For your information Emanuel, I decided to speak my story in my rough Spanish into a tape recorder. I have asked Carmela to translate it word by word and then write it accurately into proper English, so it could be reasonably understood. She did not want to have anything to do with it but, after much persuasion to have this done, here it is! Frankly, I hope Carmela has done a good job and she has not added any of her ridiculous points of views...
Good luck with your book my dear grandson!

My grandfather had kidnapped my grandmother on horseback in Galicia, Spain, and then he forced her to marry him and to immigrate to Argentina. They were never happy in their marriage and eventually my grandmother threw herself to her death from the high rocks into the sea near Mar del Plata. My loving grandfather shot himself not long after her death as well.

My parents were never happy either and eventually they divorced when I was four years old. Following the divorce, a brutal battle for my custody fumed. This is how my mother, with less resources and legal grounds than my father, finished up living with me up in the mountains of Cordoba, in an untraceable improvised shaggy hut, isolated from the civilised world.

I remember my only friend was a dirty live old duck my mother had brought me to play with, and with whom I talked for hours as I only had him to communicate all my sorrows. Despite my efforts to teach it to speak, it was a real tragedy then for me that it could not respond to me!

I also recall my mother being visited by men who sometimes gave me lollies or comic magazines to look at. I could not read them though until much later, when my grandfather came to announce an agreement had been reached with my father, it was now safe to return to Buenos Aires and I could start school.

By the time I enrolled in the first year of primary school I was already more than three years older than the normal school entrance age. I was teased, ridiculed, and bullied by other students and to top it all off, I was not bright. It took me longer to understand basic concepts, let alone read and write properly. I very much felt inadequate and second-rate amongst my peers.

Socially, I also found it difficult to make friends and play with other children, not only because of the differences in ages in my grade but because the other children started to call my mother names like slut, despicable, a whore, and an immoral bitch. At the time, I did not know what these words meant, but I knew they were offensive towards my adorable mum. It follows that I got involved in heavy swearing and fiery fights at school and outside school, which resulted in me being banned from the playground at school. My mother grounded me at home as well and I could not go out to play.

My only amusement in those days was to play with a live chicken—which had replaced my beloved duck when we moved- I was given for my 9th birthday or look through my window at other children playing soccer in the street. I clearly remember in those days, I would have done anything to own a proper soccer ball, even to hold one would have been a treat for me. My mother made a good 'soccer ball', according to her, with discarded old pieces of clothes tied up with some elastic, but unfortunately, it did not bounce much.

My grandfather helped my mother install a small shop where she sold various fabrics and sewing accessories. During the night, she sewed and repaired clothes for people in the neighbourhood. All the cash she earned except the rent and our upkeep, which was not much, she collected it in a shoebox.

My mother also had a boyfriend or two or three or more, who visited her when I went to sleep. I cannot say exactly how many because my mother sent me to sleep early most days and had told me not to come out of my room, ever!

When I was about twelve, one of these men offered me a job stuffing mattress with lambs' wool. I was not doing any good at school; my mother decided I should quit school and get the job.

My mother bought me a second-hand bicycle and a bike pump to inflate the tyres. I loved the idea of working because it was going to give me some independence and the means of transport to get to the mattress factory. And perhaps I could get some money to purchase a soccer ball one day.

I started to work for this man called Samson. Everybody called him Mr Perez, but I was allowed to call him by his first name because he was a close friend of my mum's.

Samson was huge and he was always unshaven and smelly, but he gave me sweets and he talked to me as if he was pleased with my performance at the factory. For the first time of my life, I felt proud of myself.

However, it was not to be all roses! When I think about my other extra experiences with Samson, all my body baulks even now. My head does not want to recall anything to do with this man and unfortunately it had buried all these tortuous incidents. Even hypnotised, I was unable to dredge up what really had happened to me. I need to concentrate until my head hurts to vaguely remember when Samson took me to his private office for the first time and started to touch me in my private parts and tried to kiss me. The worst was the disgusting drool that always ran down my face at the end of these sessions.

These episodes and more that I cannot recall kept on repeating almost every day, but I cannot explain why I did not tell my mother.

I have searched in my memory repeatedly, even with professional help, but unfortunately or fortunately I could not remember any more about what happened after the touching and kissing or if Samson's behaviours became more aggressive, except one day suddenly my mother stopped seeing him and I stopped going to my job.

I had many other jobs after that, sweeping floors, doing errands as an office boy around the city, working as a bellboy in a hotel, peeling vegetables in a commercial kitchen and more. All the money I earned wound up saved in my mother's shoebox, and yes, occasionally, she would buy me a chocolate ice cream from the street vendor as a treat.

My mother expanded and was progressing rapidly in her business and one day she asked me to work for her. She taught me how to serve the customers and what to say exactly to make them always happy. Her advice to me was you always had to say what people wanted to hear, especially women, no matter what age or how pretty or ugly they were.

She made me practice all sort of routine phrases like, 'You look so lovely today, dear', or 'Seeing you is like touching heaven', 'You brighten my day everyday Doña', 'You look wonderful', or 'You are always so kind and generous, my sweet' or 'It always makes me very happy to see you'. I was to repeat these learnt phrases, even if I felt completely the opposite of what I was saying. She also instructed me that these practices would help me always win women in the future as well.

Following her recommendations, I started to run the shop whilst mum did more of the sewing, also during the day. At night she would now go out with more elegant boyfriends, and I would go to sleep with my pet chicken.

I was sure mother was now saving serious money in the shoebox and one day she asked me to help her count it. According to her, we had enough pesos to buy a small property outright! She was so proud and beaming!

We looked for and found a property we thought was the best for us. It was a modest two-bedroom house with a big shop at the front. The problem was it was near the slums in the outskirts of Buenos Aires.

I could see this suburb seemed to me be poor and dirty and it was packed with criminals, alcoholics, and sex workers. When I said I was concerned about the suburb, I was told by my grandfather that this type of people also had to live and spend. 'We cannot forget we are merchants, first of all, and as such we will make these people's lives easier by selling them faithfully what they want'.

My mother decided to go ahead with the purchase, despite my opinion and soon after, we moved in there. The move proved to be a goldmine, as my grandpa had predicted, as the number of customers quadrupled. We had to employ three girls to help us serve all our clients and avoid the shoplifting.

When the shop became really crowded on special occasions, like during the Christmas season, my mother also employed an extra security officer to stop the thieves and make sure small disagreements did not turn into huge and serious brawls.

My mother's sewing business also prospered, and we graduated to a bigger shoebox for our savings. Soon, she had money to purchase another property and then another and another and another.

By then, she had got acquainted with a very prosperous Real Estate Agent, very well married Mr Rana. They were good friends, partners, or lovers for what I cared!

Rana and my mother started to do businesses together, purchasing properties for cash really cheap from people who were desperate to sell, then fixing them up—repairing, painting, or simply cleaning them—and then selling them at huge profits. I thought it was all a scam, but Rana and mother said it was legit.

My mother learnt this business super quick as she had a shrewd eye for a fast deal. She got herself the Real Estate and Auctioneers Licences and the partnership with Rana progressed exponentially.

Soon she and Rana were purchasing large properties, land holdings, and even a chain of hotels. They also started another venture in the finance business, exorbitant lending money directly to buy and sell the properties quicker at very high interest rates.

Most days I was left to run the shop on my own with the assistants, and by the time I closed the shutters I was too tired to go out. Besides, I was getting a bit disheartened; I was not able to see much money of the business for me. I earned my upkeep and a few pesos occasionally. Most of the income from the shop now went from the saving box straight into my mother's real estate business.

I confronted my mother who said we were going to be millionaires soon, I would never have to work again, I was going to be able to have the most beautiful women at my feet, at last, she had been able to prove herself, that a woman could make it in this world on her own. Other similar comments were blabbed on like this, non-stop.

She also said she was pleased with me, and as a bonus, she was going to buy me an instant camera. I felt empty and lonely, and even my mother's words or her promised miserable gift did not offer me any consolation.

Nevertheless, I also felt scared and hesitant to make any changes. I was unable to make any decision on my own. I decided to continue with my life as it was for a little while longer.

It was around this time when I noticed an old man who lived across the road at the back of his small shop, selling underwear and socks. I felt so desperately alone one night that I crossed the road and knocked at his door.

The old man introduced himself as Christos, but he could hardly speak any Spanish. He had come from Cyprus not long ago with his wife and his son Draco, who was of a similar age to me.

Christos invited me in to have dinner with them. It was heaven for me eating the homemade Moussaka with them around the table after forever eating alone my boring and stale cheese sandwiches at home.

Draco explained to me in broken Spanish they had come to Buenos

Aires with nothing except their knowledge of how to run a business. They had their memories in their suitcases along with a few clothes they had gathered in a hurry. The Turks had invaded their territory, taking their property and their money. They considered themselves lucky Argentina had opened its doors for them, but life was tough and not safe in the slums of Buenos Aires. Before coming to Argentina, they had travelled to other countries, and I was fascinated to hear of their stories.

I started to visit the Cypriot family often and soon enough I became good friends with Draco and his cousin Hercules.

Draco was obsessed with leaving Argentina and going to the United States, where he had some family, but with little income, his dreams were not easy to fulfil. Hercules also wanted to leave, but he had other plans. He had heard of a large island on the other side of the world where the meat, legumes and fruits were abundant and fresh; a continent called Australia. He wanted to know everything he could find out about travelling to Sydney, even if it was illegally.

I had trained one of the girls in the shop and I was now able to leave her in charge of our business for a few hours at the time. My mother did not know I was not at work as she was always out minding her Real Estate business.

Draco took me to the Port where he found out what he had to do to work on the merchant ships that would take him to the United States.

Hercules took me to the Australian Embassy, where we were shown films about Sydney and Melbourne. We were given lots of forms to apply for immigration to Australia. Hercules immediately applied and after a few attempts, he was eventually successful and in a short time, he migrated to Australia legally.

I loved my mother, but soon after I met Draco's family and Hercules, I realized I did not want to be my mother's slave for the rest of my life.

I started to look for a job as far as possible from her and Argentina. I made enquiries to see if with my background, I could join the commercial merchant ships, the ones that Draco was interested in. And yes, hurrah, they were looking for seamen, but I needed at least my primary school completed, which I did not have, and I also needed to obtain my Seaman's Book from the Maritime Police.

Getting a Seaman's Book involved completing a seaman's course conducted by the National Maritime Headquarters, which included survival swimming and other skills.

I did not have to think it twice. I decided to enrol at a night school where I finally struggled to complete my primary education and after that, I attended the seaman's course.

Within six months I was ready to apply for a job that would take me away from my mother and her silly businesses.

Unfortunately, without any prior experience to 'dirty' my Seaman's Book, it was impossible to get a job. I needed stamps in the book, showing clearly that I had worked at sea.

I applied for jobs to work in many small ships, without success. Finally, I organised a meeting with a few graduates from the Maritime Headquarters Course and decided to lobby ship companies for employment as apprentices.

Within a few months I got a telegram requesting me to board a small ship company, which transported fuel from La Plata to Buenos Aires.

My mother was mad at me when I told her of my decision to leave the shop. I had to help her to find and appoint a manager to keep the business running.

Part 2 - El Cuco

The job at the small shipping company was not what I had expected and at the time, with my limited resources, I thought I would be trapped again forever. The work was tedious and intense, though I applied myself to it the best I could.

Despite the difficulties encountered, this job felt a bit better than my mother's shop work. At last, I finally could feel more independent, have some money in my pocket and recover my own life.

A few months after I started this new job, I was informed without warning my work there had finished and I should report to the company's head office.

A bit timid, I went to the appointment to be told to my surprise, that I was being offered a contract for six months to work in one of their bigger ships, *Bahia Buen Suceso*, and I would be travelling to 'the end of the world', Ushuaia, the most southern part of South America and the closest city to Antarctica.

The *Bahia Buen Suceso* ship usually transported coffee and bananas from Santos, Brazil to Ushuaia. At last, I felt then ready and super happy to break away from my mother's umbilical cord forever!

My big adventure would take me along the Atlantic Ocean to Las Malvinas (The Falkland's Islands), Perito Moreno and the Antarctic. But I was one of the youngest sailors in the ship, there was a lot of training and the work itself was heavy and tiring. Besides, the rest of the crew did not accept me. Older sailors mocked me and teased me that I was weak and a sissy, because I spent most of my time off 'charging my batteries' in other words, I was laying down in my bed or sleeping when not at work.

'I am not as tall as you at all, but I am strong' I said to them one day. Pepe quickly replied, 'Are you? Then prove it! You need to be baptised sooner or later. Now … Catch this!' he shouted as he was throwing a huge roll of heavy canvas onto me. I tried to catch it, but it was too heavy to keep away from my body and it crashed and buried me on the floor. I heard a crackling noise as I exhaled a sigh, before I fully lost consciousness.

I spent four weeks recovering in the ship's hospital. The doctor told me God was on my side because I only had numerous broken ribs and a collapsed lung. He added I was lucky not to have a broken my back which it would have left me a paraplegic and unable to work ever again.

When I was rostered back to work, my teammates were silent and seemed apologetic. But soon they were making jokes with me about the incident and best of all, from then on, they accepted me as an equal.

One of the 'gangs' commented I had passed the test with honours; I was now baptised into the ship's crew, and we were now true colleagues.

They soon taught me how to remain sane on long sea journeys: playing cards, daydreaming, and drinking alcohol; whatever we could get our hands on. They also taught me about the women they all had in each port to keep them entertained and level-headed until they went back to their own wives in Buenos Aires.

I had already received many lessons from my mother about women. 'You must find out what they really like and tell them exactly what they want to hear. Believe me son, it will always work', my mother had coached me.

My mates on the ship told me women were all the same: 'Women would do anything for good sex.'

'Believe me pal, there's not one woman in the world who will be too difficult if you know how and where to touch them emotionally first, then just ram it in mate!'

I was an eager listener and ready to put my newly acquired strategies into practice! I absorbed like a sponge, and I was ready to figure out how to exercise my new skills, with women included, and as much as I could from my first trip.

On my second trip from Santos to Ushuaia, we were told to prepare the cellar to house some prisoners who were to be transported to a jail in Ushuaia.

The cellar looked and felt like a big fridge. We cleaned it as much as we could and improvised some beds with rugs, but there were no proper toilet facilities and we wondered how the prisoners were going to manage their necessities.

These 'passengers' soon boarded the ship in Buenos Aires. The open seas were rough heading south and soon these poor souls were swimming in this metal tank, filled with their own vomit and excrement.

Our daily job, after breakfast, was to get the inmates out for a shower, remove the provisional beds, connect the fire hose in place to remove the debris and hopefully the smell out to sea.

Whilst they waited in line to go back to their gaol, the prisoners had a cup of 'mate' [8] and a piece of stale bread. I thought at the time that whatever they had done, they did not deserve that treatment, but I kept it to myself. I did not want to appear a pussy amongst my peers.

I was happy when we reached the 42nd parallel south, because although it was much colder, the seas were not as rough as before, thus the place was kept a bit cleaner.

After four days at sea, early in the morning, I first saw the lighthouse, as if in a dream. Then I realized the ship was indeed entering the sheltered waters of San Jorge's Gulf that would take us back to the city of Comodoro Rivadavia in Patagonia, and to my raunchy first experience of a love affair as a sailor.

Rayen was waiting for me at the dock. I had met her during my first trip at the dilapidated Chilean Club where she was with her friends. She was tall and stout, with a thin and extended head. She had long black hair, black eyes, and a hooknose. She exuded an original beauty, drawn from centuries ago when the Patagonian Indians, the Tehuelches, still reigned in that land.

Our conversation was easy and entertaining. She had loved my jokes and my made-up stories of adventure. I had loved her smile and her wild perfume. I had kissed her long and softly. She had queried me, 'is it true you do not have a girlfriend in Buenos Aires, that big city where there are so many beautiful girls?'

'Let's dance' I had interrupted. 'Let us enjoy the time we have here today and make it memorable until my ship brings me back to Comodoro' again and to your charms'.

On my second trip, Rayen had been easy to charm once more, and her skin had been warm and soft next to my cheek. I had told her my ship would depart early in the morning the next day, as we had some cargo to be urgently delivered down south, but I promised her I would be back to her when the ship was back at the dock. We would write to each other, words of love and the hope of meeting again soon… It was past midnight when I had left her at her home, a modest tin shack, which stank of sacrifice and hardship.

Again, on my third trip, she was there at the dock, flagging her handkerchief in her best dress and smelling of wild roses. And she would be there at the local tavern for a cheap meal, where my colleagues would wink as a sign of approval. Then we would hurry to the local 'love hotel' paid by the hour, where promises of our forever love along with wild sex would be exchanged and sealed.

I would have liked to have been more honest, to have told her our love would last only until I found somebody else in the next port, but I could not shatter her dreams at that point.

And I certainly knew how to answer all her avid questions so well that I even believed them myself. 'Yes, I would come to fetch you soon… yes, I would take you to Buenos Aires, where I have a small house with a lovely garden full of flowers… yes, we would get married and have many children and we would be always happy… Yes, why not? We would take your family with us too…Eventually, I would conclude our time together. 'Listen. We are leaving in the morning for the Falklands Islands… I do not know what we are supposed to do there…maybe tender to the sheep or play a friendly soccer game with the locals… Whatever it is, I must go with my ship… sorry,' I whispered.

I can still distinguish in my mind today Rayen's figure at the dock, waving her hand, her hair in the strong wind until she disappeared. It is hard to remember her face in detail amongst so many other similar faces later, but I imagine her tears and her broken heart for the loss of her innocence and her dreams at the young age of 16…

After six months with the local shipping company, my seaman's book was indeed 'dirty' or full. I had by then earned a good track record, therefore, I started looking for a job with bigger shipping companies, a job that would then take me around the world and to more adventures.

After a few attempts in applying for jobs in different shipping companies, I was given a contract to board a cargo vessel from a large shipping line that would take me to Brazil, and from there to Europe and back.

I had a girlfriend in Buenos Aires, an employee from my mother's business, Rosita. I had often thought she would have made a great partner with whom to settle down. She was pretty, smart, and witty and many times she had made me feel as if I was touching the stars, as if I was finally in love...

Rosita would do anything to make me happy and I was tempted many times to change my mind and stay with her instead of sailing away.

But I did not want to get trapped by any woman, and least by my mother again! My destiny was to discover far away countries, other people and cultures and exciting activities overseas...

My mates were knocking at the door, and I woke, jumping from my bed without knowing where I was or where my clothes were. I never thought it was going to be so difficult to get used to those modern ships, where there were private wardrobes outside your cabin. It was my first trip in this ship, and I did not know the crew yet.

Somebody had spoken about the 'German', like a character in a mystery novel, who used to turn up in Hamburg in a new Mercedes every time the ship arrived there. It was rumoured Hamburg was a fascinating port, especially when there were people like the 'German' to talk about.

It was now five in the morning, and we needed to be ready in our posts, as the ship was entering with the help of a tugboat through the river to its next wharf.

It must have been after eight am when the second officer announced we had finished the manoeuvre and we could have a break. I felt frozen to death from the cold, so I quickly went to fetch some hot coffee from the kitchen to share with my mates, to hopefully revive us all.

'How and when are we going to board the merchandise?' I asked. The crewmate with the most experience answered, his eyes fixed in a brand-new Mercedes approaching us and stopped just below the steps to access the ship: 'There he is, the German!'

A middle-aged chubby man in an impeccable suit and a Tyrolese hat, the 'German', was now chatting with an Officer from the Health Department, and afterwards, he was avoiding some puddles of water and climbing the steps to meet the First Officer of the ship. The two quickly disappeared behind a door on the main deck.

'What is going to happen now?' I asked. 'In two or three days, we will be disembarking the merchandise we brought from Brazil and embarking our new order.'

'Do you remember when we were in Bahia Santos and two guys in white suits arrived to talk to the captain? Well, they were the ones who had the "order", he told me.

'Yes, of course I remember those guys very well,' I said.

I also clearly recalled at that time, just as we were leaving the port of Buenos Aires, the ship's officer entered our cabin without knocking and asked my roommate in a heavy Galician accent, 'Have you told him yet or do I have to tell him myself?' Right away, my roommate moved his head repeatedly from right to left and again from left to right.

Then the Ship Officer looked at me with his small dark eyes as if taking my x-ray with them and continued, bragging, 'Well, my dear Cuquito, come to my cabin after lunch, we need to talk. And you Pepe, what's up, you are late or what?' Pepe retrieved an envelope with his name from his drawer and gave it to him.

It was not much more than the Ship Officer said to me that afternoon. 'How much money do you have in American Dollars for some business? Look! Here in this ship, the whole crew is working together... our Captain is diery well connected with governments, other authorities, and heavies from other companies... All you would have to do is just play dumb and cooperate when it is needed!' He continued in his intimidating tone, 'If you happen to open your mouth or 'show the money' in Buenos Aires, your job won't be the only thing you lose.' I felt like a cornered mouse. 'You will see here, the work is automated, and most is done with levers, so it is not as heavy as in older ships. Besides, half of the profit from the 'package' is shared proportionally amongst us,' he said.

'I have $1,500 but I need $500 for some private shopping,' I said.

'Perfect', he said smiling wryly. 'Put them in an envelope with your name and give it to me. We need to have all the money together before we get back to Santos'.

We had just finished disembarking the merchandise from Brazil in Hamburg and I was anxious to know what would happen next.

Two semitrailers arrived with large boxes all duly labelled as cold meat. They were all winched on deck, and from there we manually took and arranged them carefully into the cool room leaving some space at the front.

'This merchandise is precious for us! Would you have guessed it is worth $750,000 for us?' Pepe said to me. He also explained the carpenters and the electricians were going to do some work now. 'The electricians will need to lower the power in the cool room whilst the carpenters will need to build a camouflaged insulated divider. We can then accommodate some other boxes with different types of 'real' cold meats, adequately labelled. This is in case other, more meticulous, ports, like Le Havre in France, ask to inspect the ship,' Pepe added.

More instructions followed, the ship was also picking up some 12 past ground employees from our company, now retired, who were stranded in Europe, and who we would need to look after until our return to Buenos Aires.

As we approached Brazil again, I was wondering whether these passengers would spoil our plans when we needed to deliver our 'packages'.

All my worries dissipated when Pepe explained to me the captain had facilitated a potent drug to be mixed in the passenger's dinner the night before, and he himself had witnessed all the oldies were deeply sleep by the time we arrived at Santos.

It was past midnight and the ship advanced slowly, so quietly as if it was sliding on a sea of dark oil, with only the dim emergency lights on. We had to bring the 'boxes' back into the main deck along with the ropes and a huge metal plate that would serve as a facilitating chute.

Pepe gave me some special sunglasses and asked me to wear them. They were infrared goggles which allowed us to see better and remain hidden in the dark. I could see small lights twinkling in the shadows, and then I realized it was a codified signal between the ship and another boat.

Soon a luxury launch arrived quietly in the dark. I saw two men, the first was a black man, carrying a submachine gun - 'his bodyguard,' Pepe said - and the other was dressed in an elegant summer suit carrying a large briefcase attached to his wrist with a chain. 'Look! That is where the 'dough' is,' whispered Pepe.

A sailor received the order to drop the jack that held the timber steps for them to climb onto the ship. The black man stayed on deck whilst the other disappeared behind the main gates with the First Officer.

We needed to wait quietly and for a second, I thought I would not make it; my heart was racing madly, and I had no more nails left to bite.

Suddenly, I saw a lantern twinkling again from the dark and the man, now without his briefcase and the First Officer appeared again. He made a gesture of approval to the armed man, and quickly descended the steps to their launch, which disappeared in the dark as quickly and as silently as it had come.

Instantly, I saw a moving shape at the side of the ship. It was a fishing boat, camouflaged with nets and a few fish containers. There were a few black men with ropes in their hands. The ropes flew crossing the short space, and we quickly caught them and tied them to the ship.

With frenetic movements, I helped to position the chute and others started to shift the boxes by hand as in a human chain. The first boat disappeared and then another and many more boats arrived. They were swallowed into the night with the precious cargo, I was told, of French perfumes, whisky and cigarettes, pornography, firearms, and illicit drugs.

Our job had finished, and the ship started to move increasing speed slowly, now fully lighted. On the horizon, the sun started to raise shyly, as if questioning if it could start illuminating us without any unnecessary risks. Our proud ship seemed to want to answer: 'Of course, our life continues, nothing has happened here.' It was business as usual for us.

I walked slowly to the dining room where other workers were already having their coffee. One of them asked me, 'What did you think, young boy? Surely, an easy way of getting 10 big green bucks...'

'You really want to know?' I responded.

'Well, I am thinking like the tango, 'Bailarin Compadrito' [9]:

That's exactly what I think!' I answered. They all laughed and laughed! I felt at last, I belonged there.

Back in Buenos Aires, I went to see my mother straight away and asked her to invest the US$10,000 cash in a property. She quickly bought me a nice furnished apartment in the heart of the city, where I moved in by myself at last, independent from her. She asked me about my job, but I avoided her questions and she seemed to understand I could not disclose anymore. I was too scared to speak about my experiences. I could lose my job and I suspected my life could be in jeopardy if I divulged anything.

When, in a few weeks' time, I was asked to board the same ship, I was ready to live the same adventure. As it turned out, I did quite a few trips with the same ship with increasing profits as my initial investments grew.

My funds kept adding up further as I was also bringing 'private orders' of European 'treasures' to friends and acquaintances I had in Buenos Aires. My mother kept on buying and renting properties for me. My standard of living was also improving exponentially as I was able to purchase better clothes and I exchanged my eternal cheese sandwiches for proper food from good restaurants when I was in Buenos Aires. I really felt proud of myself, as if I had made it in life.

I still remember one cold day when I realized how fortunate, I was, drinking the best Irish malt whisky and witnessing a never-ending stream of people going to work in old working clothes with their meagre lunch under their arms. They paraded constantly through the window of my luxurious penthouse to catch the over-crowded buses. Meanwhile, I reflected my life was then indeed forever easy, abounding, and sweet.

I had it made. I was still young, and I had a good chance to become a multi-millionaire soon. I thought at the time I might not to work at all shortly… How very wrong I was in my predictions.

Unfortunately, not all the trips were so danger free as the first one. From the second trip on, I noticed some of my mates did not come back to the ship, and some were taken ill in the ship hospital, and they were never to be seen again. They were quickly replaced with new sailors, and nobody dared to ask about the whereabouts or destinies of their predecessors.

On my seventh trip, the captain took ill. We were told he had a bad case of appendicitis and we had to leave him in Santos for an emergency operation. I saw with my own eyes how his stretcher was lowered to the pier and taken by an ambulance. However, there were persistent rumours that, despite his efforts to disappear changing his identity in Santos, he had been violently shot in a mafia-style fashion, not far from the port.

When I was back in Buenos Aires, I quietly tried to trace my past mates that had also been taken ill or had disappeared, but no matter how much I tried to find out what had happened to them, they seemed to have vanished without any trace. I assumed all their families were too scared to contact the police. They had nothing to say to me, they said, although I could see it in their eyes, they had great fears for their safety if they were to tell me anything they knew or suspected.

I decided to take leave of absence for the next trip, which was granted without any problem. I gave the excuse my mother needed me, being her only child, because she was sick. I also visited the Australian Embassy to see if they still needed people to migrate to their large island at the end of the world.

Unfortunately, I could not get any grants to immigrate to Australia because I did not have any trade or profession, but I could get a permanent visa if I was able to pay for my airline ticket and I was also prepared to stay there for two years.

The Australian Embassy worker anticipated I would most probably get a job as an unskilled worker onshore, which I did not mind. Sadly, they did not need any sailors at that stage!

Nevertheless, I filled out all the required forms and I also wrote to my old friend Hercules in Sydney. Hercules wrote to me straight away. He had married a countrywoman and had a baby girl. He said Australia was like a money-making machine. He had prospered quickly, and he now had his own house he was paying off and a small cleaning business employing 10 people.

I soon received notification from the Australian embassy that I had to attend a medical examination at the British Hospital, which I did immediately.

I did not think twice. When my visa application to go to Australia was accepted, I asked my mother to look after my properties, bought a one-way airline ticket to Sydney, and left Buenos Aires again.

---

[8] Traditional South American caffeine-rich infused drink/tea

[9] **Bailarín compadrito (1929)** Song Extract: Bailarín Compadrito by Miguel Bucino

'Mírate al pibe, cuando a veces oís La Cumparsita
Yo sé cómo palpita tu corazón al recordar
Que un día lo bailaste de lengue y sin un mango
Y ahora el mismo tango lo bailás hecho un bacán'

Upstart Dancer (1929) Song Extract by Miguel Eusebio Bucino, Translation. A. Paz

Watch it, when sometimes you hear La Cumparsita
I know how your heart beats when remembering
That one day you dance it in a shirt and without a dime
And now you dance the same tango looking like a wealthy man.

Part 3 - El Cuco

Hercules offered me initial board in his house for a small weekly fee. He also offered me to work with him in his cleaning business. 'But I do not know what to do' I said. 'Do not worry, I will teach you the job and all the tricks of the trade. You taught me Spanish once, remember?' he chuckled.

He helped me apply to a Migrant Course to learn English. Regrettably, I found the course extremely difficult to handle and my progress was slow, so it was really a waste of time. I could not explain whether my difficulties had arisen from my poor literacy in Spanish, or because I never had a clear mind to learn anything new academically.

The good news was, slowly I was able to communicate on a basic level with people in English. It was all formulaic, with phrases I had learnt. In fact, I was not able to engage in a real serious, lengthy conversation with anybody, unless it was in Spanish.

Despite my language problems, Australia gave me everything I had wished for and more. I learnt the cleaning trade fast and soon I was ready to work not only during the day but after hours as well.

The cleaning industry was full of Spanish speaking people and soon I made friends with many single guys. I decided I should share a flat with some of them, instead of with Hercules' family. My mates and I also shared some meals together. I spent time with them on weekends, especially going out at night to chase women.

I soon found out 'Anglo' women did not care if I could not speak much English, they loved a good drink and they were easy and eager to have a good time, particularly in the sac.

One of my mates, Abel, a Colombian national, then offered me a job to clean with him a huge church in the city, a Cathedral, I think. The work was easy and well paid, and it could be done quickly and efficiently.

I never suspected this job would come with a windfall. 'Have you noticed the diamonds and precious stones on the Virgin's robes and shawl? They will be worth thousands in Colombia. If you help me take a few of the bigger diamonds and emeralds, I can give you a good commission', Abel proposed.

I was never really a believer, but the fact was even the thought of stealing from God, brought shivers to my spine.

'I will think about it and let you know, Abel', I responded.

That night I could not sleep tossing and turning and when I closed my eyes, I had horrible visions of God throwing me into a huge dark pit full of fire where it was impossible to keep alive or get away.

The next day I did not go to work in the morning and used the day to look for another job. In the evening I went to see Abel and told him although I would not say a word about his plans, I was not prepared to go ahead with it. He looked astonished but said nothing. I gathered my work clothes and left. I never saw that week's pay or Abel again.

After two years, I had saved more than A$16,000 in cash and I felt grateful towards this country that had accepted me as I was and gave me freedom, security, safety and peace without any questions or judgements; and above all I had kept my integrity, for which I felt proud!

I still felt lonely though and I vividly recall now, that for the first time, I thought of the possibility of settling down in Australia. I thought it would be the ideal place to raise a family. However, I decided to go to Argentina for a holiday before taking any further decisions.

Looking through the window of the Aerolineas Argentinas plane and approaching Buenos Aires again, I felt triumphant and content with myself, especially because I carried a sock full of money sewn to my underwear. My mother would certainly be proud of me and my achievements at last!

At the time of my arrival, my mother had had an operation to remove gallstones and she had been very sick, but she was recovering now in a chalet near the sea. I intended to have Christmas with her and talk about her favourite subject: property investment.

I also intended to enjoy my stay in Argentina with old friends. However, I had made further plans with a friend to go on holidays to Rio in Brazil and then onto Torremolinos in Spain, where all the

Swedish single girls looking for a warmer climate were staying. These girls, I was told, were there to spend their winter holidays, on saucy adventures and were up for good, steamy sex.

My mother would understand, I was sure. After all, I was going to spend a few months with her! And how much fun I was prepared to have with my friend! And when the money run out, I would go back to Australia, where life was sweet, and money was easy and safe to make again.

In Australia I had to put up with an austere life and my loneliness, but afterwards… afterwards, well the future did not exist for an ex-sailor, only the present and the past juicy memories…

I thought of an alternative. Settle down, have a wife, children, but I had been allergic for a long time to becoming 'wife material', in those days. I honestly preferred new adventures, total freedom and plenty of free sex.

My mother was getting better, and she was happy to see me fit and healthy. I was again with her in Argentina, but the circumstances started to knit my destiny. I had my own plans, I let my mother know. However, in a short couple of weeks, everything would change for me and only my old investments would still stand still.

Angelica was her name, and the first day of the next seven years, started with the projection of a Super 8 film about Sydney and how life ran in that 'paradise' called Sydney.

As the images rolled on the screen, my fantastic mind was already looking at myself walking with those big blue eyes of Angelica's without even touching the floor in the streets of Sydney.

Angelica and I became inseparable, and our time sped its path faster and faster. The joy of our bodies made us think we could be happy together forever and ever. I would have liked her to be a virgin, but as it happened, she had experienced a few adventures of her own. I asked myself why… why… why… but surely, Argentina was not a good place for the poor young women like Angelica.

Her blurred past did not disqualify her for me to own her… She made me super happy. I had to marry her to be able to get her partner visa to Australia, so we obtained a marriage licence in Brazil, where divorce would be possible and easy, just in case our union did not work out.

My mother was horrified. She said she could have introduced me to many suitable girls of much better pedigree than Angelica! It was too late to listen to my mother's advice. I was in love!

After an eternal honeymoon in the Atlantic coast at one of my mother's penthouses, and after we got Angelica the proper visa, we made our suitcases, and departed together for Sydney.

It felt like running over a field of flowers of different bright colours and fragrances, it felt like touching the sky with my fingers and fainting there. Having her in my arms, my unsettled spirit would gradually fall sleep with a big smile...

We wrote our names in the Australian sand, but the violent sea erased them forever. It was like the troubled waters wanted to tell me something I could not comprehend. She was only 19 years of age, and I was 33 years old, the same age as Christ when he was crucified.

Angelica and I rented a small house in one of the working-class suburbs of Sydney. It would not have mattered where we had lived; the fact was we were then super happy being together.

I got a permanent job as cleaner in one of the Sydney's largest department stores and a second job where I cleaned offices at night.

Angelica tried to get a job but with no English at all, it was difficult. Besides, within a few months of being in Sydney, she felt pregnant. I was over the moon and did not mind having to work so hard. However, I hardly had any time to enjoy Angelica and baby Eva, our firstborn.

A few months after little Eva was born, Angelica fell pregnant again and this time it was a boy, baby Adam or Addy as they called him in Australia.

I had a lovely family, but my happiness was brittle. I lost my night job, and we were struggling financially.

I wrote to my mother and asked her to sell one of my investments and send us the money, but she icily responded that times were hard, and inflation was rampant in Argentina. In other words, it was definitely not the time to sell any properties, as I would not get a fair price for any of them.

Angelica started to complain she was not used to living so thriftily, she was lonely and tired, she did not have any help with the children, as she would have had back home, and she wanted to return to Argentina.

God forbid thinking of returning to Argentina then! I did not agree with her at all, especially as Argentina's inflation rate had reached 1000% briefly in a month. Even my mother, was suffering and complaining she seemed to have lost most of her fortune.

It was indeed the dark ages in finance for Argentina. It was named 'El Corralito' because the banks were closed for any transactions and people's funds were frozen in an attempt to avoid massive money withdrawals and national bankruptcy.

Some of my mother's friends committed suicide because they could not face life after bankruptcy. Others were lucky to have sold some properties for cash before the collapse of the peso and fled to other countries with their money converted to US dollars in their pockets. I was convinced it was not the time to dispose of any of my investments in Argentina!

Luckily, Angelica had found something else to do to distract her mind and get some extra cash. She started occasionally to mind the children for a woman, Carmela, who was an interpreter. Carmela would drop her four children at any time whenever she could get a job.

I quickly noticed Carmela was pretty, friendly, and smart with her money. She knew how to help her husband. She was also kind, friendly and generous with her time, always trying to help those who needed assistance.

But above all, Carmela also had a 'true family', a mother whom people called affectionately 'La Macaca' and a real father 'Paquito' who loved his wife and her clan. I secretly started to envy everything about Carmela and her family.

La Macaca and Paquito had gone on holidays to Argentina where they had a small apartment in a pretty suburb in Buenos Aires. I wrote to my mother. if she needed any help during the financial crisis, she could contact them. She did so and to my surprise they had become good friends. In one of my letters. I casually mentioned to my mother I would have loved to have a father like Paquito, always so polite and so devoted to his flock!

Meanwhile, in Australia, I was heading slowly to my grave. Despite her new activities as a child carer, Angelica continued to deteriorate emotionally. She was now crying almost every day when I came back from work, and she was continually nagging me to pack up and go back to Argentina. Our sex life also had practically stalled; she was now fat, ungroomed, tired, and wasted most of the time! I started to get concerned... very concerned...

Argentina would have been the last place I wanted to return to, but I thought of my young children, and I finally decided to do as Angelica suggested. The situation made me desperate. I felt as if my inner self was gradually vanishing, and my days were numbered.

To complicate matters more, just as I was arranging the tickets to return to Argentina with my family, my mother wrote to me to say she was coming to Australia. She had sold whatever properties, for whatever price she could get; too late to save her fortune in the middle of the financial chaos.

However, she had some cash to bring in US dollars at least, and perhaps she could have enough to purchase some property in Sydney. To my surprise, she was staying in Buenos Aires with La Macaca and Paquito, who had kindly helped her to exchange some Argentinian pesos into US dollars through the black market.

Unfortunately, she had been unable to sell any of my investments, but they were safely rented for a pittance.

I then asked Carmela if she could help me find somewhere to stay for my mother and to familiarise her with the Australian property market. She would certainly need her interpreting and translating services to get her through the maze of purchasing a property, let alone assistance with finding the professional people, like a lawyer, necessary for any transaction connected with her prospective purchase.

I could not believe when Carmela confessed to me that she was separating from her husband Giuseppe. I had always considered they were an ideal couple, with a solid marriage. Nevertheless, she said she could help as much as she could then, and my mother could stay with her as she had a spare room in her large home.

My return to Buenos Aires was not a pleasant experience. Initially, we moved into one of my vacant apartments, which was a bit small for us all but nicely furnished and in an upmarket suburb near the city.

However, Angelica insisted she wanted to move in with her family who lived far away, in the outskirts of the city, close to the slums. In the end, I gave in and agreed to move there. The house was rudimentary and old, lacking doors, proper lighting and in need of major repairs.

I could not bear the thought my children living in that dump, but I had no choice if I wanted to keep my marriage. Besides, I felt powerless and intimidated. Angelica's family worked for the police in the neighbourhood. It was openly known to all they were corrupt and involved in questionable businesses.

Before we even had time to settle, Angelica's brother offered me to take part in a questionable, shifty business. It was not easy for me to understand the process of this business. Basically, the proposal was I needed to buy with my own savings a massive number of groceries and store them somewhere. Then I had to wait for the prices to go up and for the goods to be scarce. Finally, the stored merchandise was to be sold for many times the amount of the original purchase. The whole deal was guaranteed only by bribes and corrupted transactions. I thought I had become a decent man and I was over those deals, so I refused their proposal, quickly appearing in their black books.

I tried to get a proper job, but unemployment was rampant, and nobody wanted me. Not even my mother's manager in our old shop. Angelica took to the habit of going out at night and I started to suspect she was prostituting herself or openly cheating on me.

One night, she said she was going to her sister's home with an old man she had introduced me as her Godfather. I woke up in the middle of the night and noticed she had not arrived home yet, so I rang her sister, who categorically told me Angelica had not visited her that night at all.

I waited and waited, and finally I saw her coming out of a car and saw her passionately kissing her Godfather. We had a big fight, and I threw my wedding ring at her face, as ferociously as I could. I packed my clothes into a suitcase and left.

I walked and walked the dark, smelly streets until I found a taxi that took me to my apartment in the city. I felt crushed. I had survived many mishaps in the past, but I could not see any hope in getting over this one.

The worst nightmare was that my loving and precious children were tangled in the middle of this dirty sludge, and I could not see how I could survive without them.

I made enquiries at the Australian Embassy to see what I could do… Could I possibly take the children with me back to Australia, after all, were they not Australian born…? The mother has their passports… NO! YOU CANNOT TAKE THEM! Not at all… I was told it was up to both parents, and if their mother did not consent, I would not be able to travel with them back to Australia.

I also phoned my mother in Australia to get some money to bribe the right people, to no avail. No amount of money could help me in getting the children out of Argentina without their mother's consent.

I tried and tried to speak to Angelica, but she did not conceive the possibility of the children living with anyone but her. She also warned me the best thing I could do was to disappear from Argentina by my own free will, before she arranged for me to disappear by other means.

I understood the threat well. If I kept bothering her, she would get one of her police relatives to finish me off and place me with some weights at the bottom of the River Plate or bury me alive in some concrete wall, never to see the light of day again.

My mother wrote to me about her successful stay in Sydney. She had managed to park her money safely in a Sydney property. She also asked me to go back and told me about Carmela. She was an angel: although smart, she was still innocent and naïve.

'She was the girl you should have married, not that deceitful bitch of a woman named Angelica,' she said. 'Mind you, Carmela is now free and ready to be rescued from her sorrows,' she added. She explained in detail to me the reason from her recent separation from her husband. Was Giuseppe impotent? I really found the whole story difficult to believe…

In my apartment, half clouded by bourbon and pills for my nerves, I started to dream about Carmela. I dreamt she was my woman. She was beautiful, sexy, and made me feel so extremely happy. I could forget totally about my issues when I was with her, even the pain of remembering those two innocent faces calling me, 'Where are you daddy? Love you daddy'.

In desperation, I wrote to Carmela telling her about my circumstances and asking her to be my friend, my only friend in the world. I would soon be in Australia, and I asked whether, if by any chance, she would be able to help me breathe again.

Chapter 6

HOPE & NIGHTMARES

'It does not matter how slowly you go as long as you do not stop.'
(Confucius)

'Love is a serious mental disease.'
(Plato)

Part 1 - Carmela Junior

Dear Emanuel. Congratulations on your HSC results and happy birthday also. Are you just 15 now? I would give my entire life to be 15 again, my love! And what are you going to do now? Lots of love and blessing for your future! And I hope you can get the gist of this part of my life. Any explanations, just ring or email me. You've got my email, haven't you?

My life had been most hectic since Sara went back to Argentina, since I could not count on anybody I could trust and rely on for emergencies to mind my four children.

My marital home was sold, and the proceeds were by law divided equitably between Giuseppe and me. At the last minute, Giuseppe agreed to give me a few thousand dollars more, so I had enough to purchase a decent, better home, I considered more suitable for us.

I managed to purchase a small fibro home in a nice working-class suburb. It was nicely wallpapered, and the children liked it because it had a cubby house underneath. The house was within walking distance to the local primary school and just in front of a large park.

My parents were always busy or travelling overseas and I hardly had time to even ring them, let alone drive to their house (quite a long drive from my house) to drop children to be minded. My younger sister's house was also too far to leave my children with her, and I certainly did not know anybody I could trust fully or the money to leave the younger twins with a child-carer. My older twins attended school just up the road.

I soon learnt I had to manage by myself. I loved my university course, although I could not enjoy university life because I was always in a hurry to come home to the children!

My studies were most interesting. I had decided to study two languages, Spanish and French as majors for a bachelor's degree. I had tried to learn French during my childhood, but my teacher was not qualified. The grammar rules were very similar to the Spanish ones, and the French culture was fascinating.

I attended university during the day in the morning after the older twins left for school. I took the younger twins with me to pre-school before the lectures started. After I finished all I could manage to cover at university—attending lectures, borrowing books from the library, reading, and starting assignments—I would pick up the younger twins and rushed back to be home before the older twins returned home from school.

Sometimes, if the traffic was slow and I arrived home late, I would find Chris and Cassandra playing in the cubby house underneath the house. One day I found them underneath the house playing with matches. I gave them a long talk about safety and decided to give them a key to get into the house just in case I was late, but I instructed them not to let anybody in the house, no matter who that person was.

How could I guess then, one day they would leave my parents waiting in the cold and rain outside until I came back to open the door? I was also shocked to hear many years later that my precious children had often been also 'experimenting with household chemicals and twigs', which they lit up with mirrors in the back yard. I guess it was a real miracle no accident occurred!

Life was not easy for me, especially financially, but I had done most of the three years at university, and next year I would do honours and my Diploma of Education, maybe get a permanent job with a permanent income rather than my meagre 'tertiary education allowance' and my few interpreting and translating jobs. I would be able to support my children properly and live independent of government handouts.

Giuseppe had bought a large home in the suburbs and had taken boarders to help him with his small mortgage. He never offered me any money for the children, although occasionally he arranged to take them to the park to play. I was happy he did not interfere in my life and when the issue of his alimony arose with the Department of Social Security paperwork, I did not want any disagreements, so I was happy to sign. He would give me the grand amount of $5 a week for each of the children, which was frankly not even enough to purchase them their weekly milk.

Although the children were much healthier now, they still suffered from their allergies. I had to buy special food for them and asthma equipment and medication, which were not cheap. All my income went straight into paying the bills and purchasing food and medication for the children. I was happy to eat their leftovers for dinner. During the day I used to snack on some nut and fruit packages, which kept me quite trim and healthy.

Then, while I was still missing his mother Sara, El Cuco sent me this letter. It seemed it was like pouring out his broken heart, which made me frankly, uncomfortable.

He had had to leave his home and was now living in his apartment and trying to figure out how to bring his children to Australia without their mother. He praised me and thanked me for what I had done for Sara. He also asked me for help to see if, with my knowledge of the Australian system I could find a way to bring his children with him to Australia.

Amazingly he also said he admired me as a person and as 'a woman'. Hmm… He apologised for his indiscretion and asked me not to get offended by it, but he had thought of me, and how hard it must have been to be alone with so many children. He said in his dreams he had thought of the possibility of us being together, in other words, being a couple in the near future. Really?

I felt his letter was out of context completely. He was married to the lady who had looked after my children when I needed babysitting to go to work. I went over and over in my mind whether I had given him any clues I could be interested in him romantically, but I hadn't, not even remotely.

El Cuco had lost his mind surely, in the middle of his depression and his failed marriage. I understood he had not been able to see his children and that must have played with his mind unquestionably… But he was Sara's son and at least for her sake, I should try to help him… or not? Sara was particularly centred and practical. I considered her to be my true friend, almost like a mother, as she had helped me so much to recover from my broken marriage.

Maybe I should listen to el Cuco and maybe I could help him with his children as well. We exchanged a few letters and unfortunately, the immigration authorities confirmed to me it was impossible for el Cuco to bring Australian children overseas back to Australia without their mother's consent.

Sadly, and although he had to leave his children behind, el Cuco continued to make arrangements to return to Australia. I knew Giuseppe still had a room to rent, therefore, I gave him his address and phone number, as I thought at least he would have a place to stay and some familiar faces when he arrived.

As soon as he returned, el Cuco came to see me. He poured his heart to me: he was devastated, a broken and miserable man. He missed his children totally dind his life had become unbearable. I tried to cheer him up and despite my small resources; I sometimes invited him to have dinner with us. He said the noise of my children made him feel better.

Bit by bit, either on the phone or face to face, he told me about his adventures at sea when he was younger and he showed me some letters he had written to his children but those, he would never send, as his children were too young to be able to read and understand. His writing was emotive but very erratic and showed he had some troubles with literacy in Spanish.

I encouraged him to keep writing as a way of lessening his emotional conflicts. His Spanish grammar continued to be rather atrocious at times, but his written content was poetic and expressive, and it showed me this man had potential.

When el Cuco did not come to visit, he would ring me at night, and we had long conversations on the phone. After a few months, we became the best of friends. In my family, everyone, including Giuseppe, was happy that at last, I had some support at hand.

Giuseppe seemed to get along with his new lifestyle. He had found a lady, much older than him, whom he had to practice his sex exercises, I guess. Occasionally, he would ring to announce he would take the children for a few hours. He always took them back to his house. I did not mind him having them until they started to come back teary and frightened. When questioned, especially the younger twins said daddy's lady friend was a witch, she wanted to read their future with a smelly black cloth, then lit up candles and prayed over them in the name of some demon and other spirits.

There was no way I could verify their claims, as I knew the kids had a vivid imagination and when questioned, Giuseppe denied it emphatically.

Nevertheless, I was horrified at the slightest thought of it, and I started to resent and later rejected any of Giuseppe plans to take the kids away from home, especially if he was going to take them to his house.

Just by chance, I was lucky to find through friends an elderly lady from Colombia, Isabel, who was willing to occasionally look after the children for a short time if an emergency occurred.

My friendship with el Cuco kept on blossoming. It was evident to me he thoroughly enjoyed being with the children and me. I did not have much to offer with my restricted budget, but whenever I could,

I would invite him to have a meal with us. He enjoyed playing with the children. Then after the children went to sleep, we would stay up talking, talking, and talking.

El Cuco could not understand how my marriage had ended in divorce. I finished up sharing with him my sexual fears and afflictions. He also trusted me with his stories and his many experiences in his childhood and later as a sailor.

El Cuco had such an exciting life to tell. He made me feel still young and somewhat optimistic, and before long, we were kissing and cuddling, and then becoming intimate. I felt at the time, there might still be some hope in our lives, besides discouragement and tragedies.

Giuseppe and my relatives knew el Cuco was visiting me frequently, but we chose to keep our relationship a secret for the time being.

El Cuco decided to move to his mother's flat, which was becoming vacant, and he also got a job as a car park attendant in the city. He suggested looking at my circumstances, I needed to approach the Catholic Church to see if I could get an annulment of my marriage, which of course had never been truly consummated. I eventually, and after much hesitation, I accepted to try.

The process for a marriage annulment was rather expensive, gruelling, and complicated, as it involved exhaustive interrogation and interviews with key witnesses over our years Giuseppe and I were married and involved our families, doctors, psychologists, family and friends in Australia and in Argentina. It also included endless interviews and sworn statements from me, and I suspected from Giuseppe as well. On top of all that, I was told the results were not always positive. I was a bit hesitant about having to air our dirty laundry across my family and friends, but in any case, I decided to push it forward and at least attempt it.

El Cuco's visits became more frequent, plus we started to have outings with the children as if we were already a family. My elderly friend Isabel and one of my sisters, Edith and her husband were the only ones who knew how significant my relationship with el Cuco was becoming, but they offered no advice or suggestion. The rest of the family, including my parents and my younger sister Flor knew el

Cuco was seeing us almost daily but said nothing to me.

Then one day, my elderly friend Isabel questioned us, 'Hey you two, what are you waiting for to get married?' We did not know what to respond at the time, but the question kept coming up in our conversations, especially when the possibility of having another child came up.

Not long after, I got a letter from the Catholic Church advising me, under the circumstances exposed during the process in Australia and overseas and upon payment of the final fee, an annulment to my marriage to Giuseppe was going to be granted by the Catholic Church Tribunal. I was going to be free to marry again in the Church if I wished to. Besides, and to complete our happiness, we found out I was pregnant.

Part 2 - Carmela Junior

El Cuco moved in with us and we decided to get married in a civil ceremony at home. I had to tell Giuseppe and my family and that was when all hell broke loose.

My parents were disgusted, my younger sister Flor's husband, Rolando, aggressively threatened not to see me ever again; Giuseppe threatened to take me to court to take the children away from me!

Unfortunately, nobody gave me any solid evidence as to the reason they opposed our prospective marriage. After all, they must have suspected by then that el Cuco and I were already lovers, and up to that point, they had not uttered a word against our relationship. What was so wrong now when we wanted to make amends and formalise our relationship?

At the time, I was getting a small pension and the allowance for my studies from the Department of Social Security. Within a week of our marriage announcement, two officers who I thought were from the Department of Social Security called in and wanted to know if el Cuco was living with me, checking wardrobes and cabinets to see what personal items from el Cuco were there. To my amazement, they listed some details of my private financial affairs I knew only my immediate family and Giuseppe might have been aware of. I told them we were planning to get married in the near future. Nevertheless, they announced all my government payments would be stopped as from that date.

I thought it was quite obvious someone enraged from my family had dobbed us into the authorities!

Then, I also got a visit from two suited gentlemen claiming they were from the Taxation Department to investigate my financial affairs. Fortunately, I had the guts this time to shut the door in their faces requesting a proper appointment and their ID. I rang the Taxation Department myself, to find out what I had done wrong. To my surprise, the Taxation Department had not sent anybody to investigate me!

I also rang the Department of Social Security directly and they had not sent anybody to investigate me either.

It was clear to me neither of the visits were legitimate.

I felt quite saddened and desolate that someone from my family had the nerve to do such a callous act on me personally, but above all I felt so hurt that someone who knew me well would dare to harm my children and myself and humiliate us so publicly!

I could not believe it would be my parents, after all I was rearing their grandchildren, and their English was not enough to do anything like that. My parents had never shown any concern with my private life. Why now of all sorts?

Despite our differences, I thought Giuseppe would have been incapable of hurting the children or me for that matter! We had our differences, but he would never have the disposition to hurt us, he loved his children… maybe Flor's husband? He was known to be a bit strange… Or… Or someone invisible… Whom?

These heartless actions would go on to place an irreparable wedge between me and my family, and they had certainly left an unsavoury impression in my soul. Regrettably, these cruel acts would remain a mystery to me for many years to come.

Many years later, I reflected, if anybody, especially in my family had something to say against El Cuco, they should have spoken freely to me then, as these mysteries made el Cuco and I more determined to pursue our life together.

Finally, I got a letter from the Catholic Church Tribunal announcing my first marriage had been finally annulled.

As we had planned, we married immediately in a civil ceremony at my home with my children. I was not ready to marry in the Church, after all, God had extremely disappointed me! Only my sister Edith and her husband, Isabel, and a few of my friends from university were in attendance. We did not feel like inviting Flor and her husband and my parents were away. El Cuco's mother Sara was invited but unfortunately, she could not travel so quickly, as she had to solve some business issues pending in Argentina. Isabel minded the children for the night, and we went to a Manly hotel for our one-night honeymoon.

We reported our marriage to the authorities, and I tried to increase my interpreting assignments, but it was obvious that with el Cuco's wage and no government help, we would not survive, let alone give the children a proper education.

Therefore, we decided to look for a business venture we thought would give us more financial freedom. El Cuco was keen on purchasing a franchise with an eight-ton truck run. He got his truck licence and found a truck run business with a nursery that would give us a good income.

We decided to buy the franchise from the proceeds of the sale of some of Cuco's apartments Sara managed to sell in Buenos Aires and from some money we borrowed from my father 's superannuation fund. It was good to feel that although we did not have any savings, we did not have any real debts either to start our journey together.

El Cuco 's work with the truck involved long trips to the country to pick up landscaping materials and deliver them to a nursery. The work was hard, but the pay was excellent. We dreamt of being able to move into a bigger house, in a better suburb when the baby was born!

However, within three months, the nursery was sold out and the new owners did not honour our contract. We contacted a solicitor, but we were advised to sue the previous nursery owners would take years for proceedings to start and we needed some five thousand dollars, which we did not have, just to start proceedings for the litigation.

We contacted the Department of Social Security, but we were told that to get any financial assistance we needed to sell the truck and use that money first. We tried to sell the truck, but it was not worth even half of what we had paid for it with the work contract.

We were then truly trapped with no savings, no regular income, and a new baby on the way! We needed to return my father's super money and besides, Giuseppe was taking me to court to try to gain custody of the children.

I applied to the government run legal aid service to get free legal assistance, but I was told I could not get it because I was not getting any social security benefits; and therefore, any legal costs must be paid by myself.

We contacted a local private solicitor and explained the situation and luckily, he agreed to represent me in court and get paid later, when we could hopefully be on our feet again. We also asked my parents to borrow some money again to keep us afloat to buy essential groceries and the bare necessities for the children.

In the meantime, we decided to contact some of the landscaping suppliers from the franchise and we also started ringing up nurseries to offer our services directly. To our surprise, and despite our lack of experience in the industry, we got some orders: sandstone, fencing tea-trees, railway sleepers and bush-rocks.

We knew where to get the sandstone, the sleepers, and the tea-trees but we did not have any idea how to get the bush-rocks. We were told other truck owners went into the National Parks to pick up the bush rocks, but certainly we did not want to steal them from the government! So, one Saturday, we packed the children in the truck and travelled south looking for some bush rocks.

The whole family was so excited to discover some paddocks with mossy bush rocks suitable for garden edges. We gathered some courage to call in some of the farms uninvited. We explained what we were looking for bush-rocks to sell as garden rocks in Sydney.

El Cuco's English was rather broken, but his excitement was contagious, and a few farmers got interested, especially when we told them we would pay $100 for each of the rock truck loads.

Our arrangement would be a windfall for both the farmers and us; for the farmer, we would clear the paddocks from the rocks, and they would also get some monetary gain for their work and as for us, we would only have to load the rocks on the truck to sell them in Sydney.

In other words, whenever we had orders of bush-rocks, we would ring one of the farmers and asked him to gather 8 tons or about 500 medium rocks for el Cuco to pick up. They would help el Cuco to load the rocks on the truck in exchange of some money and then el Cuco would deliver them straight to the customers in lots of 100 on the same day.

We continued to get whatever the customers asked for, bush-rocks and all, for about a month or so.

Going to get the bush rocks was extremely difficult for el Cuco, as the work was heavy, and the days were long. He started early in the morning because he had to drive for over three hours into the countryside, then load the materials, then drive back to Sydney and deliver the whole truck on the same day, because the truck had to be emptied and ready for the next order. It was also tiresome for me, as I had to organise the deliveries round the clock on top of all my other responsibilities.

After a few months, I sat down to calculate our profits. When considering the truck's maintenance and repairs, we had earned the grand total net amount of $13 a week. However, I realized if I calculated the profits from the bush-rock orders only, the earnings after deducting the expenses were more than $300 a load! It was obvious the sale of the other materials, like the flagging, logs and tea tree poles were running at a huge loss.

I explained my calculations in detail to el Cuco. I advised him we should stop delivering the sandstone flagging and the fencing material immediately and instead concentrate on the bush-rocks. I started an advertising campaign, writing personally to the nurseries, printing business cards and placing small advertisements in the local papers. The Bush Rock Centre had been born!

The orders kept coming for the bush-rocks, not only from the nurseries but now from private customers as well. I was now busy answering the phone, organising the work for el Cuco, and continuing the advertising. We did not know where to store the rocks when we had leftovers at the end of the day. Thus, we approached the local petrol station Muslim owners, who agreed to let us use part of their backyard in exchange for a small rent.

In the meantime, I managed to finish my Bachelor of Arts Degree with brilliant marks. The university offered me to do Honours on top of my Diploma of Education, which I accepted.

Soon we were able to pay my parents back, pay for our upkeep, and start saving some money.

However, not all was rosy in my life. I was summoned to the Children's Court often and to Legal Counselling and Mediation about the children's custody matter.

My solicitor informed me it was easy for Giuseppe because he had obtained free legal aid from the government.

I could not believe it! I knew for sure Giuseppe had quite a few tenants paying him rent in his house, and he used to do plumbing work in exchange for cash without writing it in the books; surely, he would not qualify for legal aid if he came clean with his income!

What a disgrace! I was furious and I rang Giuseppe and threatened him to report him to the government authorities about his lies. I also sent him a nice letter from my heart, asking him to leave the children with me. 'The children are confused, and we need to stop fighting to give them some security. I would look after them, so you would be proud of them one day.' My approach worked!

Soon after, my solicitor informed me Giuseppe had withdrawn his claim for custody, and I also learnt he had left Australia and he was now living in Argentina. He had left his legal bills for me to pay along with mine, which, at that stage, honestly, I did not mind.

Giuseppe re-married an older lady from his original Italian village in Argentina not long after. He never sent any money nor did he ever phone or come to see the children again for many years.

Years later, I was shocked and hurt to know he had visited Australia with his wife and had called in to see some members of my own family. However, he did not contact the children or me. I guessed he would have been scared of any possible child support claim I could have raised against him!

Despite our financial success, I soon noticed el Cuco was not happy. I would have attempted anything to make him happy, but he was usually sullen and upset now with unjustified outbursts of shouting and putting the children or me down for any reason. I thought he might have been overworked, so we took another short holiday to no avail. The better we were financially, the worse his moods were.

Baby Champ was born in November, and he was really a breath of fresh air in our lives. Besides, el Cuco admired my dad so much he did not mind that I registered Champ with my father's surname. As Giuseppe was not in Australia, I also decided to change the surname of my other children to my dad's surname as well.

Christopher and Cassandra thought Champ was their own live dolly, and Johny and Jack were old enough not to be jealous of the attention Champ had. We were all delighted to spoil our baby 'Champito' rotten!

In Argentina, we say, 'babies come with a piece of bread under their arm', but English babies are more blessed, I guess as they are 'born with a silver spoon in their mouth'. Both sayings were certainly true for us. After having so many financial issues at the start of our marriage, eight months after baby Champ was born, we had saved enough money to be able to purchase a half an acre block in the Western suburbs, where we could live and store our rocks as well.

The land had an old fibro still liveable house on it. In a few months, we were renovating it with all the modern conveniences, and we decided to move in there. We decided my house would be sold, and the proceeds left in trust separately for the children in the future.

I was busy with so many children to look after, trying to continue my studies and organising el Cuco's pick-ups and deliveries. It was evident I could not cope with everything, especially keeping up with breastfeeding, plus I wanted to give el Cuco my best attention. Therefore, I decided to postpone my university studies.

I was also having problems with Christopher, who did not want to go to school and was constantly truanting. He claimed the teacher knew nothing and she made lots of mistakes. He also claimed he was bored to death at school. When approached, the teacher, I would never forget her name, a Mrs Tatarinoff, informed me Chris was practically a pain in the neck. She did not know what to do with him. Lately, she'd had some success getting him to read books at the back of the class. He was at present quietly reading Leo Tolstoy's *War and Peace*, which she got from the local library.

She was explicit that she did not have the time or the energy to prepare extra activities to keep him interested. She was going to recommend transferring him to a Gifted and Talented class at a school nearby.

Cassandra, also in Grade 3 was also having troubles at school, because she could not speak properly and only communicated through her twin brother in a strange language. It had been recommended to me to separate her from Christopher at school. She had been considered a slow learner, but when tested by the school psychologist, she seemed to be of above average intelligence. Her teacher, a Mrs. Taylor, suggested all I could do was to praise her for whatever she did well, which was gymnastics. Even if I could give her just a compliment for wearing pretty dresses with matching bows in her hair would be helpful.

Christopher was transferred to a nearby school, to an opportunity class, only to encounter other challenges. He was now amongst other children, of similar intelligence to him, but using their cleverness for the wrong purposes. He was still truanting but instead of coming home, even after school hours, he was with his smart new mates getting into mischief harassing the neighbours or terrorising the local park with home-made bombs and firecrackers.

On the other hand, Johny and Jack were placid, and they started kinder garden without much fuss.

One morning, whilst preparing breakfast for my family, I stepped on a swivel armchair to get the cereal from a high shelf in the kitchen. I lost my balance and fell backwards hard on the floor. The pain was excruciating, and I could not get up. El Cuco went berserk. He was swearing and erupted in a furious rage, breaking chairs and plates; without doing anything to help me.

Again, there was nothing I could do myself as I was paralysed with pain and fright!

Christopher calmly rang the emergency services, explained what had happened to me and asked for an ambulance. I was taken to the hospital where I was diagnosed with a broken vertebra. Unfortunately, besides complete rest, there was nothing they could do for me, apart from giving me strong painkillers and sedatives.

I felt completed defeated! What was I going to do as a crippled mother, with five children including a baby, a household, a business to run and a husband to satisfy and make happy? I spent most of my time sleeping and when awake, sobbing and feeling sorry for myself.

Amazingly, I was informed Christopher had assisted again

requesting home help from an agency. Jean was hired to look after the household and the children and to also answer the phone taking the bush rock orders. El Cuco had to organise his own daily work.

The children soon became efficient at changing nappies, preparing small meals, and entertaining baby Champ after school.

Then I noticed Jean reading a children's bible to the children and praying. I truly had not thought of God or prayed since my incident with the Catholic priest all those years ago. I discussed with el Cuco that I thought perhaps we should ask Jean to leave as she was putting funny ideas into the children's minds.

After much discussion, however, we decided she should stay because she was extremely efficient.

'Where are we going to find someone like her?'

'She is really an angel,' we concluded.

Then, one day Jean asked me if I had ever known God.

'Of course, I had,' I said.

'Would you like me to pray for your healing, perhaps your complete healing?' she asked. 'He is always personally with you, my dear and He loves you', she added.

She showed me the following verses in the Bible from the Gospel of Matthew: *'Ask and it will be given to you; seek and you will find; knock and the door will be opened to you. For everyone who asks receives; the one who seeks finds; and to the one who knocks, the door will be opened'* and *'Which of you, if your son asks for bread, will give him a stone?' 'Or if he asks for a fish, will give him a snake?' 'If you, then, though you are evil, know how to give good gifts to your children, how much more will your Father in heaven give good gifts to those who ask him!'*

These words impacted me deeply. When I was alone, I could not stop weeping! I read and re-read these verses. I recalled over and over again my encounter with Jesus all those years ago during my childhood and desperately wanted to believe God was indeed almighty and merciful and He could heal me. Was He at all interested in me and my family? After all, there were so many more important issues in the world... Would it be possible if I asked my Heavenly

Father, He would perform the miracle? Jean had also asked me if I wanted her church to pray for my healing and I tentatively accepted.

'Ask and it will be given to you; seek and you will find; knock and the door will be opened to you. For everyone who asks receives; the one who seeks finds; and to the one who knocks, the door will be opened.'

I found myself on my knees crying and asking God for His mercy and healing:

'Yes Lord, I believe. You are alive. Forgive me for not trusting in you. I love you and give my life to you forever now. Forgive my sins. Guide me and save me.'

I felt like a hot wind throughout my body, and I started talking to God in another language. I knew in my spirit that I had been healed. I got up and I had no pain. I walked to the bathroom where I knew my tablets were, but I had no pain, plus I felt an indescribable peace. I was bursting with joy and gratitude to God.

I could not wait for el Cuco to return home and tell him about my experience. When I did, he said to me Jean might be a witch, maybe a white witch, but a witch, nevertheless. We should be cautious…

When I told to Jean what happened, she brought me books to attempt to explain to me the mysteries of the Holy Spirit and what had happened to me.

'You have been touched by the Lord', she proclaimed. Then, she invited me and the whole family to her church.

It took me a few months to understand my experience and it took el Cuco even more time to even accept taking me to Jean's church called *Jesus is alive.*

I felt I had been given a new life and I wanted to follow my Lord Jesus for the whole of my life.

The whole family went to the magnificent Fraser Island for a holiday break. I was still wary with my back because we were driving a 4-wheel drive and the terrain was very rugged. It seemed the pain had disappeared completely, my spirit was very much alive, and I still had a tremendous peace.

I had brought several books to the holiday that Jean had lent me. These small books were about God, his Son, and the Holy Spirit. She also suggested to me to read the Bible, especially the 4 Gospels in the New Testament. I had also kept my relationship with Jesus alive by talking or praying daily to Him, as if he was next to me.

I started to pray for a better school for the children and one day whilst looking for a Bible in Spanish, I bumped into *Calvary Chapel* primary school. I wanted to speak to the principal to see if there were any vacancies, and to my surprise, there were places for the 4 children and the fees were very reasonable.

After purchasing the school uniforms, the four children started school there. To our delight and within a short period of time, Christopher had improved his behaviour. They were all doing very well and getting exceptional marks. I could not believe it, but the teacher assured me Cassandra was motivated to learn and she was happily absorbing the normal curriculum. I was almost impossible to accept the difference this school had made. I was full of gratitude to God!

The family continued to go to *Jesus is alive* church where we witnessed many other miracles, but when the children started school at Calvary Chapel, we decided as a family to attend Church there, where God continued to perform many miracles and where we and especially the children met many people and made many long-time friends.

Other miracles happened to us quickly, like our continuous financial independence thanks to the income from the Bush Rock Centre.

The block of land we had bought was huge and we were able to properly store our rocks in our own back yard by size and price. We continued to have a never-ending demand for bush rocks. The sky was the limit for our business. We were bringing bush rocks for nurseries, and private clients, but afterwards, we were bringing large bush rocks for the Zoo and for many public gardens including the Chinese Gardens in the city of Sydney.

Although we had approval from the bank to expand the business, we decided not to purchase more trucks because labour was complicated. Nobody wanted to do heavy work and the young people we finally found to assist, were very unreliable even when we offered a good pay.

Instead, we found out about the possibility of hiring semitrailers with their own drivers to pick up and bring the rocks to Sydney to trade. The operation still demanded el Cuco to supervise the delivery of the rocks to our storeroom and then delivered the daily orders to our customers in a smaller truck, but we avoided the long travel now the different farmers were eager to collect the rocks for us all around regional NSW. After paying all our due taxes, all our expenses, and now also tithing generously to our church, our bank account kept thriving.

It was around that time when Sara visited us unexpectedly. To celebrate our success, we agreed to go on a short holiday to Queensland with the children. We noticed properties were a lot cheaper there and the returns were good. We had a look at a block of units in the Sunshine Coast and to our surprise, we discovered we could afford to buy it as an investment if we put the proceeds of my house and Sara's property together. Sara decided to sell her property in Sydney straight away and we finished up purchasing a block of units in the Sunshine Coast and another house with 2 rented apartments attached to it. These investments made us partners until she died.

At that point, and after signing all the documents for the purchase, Sara decided suddenly to go back to Argentina again.

Sara came to visit us again the following year and she was over the moon with our financial progress. She was then able to help with some of my tasks, especially attending to the children when I was forever on the phone taking rock orders or the occasional interpreting job.

Sara mentioned to me she had made a solid friendship with my parents who were by now retired and living in Argentina. Life could not be better. Even el Cuco's rages seemed to have settled down considerably.

One day, after one of my routine interpreting assignments, I made the comment to Sara that I had been deeply moved, because my client had been told she had advanced breast cancer and unfortunately, it was too hard to treat successfully. I said to her I never realized breast cancer was so real and nasty, and all women should examine their breasts regularly to see that there were no lumps there.

Sara suddenly went pale and after a while she said to me, 'I have to confess I have a lump in my breast. It appeared after I fell and bumped my chest against the rails at home. I have not told anyone because I am terrified about it,' she concluded.

The very next day we went to see my GP who examined her lump and got her to do some tests that afternoon, then go and see a specialist. She was diagnosed with breast cancer stage III on the spot. The following day, which I would never forget because it happened to be my 38th birthday, she was operated on to remove her lump along with her left breast and her lymph nodes on the same side.

The operation was a success, and she was told all cancer cells had been removed along with the lymph nodes on the side of the removed breast. However, she had to have radiotherapy treatment to eliminate any possibility of the cancer coming back. Chemotherapy was also highly recommended. 'To be on the safe side', the doctor told us. Therefore, Sara at 70 years of age, speaking little English and with only us in Australia decided to have all the treatments recommended to her for the next 4 months in Sydney.

Life went on for me with the Lord's help: the business, a new baby and the other children's lives and needs, then an increasing temperamental husband and looking after Sara, who was often sick from her treatments and/or needed to be transported to her medical appointments and tests. Sara also needed a lot of emotional support because she felt depressed due to her illness.

Around this time, we were also informed by the local Council we could not store rocks in our back yard because the zoning of our land was residential, and not industrial. We had thought all along that our property was zoned industrial, after all, our neighbours were all wholesale businesses, but apparently ours was indeed zoned residential.

A Local Council Officer notified us personally that instead of rock storing, we could subdivide the land into three blocks should we wish to. He also allowed us to keep the rocks there until we found another storeroom for the business.

I called a local Real Estate Agent to have our house and land valued to sell, and we were told with the subdivision now possible, the lot could be sold for about three times what we had bought it for. We decided to build three houses on it, as that would fetch a lot more money.

It was clear to me and especially to Sara, the Lord had yet granted us another miracle. I immediately started the process to subdivide the land by myself, with the help of a surveyor and our bank manager. The development was not so difficult, although it was time consuming. I also had to arrange to better renovate the front house on the outside and to build another two houses in the back blocks.

I had tried to make el Cuco happy for a long time but to no avail. I understood at the beginning he was missing his own children, but by now I was personally sending money monthly to their mother for their upkeep, which contributed substantially to their better education and lifestyle. We also usually tried to send presents for their birthdays and other festivities like Christmas. Sadly, at that stage, there was still nothing further we could do to bring them to Australia.

I thought we could be a family, but el Cuco had changed drastically. He was on and off getting very nasty with the children, shouting, and bashing them without any real reason.

I remember once when we moved into our new address, the children had got a bit lost and confused as to what train to take to come back home from school, so they rang up and I was able to help them. However, they still arrived home late. When they arrived and without questioning them further, El Cuco attacked them with his belt. He had lost all control. I shouted to stop, but he threatened to kill me in his rage. I was paralysed and too frightened to prevent his outburst, and all I could do was to try to calm him down with words. I understood later, I should have rung the police and for many years, I regretted not intervening more aggressively to protect my children's precious safety from el Cuco.

El Cuco even got mad with his feeble mother recovering from her chemo, throwing cups and saucers to her because she did not want to get baptised in our church!

He also often shouted at me nonstop for no apparent reason and called me whore and other nasty names if I was ever late, even when I was doing errands for the new housing project. He said all women were whores, like her mother.

El Cuco's attitude and comments towards me, my children and also Sara wounded me deeply. Our sex life deteriorated rapidly and despite my constant prayers to God for him to change and appreciate us, he did not change a bit and in fact it got worse.

One day, the shouting was so bad the neighbours rang the police. Two officers called in and said to him if his attitude did not change, he would be taken to the police station and charged with assault. I was advised I could report him and get an Apprehended Violence Order against him, but at the time, I did not know what would happen to us if I did.

I felt deeply embarrassed, thinking of the neighbours witnessing such a scandal in our family and I was sure the children felt the same way as they did not want to go out of the house. I decided there and then I did not want to help el Cuco anymore with the business. It was perhaps the heavy job that was making him so angry and unpredictable, thus the best thing for us to do was to sell The Bush Rock Centre.

We would be able to sell the houses when they were finished, and if God was gracious, maybe move to a better neighbourhood.

I was by then, lucky to apply for and get a scholarship with guaranteed full- time work as a teacher and continue my abandoned Diploma of Education at a university nearby. I looked at the workload and it seemed light and easy. Surely it would not take me much time, hence I decided to do extra subjects to get my 'official qualifications', or my second degree majoring in Interpreter and Translator as well.

Sara recovered from her treatment, and she travelled to Argentina once more to see if she could sell some of the properties she still had there. As far as I knew, she was successful in selling them all reasonably quickly at a premium price, although she never told us for how much or where she had the moneys from the sales.

When Sara returned, after six months, she did not look well. We visited her oncologist who ordered a series of tests. Her cancer had spread to her bones and lungs, and she needed chemotherapy again, but her prognosis was poor.

The treatment was much more aggressive this time, she felt extremely sick with it and lost all her hair. When the tests were repeated, the specialist told us outright he could not do anything else for her in the form of a cure. She would not survive another round of chemo. She could only have palliative care to make her more comfortable.

Sara and I both wept outside the doctor's surgery. Sara had dreamt of travelling together to Europe and she had asked me to get passports for all of us and look at some suitable tours not long before. However, her dreams were never to be fulfilled.

We tried to have a holiday at Umina beach in the Central Coast of NSW where we rented a luxury home for a week to cheer her up. But after two days, we had to leave the kids in a cinema watching a movie, including young Champ, to get some time to organise a special ambulance for Sara to take her home, because there was not a hospital in the Central Coast that would take her in with her condition. She was not only desperately sick with her cancer, but she was now highly infectious and quarantined with giardiasis!

El Cuco knew all along about his mother's sickness and the complications she was having, but he started to blame me for it. He constantly accused me of not looking after her properly and continued to call me a whore and a liar. He could not believe me when I needed time going out shopping for groceries or run errands in the Council for the house buildings.

I still had to travel to the Sunshine Coast in Queensland for issues regarding our properties there, and Sara could not come with me. El Cuco did not approve of it and went hysterical, threatening to kill me if he found out I was cheating on him, which was the last thing on my mind...

We finally sold the business at a good profit and el Cuco got a job in a local hardware store delivering building materials. I finished my studies and was offered a full-time teacher position at a school nearby. I considered myself lucky because a permanent position at my age was rare, but I believed my marks had convinced the Department of Education I was worthy to be on their payroll.

Sara, despite all my care and prayers, continued to deteriorate and she was now unable to stay on her own at home. She would scream with pain at night and many times she refused to have her painkillers (morphine tablets). I bought her a TV/video and got her lots of Spanish videos to entertain her, but she got worse and eventually she was bedridden completely and fully incontinent.

Although Sara was not a large woman, it became impossible for me to move her without hurting her because her pain was so bad that she could not cooperate any longer.

We tried desperately to get her a place in a respite facility where she could be looked after during the day, but she did not qualify because she was not receiving a pension in Australia and el Cuco did not want to leave her in a paid nursing home because of the costs.

It was clear we could not manage her pain at home, and she usually screamed and screamed at all hours. The children needed to continue with their lives and schooling. I decided to take young Champ out to the park to play for an hour or so in the afternoons most days to distract him from the constant moaning and shouting coming from his grandma's room.

After much pleading with the specialist, Sara was admitted to Westmead Hospital for radiation treatment. This would alleviate her bone/nerve pain, but after a couple of days, we were asked to pick her up in the middle of the night because the treatment was not working and the 'hospital beds were for patients who could be cured, not for the desperately terminally sick'.

We were lucky to find a Croatian lady to look after her during the day when we were all out at work or at school. However, I suspected she was giving Sara double dose of painkillers during the day because no matter what medication we administered at night, we could not settle her. She screamed and yelled that she was in pain and could not breathe. And to top it all off, the younger twins came home earlier from school one day and found her carer smoking outside whilst poor Sara was screaming and distressed inside.

I continued to ring all the hospitals to see if they could help, but I was continuously told they knew her already, and they could not do anything else for her.

The Lord sustained me and kept me sane in body and soul throughout Sara's sickness. I was able to keep the household going with an ever-increasing washing load, prepare meals, look after the children, go to work, and look after Sara as much as I could. I realized then I would never want to stay at home should I be sick in the future. I deserved better care, wherever I could find it at whatever the cost.

Eventually and after much coercing, I found a private hospital that would accept Sara as a patient to make her breathe easier. I remember promising her we would bring her home as quickly as she was better and her teary eyes thanking me.

Unfortunately, this hospital could not treat her, hence she was urgently overnight transferred without consulting us to another hospital with physiotherapy services. They were trying to relieve the fluid in her lungs that was now drowning her.

When I got there first thing in the morning, the notes had not come through to this new hospital and it was too late to advise them her cancer had perversely invaded her bones throughout her thoracic cavity! The physio treatment had been done to relieve the fluid, but the treatment had damaged her thoracic diseased bones even further. Her condition was distressing and hopeless.

My parents had recently returned to Sydney from Argentina and my mother offered to look after Sara the following night to keep her company.

El Cuco rang me at work the following morning to let me know Sara was dying, and I left immediately for the hospital. In between periods of unconsciousness, Sara desperately tried to speak to me, but was unable to do so. Her son tried to speak to her, but she refused to listen to him, which I could not understand. She wanted to speak to me personally and with some urgency.

I understood, somehow, that she wanted to give me her old wedding ring and el Cuco took it off her and placed it on my finger along with my own.

She still was not happy, she needed to speak to me, but her strength seemed not to be enough to keep her awake and she kept on falling into unconsciousness. I kept repeating Psalm 23 to her praying it would soothe her:

'The Lord is my Sheppard; I shall not want.

He makes me lie down in green pastures. He leads me beside still waters. He restores my soul.

He leads me in paths of righteousness for his name's sake.

Even though I walk through the valley of the shadow of death, I will fear no evil, for you are with me; your rod and your staff, they comfort me.'

Next time she was conscious, she seemed to have calmed down a bit but suddenly she was agitated again, and it was evident she wanted urgently to communicate with me, but she was unable to do so, as she fell into unconsciousness again.

The nurses asked us to go for lunch and a walk, as they needed Sara to be made comfortable and she had to be given her morphine injections, which were overdue, and we obliged.

We did not feel like having lunch, but we went for a short walk. When we came back to the hospital, Sara was already dead.

Chapter 7

MATRIARCHY

'These mountains that you are carrying, you were only supposed to climb.'
(Najwa Zebian)

'Throw me to the wolves and I will return leading the pack.'
(Unknown)

Part 1 - La Macaca

My dearest great grandson Emanuel; I hope you know how much I love you and how much I want to please you, so you can collect all our family stories for the book you are putting together... However, I am finding it harder and harder to write with my arthritic hands and no matter how much I want to concentrate, my mind often wonders onto another subject.

I want to tell you, there are parts in this text that I did not want Carmela to know, so I decided to give it to one of my many friends to translate. I hope it can all make sense. This is the second part of my life!

May God bless you always in your endeavours, my sweet love!

———

Reading my palm, a gypsy once told me I would die at 33, Christ's age in the cross. I was convinced that would be the case, and it almost happened. When Paquito's father died suddenly from a stroke, his mother, dear mama Doña Luisa came to live with us and our two young daughters, Carmela, and Edith. I had always been fond of Paquito's mum, the loving mother I no longer had. She was always cautious with her money; no matter how little she had, she managed to purchase all the ingredients to surprise us with divine Spanish meals and kept the house nice and tidy. She was always jolly. The entire house was filled with music, songs, and dancing: 'Granada tu tierra esta llena de lindas mujeres, de sangre y de sol,' she sang incessantly, everywhere in and around the house. The children adored her!

It was so sad when *abuelita* Luisa got ill and riddled with pain in the stomach. The worst was we did not know what was wrong with her. We tried to change her diet, reduce her beloved *café con leche* and make her have a longer siesta so she could rest in the middle of the day. But nothing helped her.

So, Paquito fetched her family doctor to come and see her at home. His diagnosis was gloomy and infallible. She had a large tumour in the liver, but she might have a chance to survive it, if she had an operation to remove it straight away.

We made arrangements to have her admitted to Hospital Salaberry near her old house in the suburb of Mataderos.

We spent all our savings and borrowed some money from El Compadre, Carmela's Padrino, so she could have the best surgeon. But sadly, we were told *la vieja's* tumour was cancer and it had already spread everywhere in her tiny body.

'It is as if we had spread a cup of rice all around her body. It is impossible to remove all the grains from it,' we were told by her surgeon. She was sewed up and sent home.

She lasted three months. We sent my two daughters to live with our Spanish neighbours and I nursed her day and night. But it had been a freezing winter and I did not care to wrap up if I needed something in a hurry from our terrace upstairs. Then I also felt sick and nauseous, and I started to cough and cough and vomit and vomit. I thought it was just a cold, or maybe I was pregnant again?

La Vieja died the day Juan Peron ordered to burn the churches. In retaliation, the Plaza de Mayo was bombed by the military in an attempt to overthrow the President. I remember the day was 16th June 1955. It was a day of mourning for many Argentinians, not just for us. Many people died in the massacre. Unofficially, they found 308 bodies including civilians, children, and many others who could not be identified.

In this chaos, we could not find anybody who would organise a coffin to take our loving mum to a proper grave. We were devastated, it was cold and raining and I was burning with temperature. In the end, Paquito found a funeral parlour open who helped us bury *La Vieja* in the Cementerio de Flores in a second-hand coffin.

I thought I would follow *La Vieja*'s fate, but God was gracious and against the odds and the gypsy's predictions, God did not want to take me yet. After more than a month in bed, numerous lung drainages and without seeing my daughters, I recovered from pneumonia and pleurisy, but sadly I lost the baby boy I was carrying.

Paquito so much would have liked to have a son at all costs, but I did not want any more children. However, despite trying to avoid falling pregnant again, I went on to have yet another daughter, Florinda, whom we lovingly called Flor. Indeed, she was the flower of our life, and a real treasure as she came to fill the emptiness in our life after La Vieja died.

Life would have been normal for me if it were not for Carmela's extravagances. She was without a doubt a problem child! I tried to give her more attention and keep her occupied. I enrolled her in piano, dancing, and languages classes, but she was never satisfied and wanted to know and experience everything.

She would not settle at school; she was clingy, and she continually complained she was bored. The teachers accelerated her by two years at school. We also changed her from a school she despised, to another and from that one, to another, but to no avail; she never settled.

In spite of all the money we spent on her, Carmela was too disconnected, she was always looking for a new adventure and many times she wanted to get involved in dangerous activities.

I must confess, despite her frustrations, Carmela had always excelled in her studies. However, as Carmela was growing up, I thought she was not a good example for my other daughters. I was so sure one of these days she would fall pregnant or end up in jail.

After she finished her Secondary studies, Carmela managed to get a job even when she was just turning 15. Not long after, she wanted to go to work in the United States. She must have been dreaming! No child of mine was going to leave home before marriage. What would the family and neighbours think, if she did?

I must admit, Carmela had a good heart though because when she finally got a well-paid job, she generously helped us with her money and time to set up a successful small family business at home.

However, by the time Carmela reached her 20s we could not hold her down any longer. She left for Australia, looking for adventures with Giuseppe, a neighbour who was a few years older than her and a bunch of other friends with the same ambitions as her.

I thought Giuseppe was in love with my daughter Carmela by the way he looked at her, but poor Giuseppe, he did not know whom he was dealing with. He would never be her suitor. She would eat him alive in no time!

Carmela had already had a nice boyfriend, Dario, whom I thought she would marry one day, but she dumped him when she got involved with my nephew Amadeo. God, I could have killed them both when I found out the news from his mother, my sister-in-law La Piruja!

I was very clever and I acted swiftly stopping the whole affair in no time!

'Tia, I love her,' Amadeo spoke. 'I cannot live without her, and she loves me too. We want to get married,' he said.

'You are a silly boy. How are you going to keep her? You do not have a good job and besides, you know you are first cousins, she could have your child with a pig's tail or worse!' I replied.

He stood there without anything to say. He was very pale and his light colour eyes were watery. He was chewing his lower lip. 'You know how much I care for you Amadeo; I always want the best for you, this news will kill us both your parents and us—lucky Tío

Paquito does not know anything about this nonsense yet,' I added.

'You need to promise me you will not see her again. Yes, never see her again,' I demanded.

I felt sorry for him as he started to cry, quietly at first, then inconsolably. 'Promise?', I insisted.

'Promise' he answered.

'And this conversation is also a secret between us. You must swear to me also that you will never tell Carmela or anybody else about our secret,' I yelled.

He looked heartbroken and for a minute I thought he was going to stand up and go, but he stayed, and I made him commit again. Then I made him his favorite hot chocolate with fresh churros and with that, we sealed our pledge.

I noticed Carmela was never again her usual self since the breakup with Amadeo, but I trusted she would get over it. So, life went on and somehow, now, I was happy she was going to Australia.

How could I possibly imagine then she would marry within six months and to miserable looking Giuseppe! Carmela would certainly trample all over him!!!

Carmela's friend, Manuel, came to visit me and confessed he was in love with Carmela, and he wanted her address to convince her to return to Buenos Aires. He was shocked when I told him she had got married the week before.

I knew instinctively Carmela's actions would have some sinister repercussions within my family. Within twelve months of Carmela's going to Sydney, my second daughter Edith announced her engagement to Lolo, her long-time boyfriend. They wanted to get married soon, apply for a permanent visa, and settle in Australia.

Inflation was rampant in Argentina and our business was just breaking even. Soon we would be suffering financial hardship again. So, we gathered some savings and Paquito and I decided to travel to Australia for a visit as tourists and see if we too could immigrate to 'that big land of opportunity'.

We closed the business temporarily, saying we were taking a short holiday and I got my sister Carmela to look after the girls and Lolo, who was becoming a permanent presence in our family!

As expected, when we got to Sydney, Carmela did not look happy. I heard her crying at night, but I had to say she had grown up quickly. She now knew how to take care of the house, she had two jobs and she knew how to cook wholesome meals for us. We mentioned to her we would like to taste life as migrants and within a week she found jobs for Paquito and me.

I had never worked for a boss, but mind you, I enjoyed making gourmet pies at this huge bakery in Bondi. I also found despite my little English, I felt comfortable and liberated with the money I was making, and the dollars kept coming weekly. As for Paquito, he also seemed to have found his niche in an old workshop upholstering upmarket lounges.

A few months after, we had to return to Argentina, after all, we were just visiting Carmela on tourist visas, but before we left, we made up our mind to apply at the Australian Embassy in Argentina to see if we, at our age, could also get a permanent visa to come to Sydney. Carmela seemed to be very sympathetic and agreeable to our new plans.

When we communicated our news to our family in Argentina, my sister Carmela was devastated, and our youngest daughter Flor could not believe us. Flor argued her English skills were certainly not good enough to continue her schooling in Sydney. Her worst problem was that now, almost a teenager, she did not want to leave her friends behind.

We persuaded Edith and Lolo to wait a year or so to tie the knot, as they were so young. But they insisted they wanted to be married and travelled to Sydney to start a new life away from Argentina and within a few months they got married. With tears in our eyes, we farewelled them, trusting we would see each other again soon.

All our plans continued smoothly. Exactly two years after my daughter Carmela left us, we departed also. We only had our suitcases with our clothes and our documents with us. Flor took some of her dolls in her suitcase too.

We had left our house rented, but our entire household items had to be disposed of. Thus, we either had to sell all our treasured crockery and linen, even some of our wedding presents, for a very negligible number of pesos or we just had to give them away. It felt to me like I was just living a bad dream, as part of our lives seemed to remain forever in Argentina, never to be recovered.

Once in Sydney, Carmela was ever so generous again to provide her largest bedroom for us until we could find a place to rent, which we did quickly, not far from Carmela's. She also helped us to purchase some second hand but almost new furniture and to move there without any hiccups.

I got a job in the city as a kitchenhand and Carmela, who was now working for an airline company managed to get a job for her father as a cleaner in the same company.

Flor was not happy at all; she was always complaining. She wanted to return to Buenos Aires, and although we understood her, we could not help her. She was enrolled in the local school, and we all trusted she would soon settle in. Carmela also enrolled us all in an English special course at night and she personally took us there until we could easily travel by train on our own.

During the day, my job was to wash the dishes in a very upmarket elegant coffee shop called *Miss Brown's Tea House*. Miss Brown noticed I had the initiative to fill in for anybody when the need arose. I even helped to fill in for the chef one day when she was sick.

Therefore, when the chef was leaving, Miss Brown asked me to replace her. I was reluctant to accept the offer because my English was still basic, but I marvelled at her trust and all my colleagues were so accepting and happy for me, I agreed to give it a go.

My new job changed my tasks completely; I had to do the orders and Miss Brown gave me freedom to be creative with the dishes I had to prepare. The customers loved my new dishes, especially the ornamental salads and my dainty sandwiches with a Spanish twist. Soon we were so busy we could not cope, and Miss Brown had to employ more girls in the kitchen and as waitresses. The business was booming and so were my wages.

Paquito was also happy with his job at the airport, especially because he could see Carmela every day. The job also came with a bonus; he was given concessions to travel anywhere in the world for almost nothing. Therefore, although it was still a year away, we could have the confidence we could travel to Argentina soon, which made Flor a bit happier.

Within the year, the owner of the unit we were renting offered us the option to purchase it. Luckily, we had been able to save some money by then to use it for the deposit, so Carmela helped us to get a loan and organise a solicitor to do the paperwork.

Socially, we made many friends of Spanish descent and other nationalities during the English course. Flor had made some friends from school and seemed to have struck a friendship with Ronaldo, a young Argentinian man also attending the evening school.

Life could not have been any better for us. However, I missed our family and friends back home, especially my sister Carmela, although I have to confess, we were settling comfortably into our new life and our new country.

I was so happy when Flor brought her school report. She had done so well that she was going to be changed to the advanced level in all her subjects. Amazingly, she had received a monetary scholarship from the Rotary Club to support her to finish her secondary studies and maybe even higher studies in the future.

Edith and Lolo had settled in the Southern suburbs of Sydney, and they seemed to have found good jobs also. They were also saving hard to be able to purchase their first home.

Carmela and Giuseppe were progressing financially as well and travelling extensively around the world and one day they announced they were expecting a baby, after so many years of marriage.

However, not all was well in paradise! Our joy at the prospect of being grandparents for the first time did not stay with us for long because Flor confessed to me that she was pregnant too.

'Flor is a child. Who is the bastard?' Paquito roared.

'She is almost 16 and Ronaldo is the father', I responded. 'He is prepared to marry her Paquito,' I added sadly.

'But...' Ronaldo is twice her age,' he whispered.

We embraced for a long time and cried and cried together. We could not believe what was happening to our precious daughter.

Flor was our baby and joy and we all loved her so much. We had so many hopes and expectations for her. We had come so far away to give her better opportunities and experiences. How could we have been so naïve and trusting? What were we going to do now?

It was providence we were away from our family and friends in Argentina and communication was scarce. What would people think? Our friends in Australia were easy to deceive. We kept quiet about Flor's pregnancy, and we would only announce it to the world once Flor and Ronaldo were officially married.

Carmela's twins, Chris and Cassandra were born prematurely at 36 weeks in December and Flor' s son, Martin, was born a month later. I loved the three babies to death! They were hard work though! But it was nice to be grandparents when we could spoil the children for a little while then give them back to their respective parents.

Nevertheless, Carmela and Giuseppe were building a house which they could not finish before the twins arrived, so they asked us for help as they had sold their flat and had nowhere to live, so they had all moved in with us 'temporarily'.

That was fine, until the babies arrived. That truly rocked our boat! We were not prepared for the noise day and night, the baby equipment all over the place, the untidiness, the nappy paraphernalia, and the sicknesses, which surrounded our guests.

Carmela turned into a walking ghost, and it was obvious she could not cope with her new family! As for me, being at work was not enough to rest from the upheaval at home.

These children were not ordinary children. Christopher was forever sick but after his recovery from an operation in the stomach, he and his sister never stopped for a rest. They seemed to be active and awake day and night and they had to be entertained constantly!

At five months they were crawling already and discovering every corner of our tiny apartment in old baby walkers, and by nine months they were walking unaided. Their new house was not ready to move in yet, so we decided to give Carmela and Giuseppe and their two little 'freaks' more space and go travelling for a while. We decided to travel through South America and Mexico, after visiting Argentina.

When we came back, Carmela's family had moved out and into their house but by then, Edith, who had not been able to fall pregnant and was trying IVF, was pregnant with twins. Edith and Lolo had bought a small sandwich business near the University of Sydney, and because Edith had to rest, Lolo needed help around lunchtime to prepare the sandwiches. I helped as much as I could, taking some time off from my own work.

However, our yearly vacation was due soon again and Paquito and I decided to travel again, this time to Europe. The fares were so cheap and thanks to Paquito's job we also had concessions for tours and opportunities to stay in good hotels for little money.

Travelling was like a dream come true. Paquito had jokingly promised me when we were young that one day, he would take me to Spain. And here we were, walking the streets of Madrid, Barcelona and Andalusia including the place where his parents had lived before migrating to Argentina, Jaen and Sevilla. We even went to relax in the Parque de Maria Luisa that Paquito's mother had told us so much about.

We had an extended holiday and we truly forgot and did not care what was happening in Sydney. This was our time!

When we returned to Sydney Edith and Lolo did not want to see us and we did not know the reason. Perhaps it was that we never contacted them to see what had happened to their dreams to have a family…

Eventually we found out Edith had lost the babies and they had also lost their business. I thought they somehow blamed us for their disgrace. If we had not gone, we could have helped them and maybe Edith would not have lost her babies.

Well, 'only the one who wears the shoe knows where it hurts most' as the Spanish saying goes wisely. What could we have done? True, I didn't contact them for months to see what was going on… But after all, they were adults, and they should have been able to pull their own chestnuts out of the fire!

I tried to encourage them to try again, and in due course, we settled our differences. I was sad to realize they were destined not to have a family. Ultimately, Edith and Lolo settled down and found comfort, giving all their love to a series of different dogs throughout their lives.

Carmela and Flor went on to have other children. Carmela produced another set of twins, this time, two boys called Johny, and Jack and Flor had Mariluz and a few years later, two lovely girls called Amalia and Teresita. The family was growing exponentially as we were approaching our retirement age.

Then out of the blue, Carmela and Giuseppe separated. I never quite knew the real reason for it, although I was aware all along from the beginning this marriage would not work out. What I did not know was within a year, Carmela would marry again this time to a guy we knew by the name of el Cuco, who had been Giuseppe's friend.

What an uproar el Cuco caused! Not since Flor's first pregnancy had there been such a scandal in our family! There was gossip that el Cuco used to bash his first wife and children, others alleged he was gay, and others whispered he was so tight with money he would not eat an egg because he did not want to waste its eggshell. I also overheard some people thought Jack and Johny were el Cuco's children, and not Giuseppe's.

I believed at the time Ronaldo forcefully went to warn Carmela of the mistake she was going to make and begged her to accept Giuseppe back. But she would not budge, the silly idiot!

It was getting a bit too much for me! We were getting closer to retirement and Paquito and I had done our bit for our children. Therefore, and without thinking too much about it, we decided to go back to Argentina to enjoy our later years in retirement.

We found out we could take our Australian aged pension with us there, which was by Argentinian standards, a small fortune. We also decided to rent our Sydney apartment, which was already paid for in full. And, with the same suitcases we first arrived in Sydney more than 10 years prior, we now returned to Buenos Aires with a few more dollars in the bank.

Part 2 - La Macaca

Once we arrived in Buenos Aires, we sold our old family home and along with our savings from Australia, we were able to purchase a small but upmarket apartment in an affluent part of the city.

We soon made friends with couples of similar ages to us near our amazing neighbourhood. They were also retired and soon we formed a nice group of retirees. We went out together, we visited each other, and we organised trips all throughout Argentina.

We heard Carmela gave birth to el Cuco's child, a boy, whom they named Champ. We also heard Carmela had changed her surname as well as all her children to her maiden name, Paquito's surname, after Giuseppe returned to Argentina.

As far as I understood, Flor sadly did not visit Carmela's family anymore due to some obscure reason with her husband. That was their own business, and I would not interfere!

We were happy! Paquito who was always complaining of aches and pains, seemed to have revived. He enjoyed the company of our friends and he even organised dinners and dancing parties for us all.

El Cuco's mother, Sara, who lived in Mar del Plata, contacted us. She was selling some properties after the *Corralito* (the economic disaster after the freezing of bank deposits in Argentina) because she wanted to invest some money in Australia. Paquito made friends with her straight away and invited her to stay with us whilst she was in Buenos Aires. We introduced her to our family and friends, after all, she was now part of our family!

Paquito and Sara became inseparable. I noticed Sara 's make-up and grooming were always impeccable, and she was always smartly dressed and wore a lot of jewellery. However, I soon found out she expected me to wash her clothes, even her underwear, which seemed despicable to me and well beyond my call of duty.

Besides, I noticed she and Paquito seemed to have some secrets which I could not share, because when I approached them, suddenly they stopped talking or changed their conversation.

One day, I had prepared a nice dinner for us in advance as I had to accompany my sister Carmela to the doctors. When I came back home, Sara and Paquito were in full 'after dinner' conversation. They had not waited for me and what matters worse was they had eaten all the meals I had prepared!

'What's going on with them? Paquito's sister asked me.

'Nothing, they are good mates,' I answered.

'I saw them holding hands… Shameful at their age,' another friend commented.

'It is nothing, she is now part of the family,' I said, trying to justify them.

Paquito and I had been planning a trip to the mountain with some friends. I asked Paquito not to ask Sara to come with us and take that opportunity to request her to leave our apartment.

Paquito objected fiercely.

Therefore, I asked him plainly, 'What is going on Paquito?'

'I do not know myself Macaca. I think I am in love with Sara, like a child again,' he answered rather fearfully.

My whole world collapsed. This was my real husband, or not? The man I was married, or not? The man I loved and cared for more than 40 years, or not? My mind was blank and my heart… I could not feel anything.

For a minute, I wished I could jump off our balcony into oblivion. God must have sustained me and wanted me to keep on living because I said nothing else, took some sleeping tablets and went into the bedroom to sleep.

The next day, I noticed all Sara's clothes which had been laying around the apartment were not there anymore, and I realized she had left.

Paquito was there. He begged me to forgive him. He did not know what had got into him with this woman. He loved me and had chosen me, to be with me, for the rest of his life.

Everything he said sounded to me rather distant and empty, like a rehearsed speech! I was surprised at my calculated calm. I thought of my children and grandchildren who adored Paquito and would be disappointed to hear of his sins, so I quietly accepted his proposal.

I promised God I would attempt to forgive him. Our lives would appear to be normal, and I would still look after him until death do us part, but deep down I knew my relationship with him had been broken irretrievable that day, forever.

A few months later, we learnt through Carmela in Australia that her mother-in-law, Sara, was diagnosed with breast cancer in Sydney. She had had a full mastectomy and some other treatments, and she was now back in Argentina to sell other properties. As far as I know neither myself, nor Paquito, contacted her whilst she was in Buenos Aires.

Then again, we learnt Sara had gone back to Australia and her cancer had come back, she was desperately ill and not expected to live for much longer. Paquito made it obvious he was dreadfully depressed. He did not want to see anybody or go anywhere, and he was always reading the Bible.

I still felt sorry for him, silly me! I asked him if he would want to return to Sydney. Surely, I could see he wanted to see Sara once more. I lied and said I was missing the children and grandchildren, and I wanted to go back.

We sold the apartment as it was, including furniture, crockery, linen and even our decorations. Our apartment in Sydney was fortunately vacant. We gathered only our clothes again in our old suitcases and travelled back to Australia.

In Sydney, we went to visit Carmela and I was shocked to see Sara looking so terribly aged. She looked at least 20 years older than the last time I saw her. She had lost her hair and she was wearing a wig; her skin was greyish; she could hardly sit straight as she seemed so weak, and she had also lost a lot of weight.

We helped Carmela with Sara's doctors' appointments and tests for her, but it was evident Sara's condition was hopeless. We visited Sara in hospital the day before she died, and I was glad I offered to spend the night with her after she had some treatment for her breathing. I washed her several times that night because she was sweating profusely and I frequently moistened her lips, which were dry.

Many times during the night she tried to talk to me, but she was unable to say any words. I guessed she wanted to ask my forgiveness.

All I could do then was to hug her and tell her everything was good between us, and God was merciful. He loved us and forgave us all.

Not long after Sara died, Paquito started his night sweats and fevers. Paquito had already been seen for heart problems, but now the specialist had ordered further tests, which revealed he was suffering from Non-Hodgkin's Lymphoma. He had cancer in his lymphatic system, and I understood, the cancer was in his blood.

I did not understand medicine much and I knew cancer was not contagious, but somehow, I was convinced Paquito got this disease from Sara! Too late to worry about it then! Destiny was already fixed, and my problem already had no solution either physically or emotionally!

We lived with Paquito's illness, his treatments, his hospitalisations, his tantrums, his eternal convalescence, his remissions, and his relapses for another eight years. Nothing medically or emotionally that could be done for him was ever withheld.

His deterioration was certain, but gradual. His physical and psychological suffering was relentless for the rest of his days. When still conscious, he often joked he saw himself in a queue waiting but his time had not arrived to go through to the other side. At times in his delirium, he would call the name Sara.

'Did he say Sara, Grandma?' Cassandra asked me once.

'You misheard him, love. I am sure he is calling me, I am his only love,' I responded with a smile.

Everyone in the family loved him and spoilt him until the end. I promised to God in our wedding vows to look after him for as long as he lived. He wanted to see the Sydney Olympics on TV in September 2000, but God called him home the April before.

When Paquito died, I was exhausted and questioned my will to keep on living. I felt old and tired with little strength to start anew. Paquito insisted our apartment be sold before he died as he thought I was not going to be able to look after the bills and other financials. And it was the truth; I had never paid a bill or fulfilled a business transaction on my own in my whole life.

With only half the pension we had before Paquito died, I felt completely at loss to face the responsibility of paying the rent and running a home. My daughter Carmela, who by then had moved with her family into a large home in one of the best suburbs of Sydney, in Killara, asked me to go and live with them and I readily accepted.

I thought I had witnessed bad things in my life. But it was nothing of what I faced with this family, living with el Cuco. In my opinion, he had a few screws missing in his brain. Some days, he was the most adorable man on earth, then other days, he threatened to kill the dogs or even worse, one of the children in his path, or any of us! For the first time in my life, I felt so sorry for Carmela…

El Cuco's mood changes, as far as I could see, were unfounded. God forbid anyone near him when he was upset for any reason! Sometimes it was the food, or the standard of cleaning in the kitchen, or one of the kids singing or laughing, or the dogs barking or shedding their hairs, or Carmela going to work, or poor me… Yes, even me coughing or breathing.

I tried to keep to my room when el Cuco was around, but I always felt sorry for the children who could not escape from his madness. When they were not bashed, they were grossly belittled and abused, no matter how well they behaved.

Carmela was worried about me, so she planned to take me on a tour to the Australian desert organised by a Spanish speaking elderly group. Her nanny Jean was going to look after the children under the supervision of el Cuco whilst we were away. Somehow, El Cuco behaved well when Jean was around and for that I was ever grateful to God!

Therefore, we finally went on this trip, and I met all these people of my age who spoke my language. We formed instant friendships with some of the ladies. I was in heaven!

When we returned to Sydney, they invited me to their social meetings and soon they asked me to apply for government subsidised housing, which at the time was being built for the Spanish speaking elderly community.

I knew it was going to be far from Carmela, but honestly, I could not see myself lasting any longer at their house with all the insanity going on there. I needed some peace and quiet at my age and I no longer needed Carmela's moral support as my depression had lifted. Besides, I had the excuse that I was going to be closer to my other two daughters.

Within a few months I was moving into my brand-new, self-contained villa in the outer western suburbs of Sydney. I thanked God for this every day! The best part of it was the backyard with a large awning where I could enjoy some shelter from the full sun and the small gardens at the front and back, which I could tend to and watch my flowers grow. To honour Paquito, I planted a red velvet rose in my front garden from a rose bush branch at his burial plot.

Carmela said I abandoned her when she needed her mother the most, as she was planning to leave El Cuco, but I did not care much. Nobody would care for me as much as I would care myself.

I absolutely adored my new place! I honestly thought Paquito's death would mark the end of my life too, but I felt younger and alive again and obviously God wanted me to keep on living for a long time yet.

Chapter 8

OVERCOMING CATASTROPHE

'In order to rise from its own ashes, a Phoenix first must burn.'
(Octavia Butler)

'Life can only be understood backwards, but it must be lived forwards.'
(Soren Kierkegaard)

Part 1 - Carmela Junior

Following your requests, Emanuel, it had taken me a while but, finally I am able to send you here another part of my life.

Wow! I am impressed! I have heard of your world achievements from the Time Magazine. Well done! You thoroughly deserved it, my dear.

And again, I am truly sorry for my delay with this text! Ring me sometime!

———

Sara's death was the miracle that allowed me to see my whole family together again. My parents came to the funeral, Edith and Lolo were there and so were my younger sister Flor and Ronaldo, whom I had not seen for so long, with their family. Many friends that I had lost touch with when I married el Cuco along with lots of friends from work also attended Sara's funeral; then, they kindly attended her wake at our home. I made a real and special effort to make this time a celebration of her life.

I had truly loved Sara as a mother and confidante. I was sad she had passed on, although I was relieved that she did not have to suffer any more. She had been always such a great friend, supporting my family and me when we needed her most. And I was so pleased everyone in the group spoke highly of her.

When everyone left, I noticed el Cuco was laughing hysterically and going through his mother's clothes.

'Puta, re-puta y más puta', he said. 'She was a whore, a hooker, a cheap slut,' he added.

'What are you insinuating Cuco? She is dead and cannot defend herself; she deserves a bit of respect,' I said.

'She deceived you all, the astute bitch,' he was laughing frantically. 'Ha Ha Ha, the devil may lose his tail but not his tricks. And you all believe her… Ha! Ha! Ha! She has been a whore all along…,' he added.

He was tearing Sara's clothes all over and to my surprise, money of every denomination magically appeared underneath hems, stitched pockets and sleeve linings, shoe soles: US dollars, Chinese Yuan, Japanese Yen, Spanish Pesetas, French Francs, Italian Liras, English Pounds, Deutsch Marks, and other denominations I could not identify.

'My mother, yes my *puta madre* has slept with many men, including your father, poor Paquito, Carmela', he shouted. 'Paquito had succumbed to her charms big time…'

'But we are rich! Look, we are rich. She left her fortune to me', he continued. 'Let's celebrate her wicked deeds!' He was now starting to sob; 'I made a comment to the bitch that I would have liked to have a father like Paquito, a close-knit family like yours. And she took it literally, Carmela. She seduced the silly man… God only knows how!' he was then weeping uncontrollably.

I felt as if a large bucket of icy water had fell on me. I could not believe it. This was not happening. I was not hearing what I was hearing. God, please take this pain away from me!

'Let him who is without sin cast the first stone.' But this was my dad who we were talking about… This could not be possible… 'And we all thought he was an example for us all!', I sobbed.

We were then both weeping and hugging.

There were no more clothes or shoes to tear up. We put all the mess in large plastic bags, piling the money according to its denomination. The next day we went to Sydney Airport to a money exchange office. We collected just under 24,000 Australian Dollars. El Cuco decided he was going to buy a new car with the money and not long after, he bought a black Pajero four-wheel drive for his exclusive use.

I sussed out my mother, who confirmed my worst fears. Yes, my father had cheated on her with Sara. Yes, Sara was and had always been a slut. Yes, my mother had apparently forgiven them both. No, she confessed, deep down, she could not forgive my father, ever. No, she was not going to divorce him, but she would not take any revenge. Yes, I swore to her nobody would ever know the truth for the family's sake. Yes, I would ask el Cuco to keep our secret— amongst the three of us only—we will take our secret to our graves. Yes! I would pray for her to find her peace.

Soon after Sara's death, el Cuco had a serious accident in his job. Part of a heavy load of steel rods, which was badly tied up, fell on his back and he had to be hospitalised for months with two crashed vertebrae. The doctors believed it was a miracle he had recovered almost fully, and he could walk without the assistance of his brace.

If his temper had been bad before the accident, it got twice as bad after it. He could still be the charming positive husband and father some days. However, other days he would not eat with us, retired to his room, only to emerge like a mad man, swearing and threatening to bash the children or me.

Despite the madness in the household, the older twins were doing extremely well at school. They had managed to be chosen to go to a selective school in the area and they were geared to get a high mark in their High School Certificate, thus get entry to one of the most prestigious universities and courses in Sydney. I felt proud for them, after all, we had been only just migrants in this country and our mother tongue had not been English.

Unfortunately, it was not the same story for the younger twins. They did not achieve enough marks to enter the selective school.

Therefore, they were going to the local public school and had made friends with kids whose parents had dubious jobs, involved in drugs or the underworld or had questionable acquaintances. I tried to keep Jack and Johny away from the streets, arranging the installation of a basketball ring to play in our own yard, but they always had an excuse to meet their new dodgy friends around the neighbourhood.

Champ had gone to kindergarten for a year but was unable to recognise a letter or the numbers in English. However, he could speak some words in Filipino, Greek, Chinese, Maltese, Arabic and so on… I found out Champ had a Filipino teacher and pupils of every nationality in his class.

'Lord please help me to see what I have to do with these children', I prayed continuously.

I enrolled Champ in the nearest Christian school and told el Cuco I wanted to move out of the area. To my surprise, he agreed. We put the properties in Queensland on the market along with the three houses we owned in the western suburbs of Sydney. And we started to look for a house in the elite Northern suburbs of Sydney, near well-known good public schools.

My life was shaken again because my father became seriously ill. His prognosis was rather poor but nevertheless it was not going to be a quick end. He was to live and suffer terribly with his disease for another eight years.

In the end, my dear dad was reduced to almost bones, a quarter of his healthy size, he could not see or talk or swallow. Everyone in the family considered him a saint. I knew he was far from that, but I never said a word about his slip-ups. We all showed our love for him!

He was surrounded daily by his wife, his daughters and his grandchildren who wanted to make him as comfortable as possible. Cassandra used to sing her gospel songs and read him the Bible; especially Psalm 23, the same Psalm I had shared with Sara before her death:

'The Lord is my Sheppard; I shall not want.

He makes me lie down in green pastures. He leads me beside still waters. He restores my soul.

He leads me in paths of righteousness for his name's sake.

Even though I walk through the valley of the shadow of death, I will fear no evil, for you are with me; your rod and your staff, they comfort me.'

I sincerely hope he found his peace...

By the time my father died, el Cuco and I had already sold our properties in Queensland and the three houses we had developed on our land.

We were blessed to purchase a large home in the leafy up-market suburb of Killara with some money to spare.

The house needed some renovations and we asked to stay in our then current home until the renovations were finished and until the older twins had finished their Higher School Certificate examinations.

I also requested a teacher transfer to be able to work nearer my new address.

Finally, in those days and before we were able to move, we got the visit of el Cuco's children from Argentina: Eva and Adam. As expected, they had grown up, but their upbringing had been completely different to my own children.

Eva had become a stunning young woman. At just 16, she knew how to dress and wear make-up, walk, provoke, and flirt with the boys. I noticed she was teaching Cassandra the arts of seducing and picking up boys.

The problem was she was soon flirting with Christopher and with her cousin Martin. We had trouble convincing her in Sydney, you do not wear see-through tops or worse still, you do not wear those types of provocative clothes to church!

'God please help me to manage this awkward situation wisely!'

On top of my daily routine with a larger family to feed and keep clean and healthy plus my work, I had an extra job, which was to watch Eva slept in her bedroom and not in Christopher's bed, playing some 'doctors and nurses' game.

I would never forget the day when I took all the kids to the 'Drive-In' theatre nearby one Saturday evening. Chris and Martin with Eva wanted to sit at the back whilst I packed Casandra and Champ at the front with me. The movie *Jurassic Park* was on the screen. I recall it was an exciting storyline with dinosaurs running loose everywhere. I was glued to the screen!

However, I noticed it was too quiet at the back of the car and when I quickly turned around and, in the shadows, I saw my three back passengers engaged in kissing, cuddling, and touching each other. I believed they all considered me cruel, 'bonkers' and old fashioned for interrupting and stopping my guests' fun!

Adam, and the younger twins were another issue. Adam settled well in the neighborhood with most of their twins' friends, but they also were the targets of constant watching to make sure they did not get into too much mischief or into the hands of the police.

I was relieved when el Cuco's children returned to their mother and glad when we finally moved to our new three-story house in Killara, away from that neighborhood.

Our home was a large house with four bedrooms and two bathrooms on the top floor, a large eat-in kitchen, dining, large rumpus room and dining room along. There was another bedroom and bathroom in the middle floor and a laundry, another bathroom, a study and a large, covered pool area and extensive landscape gardens with a family swimming pool downstairs.

The new place was idyllic and at last we had enough room to house everybody comfortably, even my mother, who was depressed because of my father's passing, was invited to come and stay with us.

Our neighbors were quiet and friendly. Most of them were professional people and their children attended the local high school that was walking distance away. Johny and Jack missed their 'colorful' friends from the old neighborhood, but I truly trusted they would soon make new, law-abiding friends.

Champ went to the local primary school, enrolling in Third Grade. I was soon called for an interview with his teacher.

'This kid needs urgent help', she said. 'He absorbs every complex concept in Mathematics but is unable to do simple additions or subtractions. And the same goes with his spelling. He speaks all the hard words correctly, but cannot spell 'mother',' she added.

'Oh dear, what shall I do?'

The teacher explained to me he needed a bit of coaching, which I could do easily using books from First and Second Grade from the local news-agency. Even though I had a heavy accent myself, any tutoring would be a great help, she explained.

So, our private little lessons started, as did a lifelong special relationship with my youngest son. Champ was like a sponge, willing and eager to learn and then put whatever he knew into practice.

El Cuco had often commented to me before, that Champ was dumb, not smart like the other children, because Champ was 'his son', thus he was gifted with little or no brains. Certainly, Champ's love for knowledge and his cleverness was proving to el Cuco how wrong he had judged him!

Within a few months, Champ was upgraded to the selective stream in his school and by the time he finished primary school, he was placed in all advanced classes in the high school.

I would have liked Champ to go to an exclusive private school because by then, I could afford it. In fact, I had enrolled him at Knox Grammar and at Barker's College for his high school, but by the time a vacancy arose, he had already cemented many friendships at the local public school and did not want to be parted with his mates.

It was extraordinary how Champ would question everything he came across with much wittiness and depth. But he sometimes exceeded my tolerance. For example, when still very young one day I asked him to do some small chores at home for me; he said to me he would do it only if he wanted to, because children had rights too. I was dumfounded! I got serious and quickly made him do his task, but the little rascal insisted he did it out of his good heart and love for me, as he still had the right to say 'No' if he wished!

Champ was not only intelligent, but he was also extremely social, and was able to make lasting friendships. He kept into adulthood many friends from various nationalities in our neighborhood: Jewish, Japanese, and Chinese, and he also seemed to have a flair for languages, because often I could hear he and his friends' playing games in other languages, like Chinese and Yiddish.

As for me, I kept on having these disturbing dreams when Sara came to talk to me, but she was unable to speak, or I was not able to understand what she really wanted. I had experienced the same experience at her deathbed, so these dreams gave me the creeps. I was now having them every night and waking up suddenly in a cold sweat.

Then one day, Sara brought a small torch in my dream, and she hinted I should follow her, but I could not trust her somehow and I woke up again in a cold sweat. The same dream happened night after night, with the same ending, but one night I recognized where we were, it was our old house, with the white terrazzo tiles and the pink carpet, and her room… and her wardrobe… and the carpet under her cabinet. And still, she could not speak despite her efforts. I could just see the light pointing to a red cross underneath the carpet and I woke up again in my sweat. I pleaded with God to remove this dream from me, but the dream kept coming faithfully every night.

Then one night, she pointed the light to the carpet at the red cross, in the corner of her wardrobe—God, she must have made a small vault underneath the floor—and I saw it: money, lots of money, piles of bundles with US dollars! God… this is what she wanted to tell me all along at her death bed; she had hidden more money somehow, her fortune in Argentina, underneath the carpet, in the corner underneath her wardrobe, a vault- completely out of sight to any naked eye. I had personally cleaned every corner of her room before moving out and I had not suspected anything or seen anything unusual.

By the time I discovered Sara's dream, we had already sold the house and had moved out. I waited until I fell sleep again the following night to verify my dream, although nothing happened that night or the following night or the following… Sara never came back into my dreams again!

I reluctantly told el Cuco about it, who agreed with me it could be very possible his mother would have hidden money there, after all, where were the proceeds of her property sales in Argentina? We had never thought about it before, but it must have been a fortune as only God knows how many properties she had spread around

Buenos Aires, Mar del Plata, and other affluent provinces. Surely. The US dollars might still be there, but we could not do anything about it now. It would be a windfall for whoever decided to demolish the house one day...

Years later, we told Champ about it, but although he was keen for the money, should it be there, he told us at the time, he would not dare to knock at the door of our old house and explain the situation to the then occupant of the house.

'Maybe, it would be an idea to purchase the house again...' he casually suggested with a smile.

El Cuco and I had always demanded the children spoke Spanish at home from an early age, and both sets of twins had always attended Saturday School to learn how to read and write in our language. However, we did not push it on Champ, because we expected him to learn English first.

Nevertheless, when he started high school, Champ insisted he wanted to learn Spanish too. This meant he would have had to choose between his beloved competition tennis, his Chinese language classes, or learning Spanish on the Saturday mornings. He chose to learn Spanish!

I enrolled him at Saturday Spanish School. Spanish was more difficult for Champ, because he had not spoken it at home, and although he understood most of what was said, he could not follow a conversation or write two sentences together. However, he certainly persevered and by the time he was in Year 10, he pestered me to send him to Spain on an exchange program.

Champ was not yet 16 years old when he travelled to Spain on his own. His flight was delayed in Singapore, and he got lost in Madrid, but he found his way around and managed to find his contact who helped him to find his way to Salamanca, the end point in his journey.

When I got his call from Madrid announcing he was lost, el Cuco went berserk and I panicked a bit, but I prayed to God for his help and somehow, I felt confident Champ was going to make it to his destination.

Champ stayed in Salamanca with a Spanish family and attended school there for three months. The host family had an older daughter and a son, Miguelito, the same age as Champ.

Miguelito and Champ became close friends, and when Champ came back to Sydney, his Spanish language performance was like that of a native speaker. Besides, Miguelito was also able to come to Sydney and stayed with us for six months. Needless to say, Miguelito's family and our family cemented a close friendship that would last despite the distance throughout the years. Champ would later use his Spanish language skills to his advantage at work in Australia and overseas.

As for my elder children, and as expected, Chris and Cassandra got brilliant marks for their HSC, and they were accepted in a Bachelor of Science (Physiotherapy) Degree and Veterinary Science Degree respectively at the University of Sydney. Johny and Jack settled down eventually and although they had missed their friends tremendously when we first moved to the North Shore of Sydney, they realized with time, leaving that environment had been the best thing we had done for them. Years later, they found out some of their previous best friends finished up in jail for various crimes and a few had been killed in mysterious circumstances.

Amazingly, I got a transfer to a school closer to home and was lucky enough to get, first a job as a teacher, then a job as a supervisor at the local Saturday Language School as well.

I had also been asked to seek another subject to teach, as there were not enough students seeking to learn Spanish or French. My Head Teacher suggested I should learn Korean, because there was a government school grant available for those interested in learning that language. I thought it was ridiculous, as if mastering another language, especially an Asian language, was a trivial matter! I rejected my boss proposal outright.

However, under pressure and to improve my qualifications and the chance of getting better employment, I enrolled part-time in a Master of Education (Computer Science and Emerging Technologies). I found the course quite challenging because until that point, I did not even know how to turn a computer on. However, I thought I wanted to try if I could handle it, and I loved it. I easily and happily completed the course in my spare time after hours, with excellent marks.

El Cuco got much better from his injury and pains following his accident, and his claim for workers compensation was finalized with some cash in his favor, which was enough to purchase outright a small investment unit in his name. He also managed to find quite a few well-paid private jobs as a contract cleaner.

Life could not have been any better for us considering what we went through. However, there was again trouble in Paradise!

El Cuco's change of moods and bad temper got gradually worse. He was constantly belittling and bullying both sets of twins and sarcastically hinting they should pay for their upkeep. My mother, who had moved in with us after my father's passing, got a fair share of his never-ending grumbles about money as well, although she was already paying us a generous board from her pension.

When bills were to be paid, inexorably there would be a heated argument because el Cuco did not want to pay anything. To avoid any more quarrels, it was decided El Cuco and myself would have separate bank accounts and all our bills and expenses would then be divided 'fairly'.

As we were eight in the household, el Cuco proposed I would pay for six: my mother, the two sets of twins and myself and El Cuco would pay for only two: Champ and himself. Even after I accepted this arrangement, the amount of the bills, especially the phone bill, was the cause for a dispute.

Our relationship as a couple continued to deteriorate even further. When we moved to Killara, we decided to buy two single beds for our bedroom. We had not had any intimacy for a long time anyway! El Cuco called me a whore and a slut just like he called his mother in the past and time and time again, he accused me of wrongdoing about any relationship I had in the past, especially with Lucho. No matter how I claimed he was not my husband so far back, he would not reason with me.

El Cuco was also rude and violent towards all the twins, especially Chris and Cassandra. They were both studying, working part time, and helping with chores at home. Yet, he called them lazy thugs and many times I know now grown-up Chris would control himself not to knock him out!

One day out of the blue, el Cuco started shouting and throwing our innocent little dogs against the walls because they had shed some hair on the couch. Everyone was in such a shock we were actually paralyzed to stop him. Or rather, we were scared any of us would be thrown around also!

A few hours after his outburst, I heard him talking to the dogs apologizing for his behavior! The dogs survived, just, but it was obvious ours was not a good and peaceful place to live!

We could not have any friends in the house as el Cuco would drive them away with his stingy and erratic attitude and even ourselves, we were all scared and were trying to avoid him as we wondered who the next victim in el Cuco's path would be.

One of my girlfriends from university came around as we needed to do some program coding for an assignment together. Only God knew how the topic of homosexuality came about, but el Cuco started to have an argument with her saying all gay people should be in hell. My friend vigorously and hypothetically defended them. After all, we were not talking about anybody in particular and she was certainly not gay. El Cuco got enraged and asked her to leave and never to return, threatening to thump her if she did not leave immediately.

Later, he said to me this was not a good friend for me and not a good model for the children. I felt embarrassed and belittled to go to class and face my friend again.

Chris left me a note one morning, which I have kept until now. He said he was praying to let God calm him down so as to avoid ringing the police regarding El Cuco's abuse, which had turned aggressive, as he had threatened to punch him. Chris could have knocked him down easily but fortunately he chose to walk away. After that, I was uneasy and tormented about leaving the house for work in the morning, thinking what would happen during the day at home if el Cuco decided to stay around!

Because of her good marks in her course, Cassandra got a

research project scholarship to study in North Caroline, USA, with all expenses paid. When she came back to Sydney after a few months of finishing her degree, even before she got her formal credentials as a Veterinary Surgeon, Cassandra was able to get a job in her field. Astonishingly, she was already known in the veterinary circles because of her research skills, knowledge, and ethics. With her income, Cassandra and Chris were able to lease their first apartment in a neighboring suburb, then a small house not far from where we went to Church.

Cassandra paid the rent and the upkeep for both until Chris finished his Physiotherapy degree and then he was able to get some money working part time as a physio in a hospital to pay for some of his expenses.

Chris went on to study medicine, which was always his dream, for a further four years at the University of Sydney with the support of his twin sister.

I could have forgiven el Cuco for his emotional abuse to me, but it was a different story to have to endure having my children driven away from home and the care they still needed from me, as they were still studying, all because of his mad tantrums.

Nevertheless, my children proved to be better than me because when I suggested we could 'all' move out and start anew in a new house, they could not bear the thought of leaving el Cuco by himself. They claimed, 'he would not have anybody in the world, mum—now his mother had passed on—to even understand him or talk to him'.

Around the time my older twins left home, el Cuco's son by his first marriage, Adam, finally decided to come to Sydney to live and we then had a bedroom to offer to him. I was hopeful the presence of Adam would calm el Cuco down in the home. How wrong I was!

El Cuco continued to terrorize everybody, including Adam, with his rage and attacks. Champ was the only one immune to el Cuco's wrath explosions.

Adam had grown into a sweet, hard-working young man. He wanted to pursue a career in hospitality, but he could not speak any English. I took him everywhere to enroll him in some English class, but he was not a migrant, as he had been born in Australia, therefore, not eligible for any support and the private tuition fees were extremely expensive. I knew he was smart, motivated, and needed to learn English promptly.

Finally, I pleaded with the local Technical College teachers to give him a go and enroll him in a hospitality course even with his limited English language. Adam was ambitious and eager to learn, and we all helped him with his English to complete his first assignments.

Adam successfully completed one course after another in the hospitality industry, and within six months he got a job in a local hotel as a waiter. He decided to live with some friends and left our 'mad' house, as he called it. Not long after, Adam applied and got a job as housekeeping manager in one of the best hotels in the city. From then on, he never stopped getting promotions in Sydney, interstate, and all over the world, and for which, I feel extremely proud.

El Cuco had bought a small caravan and enjoyed taking Champ for short holidays to the bush or fishing. The school holidays were coming up and by then Johny and Jack were old enough to be left with Jean at home, especially if El Cuco was going to be away with Champ on holidays.

I had seen a tour advertised in the Spanish paper to the Australian desert culminating in Bourke. Thus, I took the opportunity to take my mother on that tour with a group of Spanish speaking elderlies.

I enjoyed every minute of that trip mainly because I could help the old folk when they needed some interpreting from Spanish into English and vice-versa. I also thanked God for the chance to be closer to and become more friendly with my mother.

However, she must have told her newly made friends about the problems we had at home because miraculously one of these ladies helped her to find independent accommodation at subsidized rent from the government. I could not believe it! She was offered a brand-new community subsidized housing flat, and she decided to move out on her own. When my mother had moved in with us, she decided to keep some of my parents' old furniture in storage, 'just in case', she had said. It was the time then to transport furniture into her new place.

My mother's new home was lovely, but unfortunately it was very far from where we lived, and I could not visit her as frequently as I wished, nor could she visit us regularly as she was getting a bit old to travel on public transport. I missed my mother and her friendship very much and felt terribly sad and resentful about her departure.

Unfortunately, the departures of my mother, later Adam, Chris and Cassandra's did nothing to make el Cuco any better. I had asked him many times to see a doctor for his issues, but he refused to admit he had a problem. Champ started to make comments about how bad his father treated us, but I played it down, as I did not want to intensify his emotional well-being or turned him against his father.

Although, there was always a good homemade meal at the table for the whole family, by then, el Cuco refused to eat with us. He had purchased himself a large TV where he spent most of his time alone and where he would eat a sandwich or two with some cheese that he had prepared himself.

One Saturday morning, as I was leaving with Champ for my Saturday School job, I saw el Cuco in the nude shouting repeatedly out of a first-floor window 'Whore, what brothel are you working today, bitch?' I could not believe it! Some of our neighbors came out to watch him but they did not interfere.

Sobbing and reluctantly, I drove off, but I spent all day shaking at school. I knew it was not easy to arrange another teacher for my students, but I was not in any condition to keep on teaching, therefore, as soon as Champ finished his class, I asked my supervisor to be allowed to go back home and he had to ring up all the parents for the students to be picked up earlier.

When I got back home, el Cuco was in the kitchen, still in the nude and shouting obscenities to me, but now he had our biggest kitchen knife with him and was threatening to kill me. Johny and Jack were hiding somewhere, and Champ must have joined them, because he disappeared from the scene.

I did not know what to do and tried to calm him down. Suddenly, he dropped the knife, ran to his car in the garage and drove off still shouting and babbling vulgarities! I rang Chris who advised me to ring the Hornsby Psychiatric Hospital, which I did. They advised me to calm down and to ring them again when and if he returned home.

El Cuco returned home that night and he went to his bedroom to put some clothes on. He approached us and apologized to me and the children.

However, I had finally made up my mind and in the serenity of the moment, I communicated to him I was leaving as soon as I could get suitable accommodation for the four of us.

He made me promise I would not divorce him, and he wanted to make amends and be given another chance. He also revealed he did not want to lose his family, and he said, surprisingly, we were the best things to ever happen to him!

I did not have any plans to marry ever again after that experience, hence I agreed not to divorce him, but I had made up my mind to leave and I was not going to hesitate this time. He consented to selling our house and he asked me to stay until he could help us find a suitable place to live.

I agreed to stay in the home until then, but I warned him I had the Mental Hospital phone number pinned next to the phone and I would not hesitate to ring them should he ever threaten our security again.

I also gave him the name of a doctor at the same hospital to make an appointment if he wanted to try to sort out his problems. I believed he did, and he was diagnosed with severe PTSD (Post Traumatic Stress Disorder). I also believed he was referred to Anger Management Sessions, but he attended one session only because he did not want to pay for it.

He confessed to Champ all the people in these Anger Management sessions had a problem with alcohol, and he did not, which I believed, it was absolutely the truth. If he ever had some mental illness, it was never due to alcoholism or any drug addiction!

The house was sold rather quickly, and we decided to split the proceeds in equal parts. As part of the property settlement, el Cuco would keep his investment property and I would keep mine, which I had bought long ago and I was still paying it off, in Pyrmont. We would both also keep our respective superannuation entitlements.

Part 2 - Carmela Junior

A true new life commenced for me after I moved out of our house. With the share of the sale of the marital home, I bought a large and new 3-bedroom apartment in the Lower North Shore of Sydney just next to St. Leonard's station and across from the hospital where Chris was doing his internship.

The younger twins, who by now had entered the University of Macquarie Art-Law School, were accommodated in the larger bedroom, Champ in the other bedroom and I took the second largest bedroom with the ensuite bathroom attached.

The new home felt like heaven on earth to me and I suspected to my children too. We could now talk, laugh, watch TV, listen to music, invite friends over, go out, breathe easily and the list went on and on. By then I had finished my master's in education, and I had my evenings reasonably free after I organized my schoolwork. I was also free to go out, especially visiting friends and even travelling interstate or overseas during my holidays.

As my apartment was next to the station, it was a bit easier for my mother to visit us, and she did so, occasionally. I used to take her out to the local club for a meal and to a show or to the movies. During the holidays, I would also take her to the thermal baths at Moree where we enjoyed being together enormously, even soaking in the pools or playing Bingo at the RSL Club with the locals.

In the past, I had already taken both my parents to Moree a few times travelling by train. Moree is at about 700 km from Sydney, a small country town with a high Aboriginal population. It was always safe to roam the streets of Moree during the day, but we always stayed home at night for security, watching videos or playing cards. During the day we mostly loved bathing in the local hot pools, which were the main attraction there. It was said the hot spring mineral waters from the pools were good for the arthritic bones and other parts of the body. For me, it had always been a relaxing experience and a way to escape from the city and home stresses.

After I separated from el Cuco, I had the chance to visit Moree more often with my mother, now that my father passed on. I also organized trips overseas for my students to further learn Spanish. The University of Melbourne also employed me as a leader to take Spanish teachers overseas as well. I was given the opportunity to lead various trips overseas to Spain, Chile, Mexico, and Argentina. I often also took my mother with us.

The added advantage was these overseas trips were free for me and most of the time, I was generously paid for the work as well. I had the opportunity to explore many Spanish-speaking countries and become acquainted and sometimes even familiar with many overseas authorities and establish connections with colleagues from Australia and all over the world. I was always grateful to God for these opportunities, and I was always ready to witness and share His love and grace with anyone who He sent me.

In Sydney, I often celebrated birthdays and special days together with the whole family and we invited el Cuco. These celebrations always took place in a restaurant or at somebody else's home, as I never allowed el Cuco to come up to my apartment.

One day, el Cuco asked me to go with him to choose the color scheme of a waterfront apartment he was buying in the suburb of Rhodes. He said he still loved me, and he wanted to make this apartment our home again.

'The twins would soon leave, and we could be a real family, just the two of us with our son Champ again', he asserted.

I was careful not to get emotionally involved again. I already experienced his sweet-talk with disastrous results. However, I agreed to choose the color scheme of the apartment to my taste, although I did not make any promises to him about any possible future for us together.

From then on, el Cuco would ask me to go out on dates and eventually he convinced me we should go on a long holiday, perhaps to Europe on a romantic cruise through the Mediterranean, to see if we could patch up our differences.

I still felt wary, but he seemed a changed man, more genuine and a lot calmer. Jack and Johny had certainly moved on and they were now almost finishing their career and looking for jobs. Champ used to go out a lot with his friends and so many days I was left on my own, feeling lonely.

I was starting to enjoy my outings with el Cuco.

One day, he showed me a brochure of the tickets and tours in Europe he wanted to purchase for us. It would be an idyllic trip for the both of us and the beginning of our new life together. I accepted the offer reluctantly, although I wanted to pay for my share with no strings attached. At the end of the holidays, I would decide what I wanted to do with my life and our relationship, he made me promised him.

The time was approaching for our 'idyllic' trip when I asked el Cuco how the apartment was going and when, if I accepted, would he want me to move in. To my shock and surprise, he said he never offered me to move in with him, I was taking advantage of him and he was really hurt by my true intentions… blah blah blah…

I could not believe what I was hearing and in fact I felt I had been trapped once more! Oh God! Again, this one had been the best of el Cuco and his tricks… I thought I was dreaming that moment. I needed to be on my own immediately and I surely needed to think of what I wanted to do to move forward.

Shall I lose my money and cancel the booking for the trip altogether? El Cuco will never change. Shall I accept him as he is? Do I love him unconditionally? Do I want to be with him regardless of his madness, weird attitude and erratic behavior? Possibly not!

I consulted my church pastor's wife, who was an experienced counselor, Jen, and a person I could trust fully. Astonishingly for a committed church person, she was of the opinion El Cuco would never change!

I had already asked my employer for some time off to go for the impending trip and the prospect of being in Europe for the summer was tempting indeed. Hence, I decided to go on with the trip, but my heart was cold and marriage reconciliation was definitely not on the cards.

However, I promised myself I would make the most of this trip. I prayed for truth and God, as always, was faithful in taking the blanket of deception from my eyes. He showed me clearly and impartially what el Cuco was really like: an uncaring, selfish, self-loving, greedy, and shallow individual. He was riddled with self-esteem issues, and he was certainly riddled with obsessive-compulsive behaviors.

I already knew from the past that el Cuco had mental health issues and now possibly he was also suffering not only from Post-Traumatic Stress Disorder but also with attention deficit disorder. I was a teacher and had seen the symptoms repeatedly in my students. I knew how to handle a child, but it was so painful to manage it in an adult. This was still my husband I was considering. Oh God, help me!

The following words kept repeating in my mind repeatedly:

'Amazing grace, how sweet the sound...
That saved a wretch like me.
I once was lost, but now I am found.
Was blind, but now I see.'

Yes, I could certainly see the truth now...

El Cuco tried to get away from paying his wine share to people, he did not obey instructions from the tour guide and finished up being lost in the crowds and above all he had not once had a compliment for me throughout the trip. We shared a cabin or a hotel room, both with two single beds throughout the trip, but we certainly shared nothing else.

The evidence, once my emotions and my heart were detached, was plenty and I was enlightened; I observed him with his tantrums, his mean nature, his stinginess towards me and worse towards others, his unkindness, his narrow-mindedness, his immaturity, his selfishness, and his self-indulgence. For the first time since I met el Cuco, I felt embarrassed to be with him around other people and I finally knew then, as a couple, our relationship was truly dead.

Upon our return to Sydney and to save money, el Cuco proposed to take the train back to our homes from the airport. My home was close to the train station, but we were not teenagers anymore. I was tired after the long trip from Europe and would have paid the full taxi gladly, but I accepted his proposal to avoid any more arguments.

On the train trip, I told el Cuco then I wanted a final divorce and I wanted nothing to do with him anymore, ever. He looked at me bewildered but seemed to accept my request without any objections. As for myself, I felt empty, confused, and truly crushed, once again!

Chapter 9

SURVIVAL....

'It is not the strongest species that survives, nor the most intelligent, but the one most responsive to change.'
(Charles Darwin)

'There is no safe investment. To love at all is to be vulnerable. Love anything, and your heart will certainly be wrung and possibly be broken. If you want to make sure of keeping it intact, you must give your heart to no one, not even to an animal. Wrap it carefully round with hobbies and little luxuries; avoid all entanglements; lock it up safe in the casket or coffin of your selfishness. But in that casket—safe, dark, motionless, airless—it will change. It will not be broken; it will become unbreakable, impenetrable, irredeemable. The alternative to tragedy, or at least to the risk of tragedy, is damnation. The only place outside Heaven where you can be perfectly safe from all the dangers and perturbations of love is Hell.'
(CS Lewis)

Part 1 - La Macaca

Again Emanuel, I sincerely hope my manuscript is legible and to your satisfaction. I have asked one of my friends, Emilia who has been a teacher, to translate it into English for me. I had been told Emilia, once a teacher, was losing her mind a bit, so I trust she was still able to do a good job. If you feel the following text needs to be changed at some point, please do it yourself as I do not mind it at all...

I would have thought the end of Paquito's life was the end of my life as well, but in fact it was a new beginning. Paquito and I had lived a whole life together, over 55 years under the same roof, sharing the same bed and the same dining table, and above all the same memories!

Nevertheless, Paquito had left a sour taste in my heart, but this was not time to regret the past but investigate the future. I felt alive and well again! I had lots of new friends, and they all seemed to have interesting lives.

Maria, who lived next door to me, had a car, and she could take me out shopping and clubbing. She introduced me to the poker machines, and I had to say I loved the challenge of being able to get more money than I put in playing with them.

Paquito had sold our apartment because he was afraid that I would not have been able to manage the bills, so Carmela opened a bank account for me, and I had lots of money—literally, a home's-worth of money at my disposal and why on earth not? My money was also at the disposal of my new friends.

Everyone loved my generosity. We would gamble thousands of dollars in the one night, and sometimes we were lucky, but most of the time, we lost it all!

My daughters Carmela and Flor were signatories on my account and obviously they were watching my financial movements. Carmela started to ask me what I was buying or doing with the funds in my account. She confronted me and asked me why the money was going down so quickly. What a nerve! How dare she ask me? The money was mine and mine alone!

I told Carmela to mind her own business and I managed to see somebody in the bank who spoke Spanish, and soon I removed my daughters from the books as cosignatories, as I did not want anyone to spy on my account.

Carmela must have told Chris, her eldest son, about it because Chris visited me and tried to coax me into confessing how I spent my money.

'How do you spend your time outside the home, abuelita?' he questioned. I heard alarm bells in my head! Although I loved Chris to bits, I could see his intentions even with my eyes closed… In this instance, I needed to be smarter than him.

'My life is my business, Christopher, my business alone.' How glad I was when my dearest grandson plainly said he agreed with me completely and hugged me tight!

However, when alone, I thought the matter over and over. I told Maria my savings were dwindling quickly, and the gambling really had to stop. Maria did not even flinch and accepted my decision readily.

Our new way of entertainment deserved a celebration, so we went out to the local club, and we ordered Maria's favourite pizza with anchovies, we watched some people dancing to Latin music and returned home.

I think Maria continued her gambling discreetly with her own money. I felt I had been a bit abrupt but in Spanish we say, '*al pan pan y al vino vino*.' I think in English it is, 'Let's call a spade a spade'. Nevertheless, despite my attitude, Maria continued to be one of my loyal best friends for many years to come.

The complex of villas where I lived was occupied by elderly people, but I was the oldest by quite a few years. They were all pleasant, although they liked to gossip and sometimes, as they grew older and older, they fought with each other over silly things. When that happened, I just locked myself inside and turned the volume up on my TV to drown out their arguments, so I kept at peace with all of them, regardless of their issues.

All my neighbours welcomed me with open arms from the start. Esther, my neighbour on the right side was not a gambler, but she liked to go dancing to pick up men every Saturday! She would initially go to the clubs with Graciela, another lady neighbour living straight upstairs from me.

On Saturdays, I used to watch Spanish Video Soaps on TV or

videos and I usually had to put the volume up not to hear the party fun, noises, and the private indiscretions my friends were having in their apartments after their Saturday clubbing.

One day Esther invited me to go with them. I was much older than them, but as they insisted. I had nothing to lose, so I went along. We invited Maria and other ladies from the village, but they refused.

We went to the Club Marconi where they played South American music and tango in the main auditorium. Everyone was dancing and my feet started to dance, even when I was sitting down. Without realizing, I was on the dance floor with an old man, dancing and loving the moment.

Graciela and Esther, as usual, finished up with 'serious company' but they returned me to my apartment before they retired as usual to theirs with their current casual boyfriends.

I continued to go with them some Saturdays. I could have chosen to have a boyfriend if I wanted to; old men were in abundant supply there.

One night, a lovely Mexican widower and dancing partner in his eighties told me he liked me very much, he could see I was kind, generous and loved to have fun. I had already met this man, named Pancho, some time ago when my daughter Carmela and I had gone to the bush on a bus-tour. He had always seemed to me a decent gentleman. He suggested to me, we could start a more permanent relationship, mainly for company to each other. He proposed that we could commence this relationship by going to the movies or to a restaurant or just going dancing somewhere just the two of us.

I felt delighted about his compliments, but despite his insistence, I absolutely refused to accept his offer. My life was already full without any complications, and I loved it as it was! I always thought *'being free is not doing what you want. Being free is to be happy with what you do.'* I was doing what I wanted, when I wanted, and I could not be any happier! Alleluia!

By then, I had joined several Spanish groups for seniors. I was well received everywhere I went, no matter what nationalities the people in these groups were: Spanish, Chilean, Uruguayan,

Peruvian, Bolivian, Colombian and Argentinian. We played Bingo in some, learnt knitting in another, played cards in another and learnt how to use a laptop in another. Sometimes, we had guest speakers who gave us lectures on interesting topics.

The rest of the time during the week, I visited the local library and borrowed books in Spanish to read. On Saturdays, if I was not planning to go out at night, I took the bus and the train and visited my daughter Carmela, who lived in the Northern parts of the city more than an hour away by public transport.

My other daughters also visited me on and off. Flor always brought her younger brood to play with me. I was still quite energetic, so I loved the ball games in the park or the Spanish card games at home when it rained.

I thanked God every day for my life and apart from a few arthritic pains here and there, the Almighty always kept me healthy, alert, and jolly.

Paquito was my favourite 'star-visitor'. He visited me from time to time on weekends and I talked to him about my adventures and our growing family. All our grandchildren were growing up healthy and they were all very smart.

Chris was already a doctor and was studying to be a cardiologist, but his marriage to Keira was almost on the rocks. It was sad seeing him broken, but his career took the best of him, and Keira seemed to have fallen for a younger, penniless boy who had more time for her.

Cassandra was already a vet as she always dreamt to become. She was in love and about to be married. Her fiancée was a bit of a hippie with long blond hair and always wearing pink thongs. He also had a juicy story too, leaving a previous fiancée at the altar. I heard Chris would not hesitate to kill him, if he dared to do that to his twin sister!

Carmela's younger twins were as always together and they were so quiet, as if they never existed… However, they seemed to have enough brains for this world. They were both attending university and were studying to be lawyers or psychologists.

Carmela's youngest son Champ seemed to be the smartest of

them all. God had given him the gift of speaking and persuading! He would be able to sell sand to the Arabs, the little devil!

Paquito wanted me to keep talking about the other grandchildren, but I was tired, and he was getting cold there sitting by the bed. So, I asked him to come to bed under the covers to warm up for a bit and I promised I would tell him more next time he showed up.

Another day Paquito turned up with Sara, holding hands, but I refused to talk to them, and they disappeared.

Yet another day, Paquito insisted he wanted me to talk about the other grandchildren, so I told him about Martin, who was soon to be a doctor too and wanted to become an orthopaedic surgeon and oncologist.

Mariluz got involved with a questionable young man for a while and there were some rumours they were both involved in drugs. But thanks to the Lord and my prayers, she was now in a permanent relationship with a boy called Freddy. They were engaged and were expecting a child. The other girls were a real joy, very pretty, cute, and intelligent both!

It was a shame our beloved daughter Edith was never able to have any children. She would have made such a good mother by the way she treated their dogs, a never-ending stream of them, honestly, they were raised like babies. Huge Rottweilers, German Sheppards and lately, all sort of mongrels were allowed to roam around indoors and sit on their expensive leather lounges, let alone, their latest craze: they were fed their huge meals with a spoon. I felt a bit sorry for Edith. I saw then Paquito's eyes filled with tears also!

Paquito always came to see me at night, sometimes when I was watching TV or having dinner. I knew he loved my food, so I always prepared a bit more, just in case he appeared.

One night I asked him how life on the other side was. Suddenly all his body seemed to light.

'It cannot be explained, Macaca. Everything is in perfect harmony there, there is no hate, no lies, no bad intentions, no pain, no crying, no sickness. We all serve and worship our Lord there. It is an amazing place, a true paradise, my love'.

Another Saturday night, when he was having an *empanada*, he started to cry inconsolably. I got worried he would choke...

'What is this? What is the matter?' I asked. Yes, it was Carmela. He knew about her pain somehow. Carmela was a worry as always. When we all thought she had at last settled down in a nice big house with respectable neighbours, a good job and a great family, suddenly she moved out with the younger children into an apartment.

'Yes, I know what you are thinking Paquito: he is the 'devil incarnate'.

'But what does she want for a husband?', Paquito. 'Does she want a blue enchanted prince for a partner? She is certainly not Snow White, you know!'

'You should have let her be with Amadeo, Macaquita. She truly loved him, and he truly loved her too. It was real love and her true destiny, and you truncated it badly, Macaca.'

'Well, Amadeo can have whom he pleases now, he is so seriously wealthy!'

'Listen to me Macaca. Amadeo had been married 5 times already and he had had so many ladies in his life... At least Carmela had her children to live for. Amadeo never had any children. I wish I could ease their pain! You must tell Carmela what you did, Macaca, before it is too late!'

'Do not be ridiculous, Paquito. It would never have worked! He was a real bum and she certainly deserved better!'

'Look at what Amadeo became, Macaca, he is such a famous artist! Money alone cannot satisfy a soul, Macaquita. Sometimes, it is just an unexplained divine union. Love covers a multitude of sins. You should have left them alone to live their lives.'

'We better leave it there, Paquito! How can you talk to me about love Paquito? You are always so sentimental, and I find it somehow pathetic. Please go away!'

'I will, Macaca! I will indeed go away! Goodbye for now!'

Paquito took his coat from his wardrobe where he had left it years ago, put it on and left walking through the back brick-wall of the flat.

After that, Paquito did not come to visit for many years. I was missing him a lot, because as my years crept up on me, my body could not move as fast as before, and I could not go out as often as

I did before. Besides, my friend Esther started to get sick and was diagnosed with ovarian cancer. All her casual boyfriends disappeared quickly. She had a lot of pain and although her operation to remove the cancer was a success, she started to lose a lot of weight and she became feeble as she could not keep any food down.

Eventually, Esther's daughter took her away, although her flat remained furnished. I was always hoping and praying to God she would be back home.

When Esther died a few months later in a palliative care hospital, I was so miserable at what had happened. On top of my grief, I could not believe how quickly what had been Esther's precious possessions - her crockery, crystal, linen, personal decorations, photos, CDs, furniture, her personal letters, and documents and other treasures - her daughter was throwing straight into the rubbish bin or leaving outside in the street for the council rubbish pickup.

The neighbours were going through her stuff and the bins, and it was a free for all. With tears in my eyes, I managed to rescue from the street brawl some of her books and a photograph of her and me when we were happy together.

Not long after my dear friend Esther died, Graciela also got sick and was taken in an ambulance. We learnt later she had had a stroke making wild love at her advance age to one of her casual lovers and she had been left paralysed and expected to die in the nursing home where she was placed.

Her flat was also emptied in a flash, with all her contents and precious possessions thrown in the bins too. This time the frenzy was so wild I could not even get a photo of her!

The big difference was, tragically, we heard Graciela did not die and in fact, she had recovered nicely. Only God knew where she was living! Months later, I saw her at the Club Marconi one Saturday night, dancing away with an old man. I could not believe it. She looked so healthy.

When I approached her and I asked where she was living, she did not recognise me at first. Then she said in Spanish she was fine, and she preferred not to talk about sad things, although I could see tears in her eyes. Then she turned around dismissing me and kept dancing away... That was the last time we met.

After my two dear close friends—Esther and Graciela—left the village, many other Spanish people—men and women—also died or were taken away and replaced with new tenants of different nationalities. The place was never a Spanish enclave again.

Part 2 - La Macaca

Although Maria remained my friend, life was not the same. I decided to spring clean my apartment, so they would not have to spend too much time throwing my things out when I eventually went to heaven.

I found all the bills and documents Paquito had left behind and threw them out together with lots of memories. I could not believe he would have thought I would not have been able to manage my affairs without him. What a mess of papers he left behind!

I wondered now whether he, 'smarty pants', would have been able to manage himself with the new advances online that came out in the last few years.

For example, I had all my household utilities and bills organised to be paid online and on time. Besides, I was so proud to be on Facebook and WhatsApp and most importantly, I was able to use it on my laptop.

My daughter Carmela arranged for me to get me a new, smart, iPhone with all the bells and whistles. In the beginning, I was taking notes and could not convince myself I would be able to use it. However, after a bit of practice with Carmela and Flor and a few lessons in the Computer Group, I was able to master texting and communicating with people I would never have had the chance to see again, from Argentina, Spain, and other places I had visited in the past.

I would have liked to establish a sensible conversation with my sister Carmela. But I doubted she would have a computer or a smart phone, let alone use it efficiently. I did not know exactly how old she would be because our parents did not register us when we were born, except when they had the time to do it. But for sure, Carmela must have been over 100 years old, if I was almost 90, as it was stated in my official papers.

To be truthful, my sister Carmela could still talk non-stop like a parrot when I rang her at the other side of the world. However, I suspected she could not hear me, so she could not follow my conversation, therefore she could not answer my questions.

I felt really sorry for my sister Carmela. She was living on her own, like me. All our brothers and sisters had now passed on. She had lost her daughter to Alzheimer's and her only grandson had died from a shooting incident. Her grandson's wife, *La Betty*, visited her from time to time. But she was busy trying to make ends meet. She oversaw her struggling courier business, which I believe was enough just to keep the family afloat and to purchase their bare necessities. I wished I could have helped them, but I did not yet have sufficient skills to be able to organise a money transfer online or otherwise.

My sister Carmela was old but still healthy in body and mind, well, yes, quite deaf, but that was all that was wrong with her! I would have liked to be with her. Maybe I could have repaid her a bit of what she had done for me in the past! Unfortunately, my doctor had forbidden me to travel, as I had some sort of chronic anaemia that would not go away.

My daughter Carmela turned up one day with Champ because they wanted to make a video of me answering some questions they had prepared to show at my approaching birthday.

My 90th 'official' birthday was coming up soon. I suspected Carmela was organising a party for me. I said to her I did not want to put her through any expense, but she said her son Christopher was in fact the organiser and he was paying for everything, which I initially did not believe for one minute.

However, on second thoughts, Christopher was progressing in the world. He was now an up-and-coming cardiologist, and there were rumours in the family he did not know what to do with his money. He was gathering a collection of investments and possessions: properties, luxury cars, works of art, yachts, and young beautiful women.

Carmela also assured me the party would be only a small gathering to celebrate my 90 years of life, a real achievement in the South American community, where everybody was dying a lot younger than that in Australia.

In the end, we had a huge party at the Marconi Club. Carmela had invited lots of my friends from my old and newer life. Some of them arrived in wheelchairs, walkers and with oxygen equipment, and it was good we had two doctors in the family, Chris, and Martin to watch over them and attend to their natural emergencies.

Cassandra, accompanied by her husband Joel on the guitar, sang emotional songs for me in Spanish like *Bésame mucho* and I had the chance to see some of my great grandchildren, even the new ones I had not met yet.

One of my male neighbours acted as MC and he also sang my favourite song *Venecia sin ti* by Charles Aznavour. It was amazing, so much love shown in just one night!

Carmela was there and so were her ex-husbands Giuseppe and el Cuco, but somehow, someone told me she now had a new husband, her number three, an Arab man called Aram whom I met on the night.

No, I was wrong, remembering correctly, I met him before several times on outings, although I never thought she was going to marry him. Aram seemed quite formal and courteous, and he certainly knew how to give us a show with his belly dancing when the right music played on.

I was given a lot of presents at my 90th birthday but preparing for my celestial departure, I had wanted to dispose of excessive clutter, so I gave most of them away. By that time, I had certainly thrown or given selectively away a lot of memorabilia and other treasures I had gathered throughout the years, as I wanted to spare my daughters the final clean-up.

However, around that time, my family doctor gave me the good news that my anaemia was a lot better, and my kidney specialist announced due to my better than average medical condition for my advanced age, he was going to prescribe some miracle injection to keep me energetic and to keep my organs, especially my kidneys, functioning better for longer. I believe the Queen of England was given the same monthly injections! As I had my full pension, the injections were going to be free as well.

This was amazing news! I felt then I should also throw out my old furniture and refresh my flat and gardens.

So, with the help of my Russian neighbours Pasha and Lyosha, we took my old lounge chairs and my dining suite out to the street.

Within a few hours the furniture had disappeared in the hands of other residents in the village. May God bless them…

I also ordered some red bark, some new plants, and small citrus trees from Bunnings to renovate my gardens.

I recalled I was going to ask Carmela to take me to a furniture store to purchase new furniture to celebrate my new lease on life, but she did not call in that often now that she had a partner and I did not want to bother her.

The place looked naked with hardly any furniture! I brought a chair from the garden to sit on and I was having some soup on my lap when I saw a bright light, followed by Paquito, Sara and they had brought my sister Carmela also, all holding hands. What a pleasant surprise!

They were coming to celebrate my birthday as well. But that day I was not expecting them, nor did I have any chairs for them to sit down!

In the end, they had to sit on the floor and be happy just with my presence. I was surprised to find out by then I felt no real resentment at all towards Paquito and Sara, and I was so grateful to God who had allowed me to truly forgive them!

Anyway, I was so happy to recognise my sister Carmela. She was looking lovely and young in her favourite dress and a large pink bow on her long curly hair. They all seemed to have new revitalized celestial bodies! We embraced and kissed each other and before they disappeared through the walls, I made them promise they would come back soon.

When my daughter Carmela finally came to accompany me to buy the furniture, I told her about my heavenly visitors. She did not look surprised, but she smiled! I think she believed I was becoming senile and quite demented! She casually mentioned she knew about her aunty Carmela's passing but did not want to tell me, because she did not want to upset me!

Anyhow, I felt quite happy with my purchases! My place looked so lovely and uncluttered with my new dining suite, a two-seater and two lounge single chairs to match! I also bought a matching electric reclining chair for me so I could sleep if I felt tired when watching my new smart TV. This wonderful electric chair also made it much easier for me to stand up quickly if I wanted to.

Despite my children's protests forbidding me to do any heavy work, I dug up the front and back gardens and removed all the weeds and I also fertilised and pruned all my existing plants. I planted my newly bought Meyer Lemon, the Birds of Paradise, red camellias, Thai orchids, and some other Australian natives. I also pruned and fertilised the red rose I had grown in the front garden from a cutting of the rose bush at Paquito's gravesite.

Finally, I placed into the garden beds the red bark mulch I had delivered from Bunnings in bags, and all by myself. I did this with the help of a small wheelbarrow and a spade on the garden beds. I could not recognise my gardens and looked forward to seeing what their transformation would bring, with the approaching spring.

I felt exhausted and in need of some company to show my accomplishment. However, the problem was that not many people visited me anymore and many times I wondered whether the dead were more kind-hearted and considerate than the living.

My daughter Flor used to visit me more often in the past. But now she had finally broken free of her husband-imposed confinement just when her younger daughters were already grown up. I was so pleased she had now given Ronaldo the 'big sack' at last.

At last, Flor had also decided to finish her secondary schooling –her HSC. She was studying day and night and she must have got high marks because she was offered a place at university to get into an Accountancy and Law Combined Degree.

I suspected her relationship with Ronaldo had gradually been breaking up throughout the years. He had been sick from jealousy and possessiveness in the past. I was so pleased she was now free, and I thought it was not peculiar when Flor started to come on her own and she started to take more care of herself. She had lost some weight, kept her hair nice and tidy, and she even ventured with some makeup.

I believe when Flor was just about to finish her Degrees, Ronaldo finally moved out of the marital home. I asked and asked and asked Flor what the matter was, but she would not tell me or anybody.

Finally, the last person I would think of undoing the tangle, did. Yes, it was Paquito. During one of his renewed nocturnal visits, he was the one who would explain to me what was behind Flor and Ronaldo's split.

Ronaldo, as he usually did, had gone to America on a business trip for his employer. One of their girls wanted a particular perfume and Flor thought Ronaldo could purchase it duty free. She could have sent him an email, but she thought she would like to give him a surprise!

It followed that Flor rang Ronaldo's employer to get the details of where he was staying in the States to get in contact with him directly by phone. To her dismay, Flor was told Ronaldo was not on any business trip but instead he had taken a few weeks holidays and they did not know where he was.

When he came back home, Ronaldo was confronted with the news, and he had to face the music confessing he was having an affair with his secretary, and he had gone away on holidays for a few weeks with her.

Paquito looked agitated and sad. I wanted to calm him down and I made him a hot café con leche as he liked it and offered him his favourite cookies, but I did not know if he was allowed to eat in that state...

'The bastard', he cried, 'I always knew he was a bastard'.

Paquito finally calmed down before disappearing again and promising to come back soon.

A few weeks later, Ronaldo had the nerve to drop in to see how I was. However, he did not dare to tell me any more details about his appalling behaviour. He was apologetic and begged me to interfere in his favour for Flor to take him back, but I told him Flor was my daughter, and if I had to take sides, I would always take her side not his. I told him I found him irresponsible and disgraceful. He was politely but firmly advised to never come back to see me or phone me again.

I heard people saying, 'Time always heals all the wounds'. I hope Flor's pain was healed because she fully deserved to be happy and find her lasting peace in this world.

From what I know, she graduated and was offered a job in a prestigious Accountancy Firm. However, her visits to me started to dwindle and in the end, she was always busy, so when she visited, it was only for a short while, to have a quick lunch with me or to drop a small gift for Mother's Day or Christmas.

My other daughter Edith and her husband Lolo had no family of their own. They tried adoption but it did not work, so they bred a series of dogs, which they loved and treated like humans. Edith and Lolo were also busy always with their creatures, if not working, so when they visited, it was not for long.

Besides, I could not visit Carmela anymore because it was hard for me to negotiate public transport and she did not visit or call me either because she was always busy with her work and her personal life.

Most of my closer friends and acquaintances had already died except Maria. She was going insane with her family's demands. Her sons and family usually all came to eat at her tiny flat and left the children there to be minded. I felt sorry for her because she had no way of escaping the abuse as she could not drive or go out on her own anymore.

As for myself and at over 90, after I finished my daily routine of thorough cleaning and washing and tidying up everything ready for my imminent parting, I sometimes felt a bit lonely and had to wait patiently for the dead to comfort and entertain me at night whenever they felt to appear.

Chapter 10

RESILIENCE

'Success has a price tag, only those who are willing to pay its price will
reap its benefits.'
(Aniekee Tochukwu Ezekiel)

'Be not deceived; God is not mocked: for whatsoever a man soweth, that
shall he also reap. —GALATIANS 6: 7'
(Paul the Apostle)

'All human wisdom is summed up in two words—wait and hope.'
(Alexandre Dumas)

Part 1 - Carmela Junior

*My story hereby continues Emanuel. It has taken me such a long
time to write. Possibly this is my last recount.*

*By the way, it was so nice to see you at your latest product
presentation and I thank you so much for your invitation and
arrangements for my transport. I certainly enjoyed the limousine,
the champagne, and the attention.*

*Your gadgets are super amazing! You must be so clever! Do you
think I could have a sample to try?*

You certainly made your grandma super proud!

*May God continue to bless you in the future! I wish you success
always, my dear grandson!*

When I divorced Giuseppe, I swore I would never divorce again. I did not want to go through the pain and anguish again.

Over the years, I had prayed to God to save my marriage to el Cuco, but no matter how much I tried and pleaded, the Lord could not grant me that wish and I regrettably, had finally accepted our wretched relationship was over.

The Lord had asked me long ago to take up my cross and follow Him. It took me half my lifetime to appreciate my purpose and what He had truly meant! I was gradually but irrevocably understanding that my life had not been easy going or sweet. However, instead of a good life and marriage, the Lord had granted me so many blessings, mainly in the form of my children and grandchildren and He had also given me special brains to succeed in business, so I was never short of money or lacked anything I needed.

Cassandra loved her job as a veterinarian, but she loved God more. I used to pray she would find a good husband who would not take advantage of her innocent, kind, and generous nature.

Cassandra eventually fell in love and married Joel, who eventually became a pastor in our church and had two gorgeous children; a girl Anastasia, who looked just like her dad and then Jacob, who everybody thought looked just like me.

Although they did not have much money, they were happy, and God provided everything they needed. At some point, they wanted to buy a house close by, but prices in Sydney had skyrocketed because of the large influx of rich Asians coming from Hong Kong and other Asian cities. When Christopher learnt they were having financial struggles to get a decent house, he helped them financially to purchase the house they had chosen in a nice suburb. My heart still jumps for joy when I remember how generous Chris could be!

Chris had become a famous Cardiologist and his name was becoming recognised all over the world; but sadly, he was not so lucky in love. His childless marriage to his sweetheart Keira had failed after seven years. I thought Chris had not given his wife the time she needed because of the demands of his career, but even that was not a good enough excuse for Keira to run away to London with some other punk. Poor Chris! Keira eventually came back but Chris did not want anything to do with her anymore. I could not blame him; I would have done exactly the same!

Pity! I liked Keira, but regrettably, she did not know the life she would miss. Keira could have had in Chris a husband who adored her and spoilt her with everything she wanted, but I had to assume that, at that stage, she had not grown up yet or she had real shit for brains!

I really admired Chris! He was getting very wealthy, but he never forgot his humble beginnings and he had a generous disposition. He would give a helping hand emotionally and financially to anybody in and outside the family, if needed. Plus, now he was dating the most beautiful women I have ever seen in my life! I prayed to God that Chris's heart eventually be healed and he could find true love at last.

Chris had also become an athlete and at some point, he asked me to come to New York with him to support him, as he was participating in the NY Marathon. It was amazing. He took me business class to America, the best hotel, the best restaurants, and tours. I would always be grateful for this trip with Chris as we had such a special time together.

Johny and Jack graduated with brilliant marks, and they got good jobs at first and then with the financial support of Chris, they moved out and set up a successful legal practice in one of the best suburbs in Sydney. They eventually married another set of mirror-image twins they met online and were producing a series of twins. Oh boy, it was always hard for anybody to tell these kids apart, but thankfully, so far, they were cooperating with their identification, because they did not want anybody to confuse them with each other.

Adam married a girl from New Zealand and had a son who looked just like Champ. I knew Adam was shrewd with his finances and lately I heard he and his wife were managing a large chain of hotels in the United States.

Eva married very young in Argentina and had a daughter, but the marriage did not last. She had then married again and had another daughter from this union, and I heard she was very happy and her girls were very cute and smart.

Champ had still been living with me. He had had some study hiccups in his second and third year at university. He had chosen to study Aeronautical Engineering and he had to do a lot of difficult and time-consuming assignments. Every day he needed to solve rather complicated mathematical and computing problems, while his friends were cruising with other easier and more palatable courses.

At that time, Champ was also heavily involved with the church and its homeless youth program, counseling and feeding young people in the streets of Chatswood, a reasonably affluent suburb in the north of Sydney. I need not to say he was very fond of the ladies as well, with a new girlfriend every second week. A string of girls was always ringing him at all hours of the day or night for some spiritual advice and affection.

Nevertheless, Champ confronted me one day and confessed he wanted to be a church pastor and he had to abandon his present studies and embrace a theology course full time.

'I am sorry Champ, but I cannot support you with your plans' was my response.

'Why not mum? It is what God wants me to do,' he insisted.

'I have promised God, I will support you in your chosen career, and that is Engineering Studies. I suggest you finish that first, then when you can start getting your own money, you can choose what you want to do,' I advised him.

It was extremely hard for me to say because nobody, including me, had ever denied any wish Champ had. He was spoilt by the whole family!

I thought he would get mad at me, but instead he nodded his head and went quietly to his room. I heard him praying that night and many other nights after that. Some days he would fast breakfast or lunch as well. However, after our conversation, Champ changed forever.

His involvement with the church continued, but he seemed more focused at university and his marks improved significantly. At the end of the year, he announced he wanted to be baptized in water and he also said to me in confidence he would stop going out with girls unless he thought he was going to settle down. Wow! That had to be a miracle! He was not even 19 years old.

In any case, Champ's outings declined considerably during the following year and by the time he was finishing his degree, he brought Joy home and announced her as his girlfriend. I was indeed surprised! Joy had been his friend ever since they were children and they had always fought like cats and dogs in the past.

Champ had always said he liked tall dark and slim Latino type girls like him! Joy could not be any fairer or physically distant from his ideal girl; yes, she was tall but although she was not chubby, she was certainly not slim, and she was very blond with celestial blue eyes. Wow! I would have never dreamt of her as Champ's choice for a partner. But Joy definitely loved God as much as Champ and now they were together and very much in love.

Champ went on to finish his degree with honors and he was then offered a paid internship with City Rail as a junior engineer.

In the meantime, my mother used to come to visit, and she always asked me why I did not find another partner.

'Champ will go, and you will be alone. You were so, so, so, unlucky in love. I will not be on this planet forever for company, my dear. You need to find another man,' she would tell me continuously.

At the time, my mother must have said something to Johny and Jack, because they came one day and suggested I joined the RSVP dating site.

'Mum, that is how we get our best girlfriends. And it is so easy to join. All you have to do is fill in your profile including a list of what you would expect to find in a future partner', they insisted.

I was now free and although I often thought of Amadeo and prayed to God for him to be happy, I was reasonably happy with my life just being alone.

I would have liked to share my new freedom with my mother, go out together, enjoy our times together, maybe travel to places together, but she had already found good friends of her age and had moved on.

It was also true I felt lonely sometimes now Champ visited Joy at her home more often. Therefore, one day, when Jack and Johny were visiting, I asked them to help me fill in my profile on the RSPV site. I was as truthful as I could be. Yes, I was 57, a committed Christian, a university graduate with a well-paid job, well-travelled and I had a nice apartment fully paid for. Yes, I had so many children, but they were all independent. I had nothing to lose…

Furthermore… I wanted a man about my age, a Christian, a university graduate with a well-paid job, well-travelled and with his house paid for. Adult children would be fine!

I posted the profile, but I did not attach any photo of myself.

Within a week, I had about 20 potential suitors in my inbox and 10 free kisses to send out. All I had to do was to send a kiss to the ones I thought might be suitable, which I did. They all wanted to meet me or at least they wanted my private email address.

When I told Cassandra about my adventure, she was horrified, and she offered to come with me to watch and make sure nothing would happen to me if I intended to meet them. She came to all my dates, except later, to the one with Aram.

Theophilus said he was a doctor in medicine. We met at a café in Chatswood. He was too arrogant. He boasted about himself and his achievements all the time we were having our coffee. I did not like him at all.

Pete was from NZ. He said he was a committed Christian and I agreed to meet him, again, at Chatswood. When I met him, he could hardly talk and he could not remember what church he went to, plus he apologized because he had just lost his front teeth and he did not have his dentures fitted yet. Wow! Definitely not my type! I never saw him again!

Bret was a widower, and he did not cease to shake the whole the time we were having our coffee. He was obviously full of drugs for some mental disorder he had. I have been through that before, thank you very much!

Luigi brought me some *kinotos* (kumquats) from his garden. As soon as the coffee came, he started to sob and confessed he missed his ex-wife. He said I was understanding and caring, blah, blah, blah... I offered him a packet of tissues I had in my bag and sent him on his way.

Ricky seemed lovely and a lot of fun, but by the end of our conversation he had confessed he had his doubts about his sexuality. No. No. No. Thank you very much!

Carlos spoke Spanish but he seemed disturbed. When questioned a bit further, it was about one of his children, who happened to be in jail. No, no, and no! I could not handle any more problems!

Robert was a university professor, but he was still living with his wife and openly looking for a fling.

Eddy was a lot younger than me, and he was handsome! When I questioned our age differences, he said he did not mind... He was looking for an older woman with money who would leave him her fortune when she 'kicked the bucket', obviously the sooner the better! OMG! At least he was honest!

The list went on for about four months, with Cassandra faithfully attending and often giggling during my dates. She was always sitting nearby, watching me like a hawk.

Aram had sent a kiss back and wanted to meet me for coffee. I said I wanted to know more about him. He said he was Assyrian, born in Lebanon. I said I did not want anything to do with Muslims. He said he was a Christian.

'Assyrians were one of the first nations who recognized Christianity and Jesus spoke Aramaic, my own ancient language,' he protested.

He sent me a photo and if it was a recent one, he seemed to have all his teeth intact and looked reasonably normal. We exchanged a few emails. He was an engineer, had been divorced for a while and had an adult son. Tick! Tick!

Aram worked in Campbelltown and lived near the city, close to the school where I worked but he could not get there till late. He insisted he wanted to have a coffee with me. We agreed to meet at *The Shed* at Randwick at 6pm the following day.

My schoolwork was supposed to be finished by 3.30pm but I

had a few lessons to prepare and had to look over the work of a new teacher. I told my friend Norma about my date. She said I was mad to wait. It was cold, raining, late, and he should be making the effort to come earlier. I sort of agreed with her. We should meet in Chatswood, like the others, with Cassandra's blessings.

Besides, it was true; it was cold and raining… I should go home and forget about this guy! Soon it was 5.45pm and I got ready to go home. 'What if this is the one?'

'With such a name, Aram, this is not 'it', surely! Impossible,' my friend Norma said, and my gut feeling confirmed it!

If I get parking easily, I will give it a go, I said to myself. *Yes, here it is, a parking spot at the shopping center car park, and it is rare at this time on Thursday! An omen? Maybe. Carmela, you do not believe in omens or luck! It could be a divine appointment, maybe then, from God?*

Aram was there already sitting with a double expresso cup in front of him. He suggested I have a hot chocolate to warm me up! I liked his initiative and the hot chocolate. He was cheerful with a mouth full of teeth, not crying and I did not notice any obvious shaking. Tick! Tick! Tick!

We exchanged a few pleasantries. *Hmmm…* He was respectful, educated, with a husky paused masculine voice. He looked similar to his photo, maybe a few years older, but I found him ugly, very, very ugly! He reminded me of an ugly somebody. Yes, Charles Aznavour, the French singer I loved in my youth. Ugly, but with a great voice! Ticked… Hmmm… Not sure…

We are both Aquarius, born three days apart! Yes. No, I am his senior! We arrived in Australia a few days apart on the same year. He seemed genuine.

I sort of liked him, but possibly I would never see him again. How wrong I was… I saw him in the car park! Was he checking out what car I drove or was I imagining that?

He kept on contacting me through the dating site. My mother was coming the following weekend to visit. Aram wanted me to go out with him to a restaurant for dinner. I explained I had to entertain my mother on Saturday night. Aram said he did not mind my mother coming to our date.

We all met at the restaurant where we had a meal. My mother liked him a lot.

'But it is me, who has to like him, mum.'

He smiled and stared a lot, maybe he smiled too much? He was polite, and he insisted on paying the bill for us! We exchanged personal emails and he accompanied us to take the train that would take us home.

Aram and I continued to exchange a few emails just to get to know each other better. He said his wife had left him after 25 years of marriage, he was a family man, and he was looking for a permanent relationship. *Hmmm... Not sure...*

Aram wanted to go out again, but my mother was staying with me for the weekend again and I already had tickets to see an 'Elvis' show with her at my mother's local club on Saturday. My mother loved Elvis!

Aram asked me if he could join us for the show. I said I did not know whether there would be any tickets left as I had bought ours weeks ago.

I don't know how he got the ticket, but he was there, smiling, at the club entrance to greet us that Saturday. He was pleasant to be with, a real gentleman, well dressed, a bit short but well spoken. He bought us drinks and some snacks whilst we watched the show.

He invited us both to a Kurdish Street festival the following day, and my mother accepted for both of us straight away.

We met in the city and walked the streets and enjoyed the Kurdish festival, tasting different traditional foods and drinks. We met a young Assyrian couple with their children there and they all greeted him enthusiastically with kisses and hugs. He introduced us as good friends.

We looked at some shop windows all nicely decorated. My mother mentioned she liked this particular and unusual porcelain teacup and saucer with exotic flowers. He immediately walked into the shop and bought it for her. We tried to dissuade him not to buy it—

we could pay for it—but he insisted it was a present from him to her with all his love and respect.

On the train back home, my mother counselled me, she said she liked Aram a lot and I would not find any better-quality man than him. He was clean, respectful, lonely, and surely in desperate need of some company. She also repeated that I was still young, and life could be long and desolate on my own. According to her, I had nothing to lose pursuing a relationship with short and smiling Aram and that I should definitely give him a go.

My mother did not come the following weekend and Aram invited me to a picnic in the Central Coast. I gave him my address outside my building, so he could pick me up in his car. I prepared a Spanish potatoes omelet—tortilla - with some salad, and he was bringing the drinks.

Although it was winter, it was a sunny day, and it was not cold. We had a picnic lunch under a tree in a large park at the Entrance. The place was scenic and peaceful. Everyone there was enjoying the blue skies and the balmy conditions including colorful lorikeets; we even spotted a large white cockatoo that was looking at our food basket suspiciously.

I was a bit surprised at how perfectly Aram had prepared for our 'casual' picnic. He had brought a picnic table, an impeccable white tablecloth and two folding chairs, paper plates and disposable cutlery, some fruit juice and two mangos already cut up to eat in a plastic sealed bag. He seemed too domesticated for a male, tidy and very clean! And he seemed to enjoy my food as well.

After eating, we went for a walk, and he shyly held my hand. We had a coffee in a quiet café, and he said he liked me. He had gone out with other women and some of them he had taken to his bed and some of them had taken him to their beds. He had not found one lady nearly as suitable as to make her his permanent partner yet.

We sat down at a park bench. I told him part of my life story and he seemed interested. Was I dreaming or did I notice he was having difficulties maintaining eye contact with me? Instead, he seemed to stare at some people sideways.

My children all kept ringing me during the day to ask me how I was. I felt a bit embarrassed but pleased to learn they all cared about me.

Back in the car and before we drove off, he said he liked me again, hugged me and gave a light kiss on the lips. When we got home, he asked me if he could see me again the following weekend and he also said I could call him Ari which was the name people called him in English.

We emailed each other during the week, and I found although from different cultures, we both held similar values and beliefs. I tried to be as truthful as possible and prayed to God he would be truthful too.

Our relationship continued to grow, and we continued to see each other at least on the weekends, sometimes with my mother and sometimes the two of us alone. One Saturday we went to a club to dance, and he held me in his arms during a slow song. I loved it, but I could perceive he was not feeling that comfortable. I also noticed he kept on talking to himself some words I could not recognize. When prompted he said it was his own 'silly language' he used if he felt a bit anxious: 'patchis' 'rataji' 'chispij…' It was not Aramean, nor it was Arabic… He used it with his nephews also… I found it hilarious! It reminded me of my older twins' talk, many years ago.

Although I still considered him rather ugly physically, he was not dark, but his features were very angular, his steely grey eyes depicted some deep sadness, and his peculiar mechanical smile… I could not pinpoint the reason yet! What was I getting into?

I was surprised I still felt attracted to him. I somehow sensed I could trust him and felt secure with him. He seemed so methodically, systematic, and formal. For once, I really needed some structure in my life.

At some point later, Ari introduced me to his close nephews Youel and Abrahim and their families, and they all seemed simple, unstructured, and casual, nothing like Ari, but they all seemed very warm and generous people. I enjoyed being with them. And they cooked the most delicious Assyrian and Middle Eastern meals.

Finally, I reluctantly let him up to my apartment and introduced him to my son Champ. Champ liked him instantly. He thought he seemed honest and genuine but a bit stuffy and somewhat odd. Champ also confessed to me he could not pinpoint exactly what was peculiar with him though. He might be trying to impress us all...

Aram wanted to take me away for a weekend somewhere, but I said on Sundays I needed to go to church with my family and then I rested for the day as it was the Lord's Day.

Aram—or Ari as he wanted me to call him—said he went to his church—The Assyrian Apostolic Church of the East in Sydney—only sometimes. I had already found out his church was ultra-traditional, and my church was a contemporary Pentecostal, of the 'born again' Christian movement Church, indeed very casual.

I tried to explain to Ari that our church aimed to have an intimate and personal relationship with Jesus Christ. We expressed our love to God through contemporary Worship and submission to the teachings of the Holy Bible, but it did not have any 'rituals' as such.

When Ari said he was very interested in visiting my church, I was shocked, and I told him it would not be possible. I tried to justify myself, saying the service was conducted in a school hall, not really in a church building, it was most likely not suitable for him...

However, I felt convicted, because the real reason I did not want him to come was I was starting to like him, and I did not want to drive him away because of our different church approaches to worshiping God. I just needed some time, at least until I had a chance to explain what my church was like and what he would get from it.

I rang Cassandra, my daughter, and told her about the situation. She advised me it was not proper to deny anybody the chance to get closer to God, she explained.

'Whether Ari approves of our church or not, it is up to God to decide, not us', she added.

I felt even worse after that explanation. I knew what she said was what I also believed, and she had been right. Therefore, I rang Ari up and said to him if he wanted to come to church, I would take him there next Sunday morning for our regular service. He accepted enthusiastically.

Ari was a bit taken aback by the volume of the music and especially, the fact that there were no crosses or statues in the school hall. He was also taken aback also by the exuberant friendliness of the people in the congregation - 'patchis' 'rataji' 'chispij'—but he got really interested in the sermon and he asked me to take him back the following Sunday.

I brought him back to Church Sunday after Sunday. I noticed he was wearing discreet hearing earplugs during our worship. He mentioned the loud music perturbed him somehow.

However, most Sundays, he was fighting back tears during the singing and especially during the sermon. After a few months, when the pastor asked if anybody wanted to give his or her life to our Lord Jesus, I was stunned when Ari ran to the front of the church for prayer.

I had already said to Ari I had lived for and served Jesus for a long time, more concretely since I had His miraculous healing and touch those years ago and anything was possible with Him. I believed He was always looking after us and if it was beneficial and at His perfect time, He always gave his people the desires of their hearts.

Nevertheless, I had never witnessed so many small miracles in a person as those happening in Ari's life. He appeared to be much happier and at peace with himself and he was much more open to talk about his past and other disappointments in his life.

Part 2 - Carmela Junior

Ari made it clear to me from the beginning of our relationship he was looking for a permanent relationship, and now God was involved, he hinted he wanted to marry me. - *patchis, rataji, chispij...*

Gradually, I introduced all my children to Ari and initially they all seemed to approve of him just like my mother had done. Casandra was a bit more suspicious, and she suggested I should wait at least two years to make him my permanent partner. This way, I was going to be able to see in the long term and I felt more than inclined to agree with her.

I had organized an educational excursion with my students to Argentina, and the trip was coming up. I thought being so busy and away from Ari for a while was going to give me clarity of mind to make a more informed decision.

Besides, I would have the chance to meet Amadeo. Of course, if he wanted to see me. That would give me the chance to test what was really happening in my heart, after such a long time!

Amadeo agreed to meet me in the heart of Buenos Aires, the city that had been home to both of us once, one lovely evening.

Nothing would prepare me for what I saw after almost 40 years of not seeing each other. The handsome prince from my dreams had become grossly obese, he had a few grey hairs on top, but he was almost bald. He could hardly walk, except with the help of a cane and his sharpness had mellowed into a series of incoherent stories about some people I did not even know.

He took me to a vegetarian restaurant to share a meal together and there in the quietness of our chat, I could still faintly perceive in his eyes, our powerful connection, the loving wholesomeness of his soul and the reason I had loved him so much.

I tried to ask him why he left me all those years ago, and his eyes filled with tears. He mumbled something about my mother interfering, but his explanation did not make any sense. He implied my mother had told him to break up our relationship, she had explained it was wrong, a sin in fact, and the whole family would have been damned forever if he did not act instantly and split up from me once and for all. And what the neighbors would think? What if we ever had children, they would be born with monstrous pig's tails or worse...

What...? Was I hearing right or was I trapped in a nightmare...? My mother interfering... Worried about what other people might have thought? Some sort of a cultural curse threat?

Amadeo was babbling again... After our truncated relationship, he had dedicated his life to pursing God through the Sufi religion and he was still on his journey to achieve spiritual satisfaction.

God had given him a brilliant career and financial freedom. However, despite of having many relationships and five failed marriages, he had not found personal happiness with any woman, nor had he had any children. My sadness was becoming unmanageable.

We decided to walk up the road to what was once our favorite coffee shop. I felt it was already sad enough, talking about what it could have been our life together. Therefore, I decided it was too late to tell him anything about my abortion so many years ago. If it would have come to fruition, our child would have been almost 40 years old... And only God knew where we would be then. Certainly not sobbing in an old coffee shop.

I left him in a taxi, in a city street in Buenos Aires that was going to take him to his mansion up the coast by the River Plate. I wandered around the steamy vibrant streets of the city for hours like a tramp, without knowing where to go. I could not breath freely... I felt lost in Buenos Aires, the city where I once belonged.

I walked and walked with a bitter taste in my mouth, a deep hatred towards my mother and the certainty I could not possibly come back to live there, not now, not ever.

The rest of my life was somewhere else, so far away, in Sydney, where I had my routine, my children and my grandchildren and where I could, at times, could breathe more easily...

The school excursion was a resounding success. Ari and I had kept in touch by phone and by the time I came back to Sydney, I was really pleased to see him again—*patchis, rataji, chispij, aniloc...*

However, I had organized another trip to lead an excursion for teachers to Spain. This trip was during my summer holidays, and it was going to last six weeks.

I had done these trips before, so I had a lot of practice managing the teachers, sometimes in disarray away from home.

'Irma snores and I cannot go to sleep'; 'No, Elena, you cannot steal sandwiches from our breakfast spread'; 'You need to go to class. This is a scholarship for you to improve your Spanish, Raquel, not a holiday. If you go away again, I will have to send you back home to Brisbane.' Nevertheless, I usually enjoyed such odd experiences enormously.

However, this time, I could not focus fully on my job because of the teachers' silly complaints. Their jokes and mischiefs started to annoy me.

Despite being in touch by phone and email, I started to miss Ari's companionship, his chats, and his peculiar humor.

I started to fantasize about what my life would be like with him. He treated me like a lady, almost like royalty. Wow! Perhaps, my mother was right, for the first time in my life, I had been given the treatment I had deserved all along.

Ari was also missing me. He told me he intended to travel and meet me in Spain, but after all, this was not a holiday for me either; I was working. Therefore, I refused to accept his plans and persuaded him to stay in Sydney. We would have to wait to be with each other when I returned.

Within a few minutes of arriving back to my apartment in Sydney, there was another big surprise waiting for me.

About 12 giant vases full of red roses were delivered to me along with 12 love letters numbered from 1 to 12. My surprise turned into panic when I saw who was sending me the flowers: yes, it was el Cuco!

El Cuco had learnt about Ari. He could not believe it! He was conscious of what he had said to me on so many occasions, including that I was incapable of finding or holding a good relationship.

Yes, the bugger, he would say anything to put me down. Now he regretted it wholeheartedly! Hmm No... Sorry... I did not trust him.

El Cuco's letters were melodramatic: he thought I was holding onto my promise many years ago I would never marry again! He warned me, 'all new brooms sweep the best at the beginning, when they are new'. He thought better to be the devil you know (him) than the devil to be discovered (Ari). El Cuco said a new relationship would absolutely not work for me. I should remember we had a son together... *Blah Blah Blah...*

He was saying he loved me and wanted to be with me again forever. He could not live without me and without our family. Hello? Really? This was the opposite to what he had said during our marriage...

His letters were repetitive, seemingly sincere, but impetuous. He was so sorry for ruining my life in the past. He was now prepared to show me how much he had changed, and he would still change in the future. He wanted to make me happy, at last!

This was the outcome I wanted from him, although this was many years too late. I had pleaded to God to change el Cuco so many times in the past, to save my marriage, to enjoy life. We could have had everything...

But now, I had heard it all before and I was not prepared to sacrifice a good relationship with Ari for an uncertain and perhaps doomed relationship with el Cuco. Thank you very much!

El Cuco tried to contact me by phone or text me over the next six months or so, and he tried even to persuade my children and my mum to interfere in his favor, so he could have a chance to talk to me face to face. He left me messages trying to manipulate me into helping him. He said he had a bad tooth ache and he needed me to get an urgent appointment with our dentist because he had lost the dental clinic number.

But I was firm and sure this time in deliberately not responding to any of his calls, tricks, or silly requests.

Ari felt we wanted to be together intimately, '*patchis, rataji, chispij. aniloc...*' but I did not want him to share my bed, nor did I want to share his. Therefore, we decided to go on an extended holiday to see how we got along in that department, not that at my age it mattered to me much. He also wanted, if I found it appropriate, to talk freely and without any interruptions about our future together.

We decided to book a cruise around the Pacific Islands for two weeks. Ari seemed fascinated and proud when talking about his work. I noticed his favorite conversation with anybody we met on the boat was how electronics were produced. If there was any other topic addressed, he just kept quiet until he could bring his complex technical processes into the conversation. Most people seemed interested as well, so there was no issue there.

Ari did not want to talk much about his past life, or his young son, and I thought the reason was that he was still hurt. I suspected the real cause of his marriage breakdown was that unintentionally, he had left his wife to her own devices whilst travelling extensively overseas with his work. But when we referred to our future life together, our conversation flowed easily and extensively.

I agreed with his wish to write down in a book all the decisions we were considering together and those that were important to both of us. I had a good memory and I usually act on a project as it develops, sometimes on the run. However, I agreed to document all our decisions; if we were ever together for good, we would not travel on our own. We would share the house responsibilities; we would share bank accounts to pay for the bills.

Above all, Jesus would be the Lord of our lives always; we would go to church every Sunday, we would take care of all our children if they needed anything, we would travel until we were that old that we could not travel anymore, we would not have any pets whilst we were still travelling, and so on and so on.

As mentioned, Cassandra had advised me to wait about two years before we decided on anything too serious…

Ari officially asked me to marry him, 'within the hour' of the two-year anniversary of our first date. I readily accepted his proposal. For the first time in my life, I got an engagement ring with a big diamond on it.

Champ also proposed to his darling Joy, and they had a big engagement party where all my family was invited, and we took the opportunity to announce our engagement too. Everyone was happy and wished us well. Life was good! All we had to do was to organize our wedding.

Ari wanted to be married in his church, but the Assyrian Church could only offer us a 'blessing' because we had both been married before.

After his official research, however, Ari discovered he would be allowed to marry again in his Church, because although it was his second marriage, the reason for his divorce—his wife's unfaithfulness - was somehow an exception to the church regulations.

It was a different story with me. I had been married twice and I was not Assyrian. We had a meeting with the Assyrian Bishop in Sydney and took all my previous marriage certificates and divorce documents, including my Catholic Church annulment from my first marriage.

The bishop took photocopies of every document. He explained to us he had to travel to the Middle East in the following weeks, and he was going to meet their *Catholicos Patriarch*—head of Holy Apostolic Catholic Assyrian Church of the East for other businesses.

The bishop told us there might be a slim chance for us to be married in the Assyrian Church because I had an official annulment from the Catholic Church of my first marriage and my second marriage was only a civil marriage, therefore, it had never been officially recognized in a Christian church.

Our union had to be approved by the Assyrian *Catholicos Patriarch* first. We felt we were in the right place, at the right time, that day. All we had to do was to wait patiently for the bishop's news in about a month's time.

Around that time, we also decided that once married, we would live in my apartment until it became clear where we would like to spend the rest of our lives together.

Nevertheless, there was an elephant in the room.

My younger twins and Champ expressed their worry that, 'Ari might be… hmm might be, hmm… might be just a gold digger.' Their worry was not unfounded. After all, I had my apartment paid for and my investment property almost paid off. I had a good job, and I was quite free from financial worries. I was in a much better position financially than him, they claimed. They were rather concerned, and it needed clarification …

Ari must have heard our conversations through ESP because when he came to see me next, he said he wanted to marry me for what I was and not for any financial gain, '*patchis, rataji, chispij, aniloc…*' What a relief!

Ari suggested we should start a financial plan and pre-nuptial arrangement options were written for consideration. In the end, we decided whatever we had in cash before marriage, we would keep in our own private bank accounts. About our properties, whatever each of us had, would remain in that person's name and their heirs when we eventually passed on.

However, whatever we were going to earn together after marriage, we would open a joint bank account to use together and if we purchased any property with funds from our bank account in the future, it would be equally in both our names.

I agreed to his suggestions as they were clear and fair, and Jack and Johny helped us find a specialist solicitor who drew a pre-nuptial agreement or a 'financial agreement' between us. The same solicitor wrote new wills for both of us to seal our plans.

Soon after, we got word from the Assyrian Church that we could have a church marriage, should we wish to.

We decided to get married the following June and we booked a date in the Church. We wanted our wedding to be very low-key, but in the end, we had a party of about 35 guests in the church and at the reception.

At 58 years, I was as nervous as a bride in her twenties, and I sincerely asked God that day to secure our lives together and forever.

We had yet another issue to solve as a matured married couple. Ari had been living with his now 19-year-old son Bobby, since his wife left him for another man. Bobby was having serious problems with his sexuality. - '*patchis, rataji, chispij, aniloc…*'

Ari suspected he was gay, as he had discovered he was using heavy make up at night when he went out. However, Ari did not dare to face him or ask him outright the reason for this behavior.

Ari felt terribly embarrassed about his son's sexual tendencies because in his culture, this type of lifestyle was not accepted. I thought Ari felt somewhat responsible for his son's issues.

Bobby certainly looked, spoke, and acted a bit strange to me but he was so young. Maybe he was just confused. I had never had any formal experience with gay people, but I knew from my teaching that children liked to experiment entirely with their sexualities.

I suggested to Ari, under the circumstances, it might be safer and better for Bobby to live with us at the start of our married life. We could then keep an eye on him, and this would also give him a bit of control and peace of mind.

The twins had already moved out of my apartment long ago to be closer to their jobs in the city. My youngest son Champ was going to marry his beloved Joy six months after us. He had moved out of my unit a few weeks before we got married, as he wanted to check out how he was going to manage on his own.

Bobby moved in just before our wedding and had taken Champ's bedroom. Bobby got a transfer to work at the local Bunnings during the day but in spite of now living in a 'normal' household, Bobby persisted with some weird behavior when going out at night and this continued to bother Ari, *'patchis, rataji, chispij, aniloc…'*

We had been invited to some of Ari's Assyrian family parties and other Assyrian/Lebanese events. I was astonished at the way these people celebrated birthdays, weddings and even funerals. Women would dress in their best costumes and wear their best jewels, therefore, although I liked to dress simply, I decided to buy myself a new wardrobe for these occasions.

The Assyrian 'parties' and festivities were very big, and when I say big, they were indeed huge. A party usually had 300+ guests gathered in a massive function room, and I always thought the food was nicely prepared, but it was too much, and it surely appeared to be organized for multiple events. There was always so much left at the end, it seemed to me a real waste.

There was always a lot of men singing and belly dancing to roaring Arabic music and Ari always featured well in these groups. After watching *My Big Fat Greek Wedding*, I thought only the Greeks knew how to party. Believe me, the Assyrians did just as well, or better.

Keeping to our promise, Ari continued to work in Sydney for a couple of years and when he was asked to go overseas, he found an excuse to reject the offer. As for me, I had to stop all my jobs that required travelling abroad.

Our life was nice and easy! We were finally looking for a small house to buy together in Sydney, when I stumbled into a magnificent well-situated and affordable block of land. My real estate skills alerted me we could build not one house but two houses or what is known as a duplex in Sydney. I explained the opportunity to Ari and together we decided to investigate further and perhaps give it a go!

Ari invested the proceeds of the sale of his marital home, and I sold my investment unit, so we only had to borrow a small amount from the bank to cover the costs of our project. I had had plenty of experience with developers and I had also had plenty previous advice from Sara, my ex-mother-in-law, about new real estate projects.

Besides, we prayed as a couple God would guide us and for Him to look over our plans as if it were His own project. Thanks to God's unfailing Grace, our relatively complicated project was conceived, and the duplexes were being built relatively smoothly.

However, I noticed Ari got too anxious and agitated if something did not go completely as expected. I kept on advising him to look at the end-product, 'the whole picture' and what it would mean for us, rather the temporary "normal" building hitches.

By that time, Bobby decided he wanted to move out, and Ari supported him with the deposit to purchase a small apartment in the inner Western Suburbs of Sydney. Bobby had by then met Max, a young Indonesian young man and it seemed they were then working on a steady relationship. Ari still did not approve of Bobby's sexual orientation and the truth was that it was difficult also for me to follow Bobby's erratic routines at home, so it was good when he finally moved out and became independent.

Ari was then asked at work to transfer to Darwin. They needed him to re-structure the factory there. The dilemma was I was still working as a head teacher in Sydney and the duplexes were still to be finished, thus I could not go with him.

Therefore, he requested a special arrangement from his company: he would work only Monday to Thursday, and he would come home for the weekend. He would also work two weeks and he would have the third week off. It was the perfect contract and a blessing; except we did not realize we were gradually getting older and older.

That predicament had consequences, especially for me. I somehow got sick and then sicker and sicker and needed a hysterectomy, followed by an operation on my eyelids that had drooped and prevented me from seeing clearly.

These medical hiccups were followed by cataracts, followed by a shoulder reconstruction, followed by a carpel tunnel operation in my wrist, followed by a major hip replacement operation and then a long rehabilitation.

I was honestly experiencing a never-ending stream of medical issues! And my body was not so accommodating to so much anesthesia and 'improvements'.

I soon learnt by force that when you were well, social interaction occurred almost automatically. However, when you are sick and imprisoned on your hospital bed or to your home, social interaction declines sharply or simply stops.

Ari took as much time off as was reasonably possible for him to be with me and he helped with my confinements. My children, my mother and some friends came sporadically to visit me. For the rest of my family and friends, they were all too busy, or just did not think of my situation and seldom came to see me and didn't even call to see how I was. Everybody was just too occupied with their lives, including my mother. I was not surprised, as my mother had already disappeared in the past when any of her daughters needed her most.

Apart from my daily Assyrian nurse who used to come and check on me during the week and my daily *Meals on Wheels* volunteer, I usually had nobody to talk to, except one companion day and night; the Spirit of God. He accompanied me for many long days and for quite a long period of time!

Opportunely, although my body was incapacitated and I struggled moving around, my mind had a long time to think over and over again about my many concerns. Finally, my soul also had ample time to ascertain and understand what my darling Ari had then been fulfilling in my destiny.

Ari continued his commuting between Sydney and Darwin. He was then having issues with his employees as they were 'annoying' because they were not following his 'instructions to the letter,' he said. He confided to me he had lost his cool a few times with them and sometimes he had lost it also with his bosses as well — *'patchis, rataji, chispij, aniloc...'*

When Ari was home in Sydney, we made the most of our time together, although I was quite incapacitated and could not go out. Life for me had become lonely and it made me realize as I grew older, I did not want to spend my life in a high-rise apartment.

The duplexes were finished and one of them, especially, had been built to my taste. It had nice timber fittings, a huge main bedroom with walking wardrobes and an en-suite bathroom. The kitchen was a dream, as it had been designed with all the latest conveniences and it led through large sliding glass doors to an interior entertainment patio and then the backyard. The double floor homes also had amazing views to the valley from every window. I felt so happy with the anticipation of us moving in there!

However, my dream was to be completely shattered because although I tried to convince Ari God would help us, he was adamant in his belief it was impossible for me and in my condition to negotiate the many stairs in the new building, let alone manage the maintenance of such a large home.

The brand-new duplexes were finished but we had to rent them both out since we had no choice but to indefinitely postpone our plans of moving into our dream home.

Chapter 11

NEW HORIZONS...

'I looked up to the stars and wondered which one I was from.'
(James McCue)

'The most interesting people you'll find are ones that don't fit into your average cardboard box. They'll make what they need, they'll make their own boxes.'
(Dr. Temple Grandin)

'I said I love you that's forever. And this I promise from the heart. I couldn't love you any better I love you just the way you are'.
(Billy Joel)

Part 1 - Aram

I promised I will finish this today, Emanuel, and here it is, on the dotted line, as promised! Thank you!

I was born in the mountains of Northern Iraq, but I was always told I was Assyrian. I believe my parents lived in a small Assyrian village near the Turkish border, but in 1900s the Ottoman Empire (the Turks) ordered the systematic extermination of all Christian Assyrians living in what they considered—wrong—wrong—wrong — their historical homeland. Many historians and all Assyrians considered this slaughter a, 'true genocide'. I was told that during World War I the Assyrian population was reduced in number by two thirds.

I believe my parents were blessed to have escaped this horror. They were displaced and persecuted all their lives, and in the process, they had to leave behind many loved ones, all their possessions and their memories, never to be seen again. This fact impacted the rest of their lives and ours as well.

After so much suffering, my parents eventually settled in Beirut in Lebanon and raised seven living children there. When my mother realized she was pregnant with me, she thought she was past her childbearing age and wanted to get rid of me, but my eldest sister, Nina, who was already heavily pregnant with her third child, persuaded her to keep me. This is how I came to have three nephews, Abrahim, Hano and Youel, sons of my elder sister, who are older than me! Mind you, I was always the 'runt' of the pack regardless.

We were poor in a foreign land and my family was not welcome in the neighbourhood because we were Christians and not Muslim like most of our Lebanese neighbours.

My father worked as a kitchen hand in a small shop but what he got was not enough to feed everyone, let alone give us an education. We all lived together in a small rented flat and went to the local Church of the East school.

Abrahim, Hano and Youel grew to be tall and strong like all our relatives whilst I was always the smallest—like my mother—and the weakest of the group. To make matters worse, I was also colour blind, like my father.

I was also 'peculiar' when compared with other Assyrian children, or so they commented.

My world and routine always needed to be in perfect order, and this was to prevent me from withdrawing or exploding into a rage.

My teachers also told my parents they found me 'socially awkward'. It was hard for them to communicate with me effectively or for other children to cement any meaningful relationships with me. In any case, the teachers gave me a list of instructions, which I always followed to the letter. They also trained me to always smile and look up at people's eyes when I was talking to them.

To compensate for my poor social skills, it was also discovered God had given me a special gift, a quick and talented mind. The church priests and teachers realized I was above average at school, especially at Maths and Languages including Aramean and Arabic.

My teachers could not believe when I got first place in Arabic in my final high school assessments, especially because Arabic was not my first language!

They all praised me profusely and tried to hug me, but I disliked physical touch and felt uncomfortable. The teachers must have picked up my vibes because they had long ago already left me alone.

Furthermore, when I finished my basic education and because I achieved such high marks, the priests offered my father a scholarship to send me to a private college for further studies in Electronic Engineering. I continued to excel in my studies, of course, as I always did everything my teachers asked me to do to perfection.

At the College I met many young people, some of them also Assyrian, but they were all from more affluent families than my own. Although I always had better academic results than them, I felt intimidated to explore their friendships further. Destiny had its way though, because I would never have dreamt that I was going to meet them later in life and befriend them in Australia.

Unfortunately, all the main breadwinners in my family passed away suddenly—my nephews' father and my own father died within a few months of each other. In an already hostile environment, my life got even harsher, and survival was more difficult.

Apart from extreme poverty, we started to get persecuted even further in many ways because of our religion. Our rent went up and even when some of us were well qualified, the best jobs would go to the Lebanese Muslims. Besides, everybody in our community was afraid of what could possibly happen next in the country. Then one of my brothers was killed, we believed, in a crossfire between government forces and Palestinian soldiers.

Under these circumstances, my Aunty Nina, and my nephews, with other members of my extended family who knew our church leaders very well, decided to initiate the paperwork to immigrate to Australia.

Other Assyrians compatriots in the neighbourhood had already chosen to immigrate to Canada, Europe, or the United States, but we chose Australia because of its better climate and because there were good connections in Sydney with our Assyrian church. My nephews with my Aunty Nina and other sisters started to organise their passport and would travel first and they would try to settle in. Then they would attempt to bring the rest of the family, including my mother and me.

I had just finished my studies and had started my first job as a cashier in a service station, when I was urged to prepare our passports and corresponding visas to enable us to migrate to Australia. We were promised our airline tickets would be bought in Australia and be sent to all of us soon.

Within a few months, my mother, my other sisters, other nephews, a niece, and myself, with our shabby suitcases made the trip to Australia. Everyone went to Melbourne, except my mother, my sisters and myself. We decided to stay near our Church of the East in Sydney, where other nephews had already settled.

At the beginning, we all lived in the same flat, but as my nephews got better jobs and then got married to Assyrian ladies, we separated. I stayed with my mother even when many years later I got married myself and decided to move nearer the city.

Life in Lebanon had always been subdued for me. I was rather shy with girls because Lebanese girls would not go out with me, whilst Assyrian girls were forbidden for us unless we were prepared to marry them.

Australia was completely different. My nephews took me to the local club on the weekend. I knew how to belly dance and all the girls, especially the English-speaking ones loved it and wanted to go out with me! I enjoyed the fuss and the great freedom this new country was offering me.

I soon got a job in the electronic department of a large security company, which was close to where I lived. I had to 'refresh' my qualifications and once I got the proper documentation, I was given a pay-rise and permanency status in the company.

I also had many casual spicy relationships, but my mother wanted me to marry a decent Assyrian girl and settle down. I avoided the subject, as marriage did not appeal to me at all at that stage.

I was approaching my 31st birthday and had already been promoted a few times in my job, when I met this gorgeous English girl called Valerie.

Val was very pretty, young, clever and a lot of fun. I taught her to belly dance, and we became the best dancing partners. We drank quite a bit, especially Scotch Whisky, but she loved me even when we were sober. She said I was cute, a bit eccentric, but very handsome! We soon became best friends and also lovers!

I introduced Val to my family, and they seemed to like the fact I had a girlfriend at last. I proposed to her within a few months of meeting her and we got married in the Assyrian Church, followed by a great party in a reception hall nearby.

By then I had saved some money and I decided to purchase my first home nearer the city and closer to my job. I took my mother with us. Mother was pivotal in teaching my new bride how to cook my beloved Lebanese and Assyrian dishes and to teach her our ways.

Val was happy and so was I. However, my relatives were growing their families, bursting exponentially with children. As for myself and despite my precise efforts in bed, Val was not getting pregnant. We went to see a specialist, who said she had some hormonal problems and gave her some tablets to take, but nothing happened. I got concerned although the specialist had cleared me of any issues in that department.

Whilst I was expectant of pregnancy news, month after month, Val did not seem to mind much about the issue.

We had been married seven years, a record time for an Assyrian married couple to have had a child, when Val announced she was finally pregnant. I was happy when Bobby was born! He was a bundle of joy, although I did not have much time for him at home.

My destiny was now to provide for my family, for him and Valerie, so nothing would be lacking in our household.

I kept on getting promotions at work, and I had already paid my house off, but I was happy to work overtime. I would have more money to support my family. I mentioned to Val I would have liked to have more children, but I was surprised with her response. 'One is too many,' she said. I felt disappointed but for the time being, I felt content… so I left it at that.

My company was overtaken by a multinational and was moving to the outer suburbs of Sydney. I was asked to accept yet another promotion, but I rejected it and instead I accepted a redundancy package. The package consisted of a large amount of money, which I immediately decided to roll over into my superannuation, against my family's advice. My nephews had had similar experiences. However, they had used their redundancy package to purchase investment properties.

I left my job on a Friday. I was planning to have a short holiday before I started looking for a job. However, an executive from my company called me on the Saturday and offered me a contract for six months as a technical trainer in Scotland. I could not believe my ears!

They offered first-class airfares, first class accommodation, all expenses paid, and the salary would be about three times as much as what I was getting just the day before. I was to sign the contract on Monday and leave immediately. As soon as I finished the conversation, I was already packing my bags!

After Scotland, other contracts were signed, to England, to India, to Indonesia, to New Zealand, to China, sometimes in Australia, in Perth, Melbourne, Perth, Brisbane, and back to Scotland and so on. I was travelling constantly, with some periods of vacations in Sydney mainly during the Christmas or Easter Seasons.

I used to ring Val and Bobby almost every day and I felt happy they were living with my mother; thus, they could have each other's company. Val seemed happy too, enjoying the new comforts my new salary brought to our home. We were able to renovate the home, buy new expensive furniture, wear expensive and fashionable clothes, and send Bobby to an expensive private school.

Once, I asked Val and Bobby to join me in England, so Bobby had a chance to meet Val's family. I bought tickets—first class, of course - and accommodated them in the best hotels. I even got them a car with a chauffeur, thus, they did not have to wait for me to be free to enjoy their time away.

Life was excellent and time went quickly. I wanted to give Val a surprise and I requested an extended holiday in Sydney, so I could spend more time at home with her and Bobby.

Besides, my mother had been ill, and I thought Val would appreciate the help from me, as she was my mother's main carer. To my surprise, she kept asking me when I was going back to work overseas. When I wanted to make love to her, she rejected me outright.

I realized maybe she had got used to another routine with me away. I decided I should spend as much time as possible at home and organise shorter contracts closer to home, and maybe even some in Sydney.

But I noticed Val was getting more and more unsettled and unhappy. She shouted at everybody who crossed her path. In the evenings and almost daily she got dressed in her best clothes, she did her make up and left us all watching TV. When I asked her where she was going, she said she was going out with her English friends. She also said she was getting bored with our 'Assyrian ethnic family and friends'.

Furthermore, as my mother was getting sicker and harder to manage, I thought she might be the cause of Val's grievances. We found a good nursing home for her to be more comfortable and to give Val some respite.

I thought my mother's confinement would do the trick and make Val more relaxed, but she became more and more argumentative and demanding; swearing, and constantly asking me when pay day was coming and when I was going to travel far and away again. I honestly thought this dark face of hers was only temporary and our marriage was as solid as a rock, and all would be good again soon.

I had had some pains in my chest for a while and one day I collapsed walking back from work in Sydney, in the company' s car park. I was taken to hospital and after some tests I was told I had three blocked arteries in my heart.

I needed a triple by-pass—if I decided not to have the operation, I had a 90% chance of dropping dead at any given moment. I chose to live. I still had very many things to live for!

My operation and rehabilitation went well, and I was back at home again. Valerie was worse than ever. She hardly spent any time at home, and I had to employ a housekeeper to take care of us. Valerie said she had to meet her English friends in town almost every day. I did not know what they were doing but I always trusted her. She just wanted to have a bit of 'English' fun at the pub with her friends, have a few beers, laugh, and laugh loudly at the jokes I could ever hardly get…

I was convalescing at home and hopefully I was going to go back to work soon. I tried to help with shopping, the washing, and the house chores as much as I was able, and in the end, all Valerie did was the cooking when she felt like it; otherwise, we would get KFC or other take-aways from the shops.

But all my efforts in the house were to no avail. Val hardly talked to me and when I asked her where she was going, she would shout that it was 'her own business'. If I got a meal from her in the kitchen, it was practically thrown on the table in front of me and I was left to eat it alone.

We got a call from the nursing home saying my mother's condition was getting worse and she was not expected to live beyond that day. I was shocked to learn Valerie had not visited her for weeks during my medical confinement. When I asked her what had happened, she swore at me, she called me a freak and shouted my mother was not her mother after all and I would be wise to leave her alone.

I justified her behaviour, thinking maybe she was going through menopause as I had heard it was normal for women to temporarily change their moods.

My mother died but Valerie's manners at home did not change. When I was finally ready to go back to work, I requested to be given a job in Sydney, so I could be closer to my family.

Not long after, coming from work, I found a note on our bed. 'I do not love you anymore. I left you. Please understand.' She had taken her clothes and all her toiletries and had left Bobby doing his homework in his bedroom.

I could not believe it! I rang my nephews' wives and some of her English friends, but nobody knew anything about her whereabouts. I drove the streets of Sydney like a maniac, looking for her. It seemed to me she had truly disappeared from this world!

I started to shake badly, and I felt the world had finished for me. I needed some money, so I went to the bank to get some cash. To my dismay, all our accounts had been emptied and I could only withdraw $200 from my personal account. I went to see a private investigator who listened to my tragic story, and I gave him all her details.

The private investigator came back to me a few days later. 'The usual,' he said. 'She has moved in with a man she was having an affair with. She lives on the other side of town. She is fine!' he added.

I was shocked, I could not breathe! How could this be happening to me? I prayed to God to get her to see what she was doing, for her to come back to us, to her family…

I prayed on my knees repeatedly asking for mercy, 'God let her come back to me.' 'What am I going to do? I am completely ashamed and lost.' 'Please let her come back.'

I would never have dreamt this was going to happen to me. Why was I not given a warning?

In the Assyrian community, this would never happen to a good, decent man. What else did she want? I was not perfect, but I had no major bad habits and I had always been faithful to her. 'Dear Heavenly Father, please listen to my prayers and let her come back, if not for me and my reputation, for our son's sake!'

But God was not listening to me because she did not come back. My son Bobby was soon to turn 18 and he was finishing his last year of his secondary schooling. Despite spending a lot of money on private schools, he had never been a top student. But I had dreamt he could find a good course at TAFE after his HSC to pursue his chosen career, which at the time I vaguely thought, must be computer design.

Bobby was as shocked as me about his mother leaving and I noticed he was hardly home and when he went out at night, he would wear make-up and lots of perfume. I thought maybe he needed the makeup to cover his pimples. But then one day, I noticed not only was he wearing his usual make-up, but he also had false eyelashes, heavy mascara, and lipstick.

'What are you doing son? What is this make-up?'

He said simply, 'I like it, dad, and I am doing it because I am gay!' 'Isn't it obvious? I thought you knew!'

I had understood Valerie leaving us was bad, but God, this was much worse! I wanted to go to bed and never wake up! I shook and shook! I cried and cried until I had no more tears. I could not go to work like this. I wanted to die.

I rang Abrahim and he came around and took me to my doctor who prescribed tranquilizers and told me to take some time off from work. My life became a blur, and I could not see any way out.

When Valerie finally rang, it was to ask my permission to come home and pick up the rest of her personal stuff. She asked for me not to be there. She also had the nerve to ask me for some money to pay for a gynaecological procedure. I had no words to protest or request an explanation for her conduct. I agreed to everything she demanded. I felt crushed.

Not long after that conversation, Valerie sent me a letter through a solicitor requesting the house to be sold. She said she wanted to claim 70% of the value of it and she was entitled to it, as she had contributed to our household for so many years by cooking, cleaning, and looking after us and my mother.

That letter was the key for me to wake up from my desperation. I searched for our bankbooks to see how much money she had taken. After all, I had worked all along, and I had had good contracts for many years after I had paid off the house completely. She had never had a job. Where was my money?

My investigation was simple; the money had come in regularly from my employer on pay day but as soon as it came in, there were cash outs, cash outs and more cash outs for years in the bank statements. God, we must have been eating diamonds and sleeping with gold sheets for such a lot of money to be spent every week.

The last withdrawal from our accounts was just a day before Valerie left and it was for $3000. I rang the bank to enquire if such a large amount was allowed to be withdrawn and the bank informed me my wife had increased the daily cash withdrawal limit amount years ago.

Then I realized I never checked my bank accounts. Valerie took care of all our financial affairs! She was my wife, after all! Good Heavens! How could I had been so blind...

The next morning, I made an appointment with the solicitor Abrahim had recommended.

I took all the books and the report from the private investigator to the solicitors. They said they would engage another professional investigator to see where the money had gone. There was an amount of about $750,000 missing, at least, which the lawyer said seemed indeed bizarre. He also considered it a bit dubious that someone could withdraw such an amount of money without me becoming aware of it.

I also went to see the clairvoyant Abrahim's wife recommended. She told me my wife had planned her escapade for a long time, in fact, many years and that the man she was with was not the first she had cheated me on with. She also said it was better for me to leave my wife alone and look somewhere else for comfort. There were plenty of women for me in the horizon, according to her.

I was really confused. My wife... unfaithful to me... I could not comprehend it. I went to see another clairvoyant who more or less said the same thing.

In the confines of my home at night, I was still praying to God for Valerie to come back. But she did not come back! She was not going to come back, not then, not ever.

I closed my bank account and decided to go back to work. I was truly lucky to be sent on a contract to work in China this time, where I would meet many ladies eager to become my partner and lover and come to Australia to live with me, with the prospects of a permanent residency.

I must admit, I loved the attention and the fuss of these ladies, but my heart was broken, and I did not trust them.

I rang my son Bobby regularly and he seemed to have got over his sadness. He had found a job in a larger hardware store and was surviving reasonably well at home without his mother and with the help of the housekeeper.

I came back to Australia to finalise my divorce and property settlement. I had worked hard to make my home comfortable over the years and I had many good memories of our family there. I had put so many hours labouring and dollars maintaining it to make this house our cosy home. I was devastated. I would have liked to have kept the house, but I had a court order and the house had to be sold. Besides, I had no money to be able to purchase it outright or even any amount for a substantial deposit.

The house went to auction and fetched a record price. I got 50% of the proceeds, thanks to my solicitor's negotiations. However, the money missing from our bank accounts was never recovered, as it just seemed to have disappeared into thin air. Despite exhaustive investigations, my lawyer could not find any account belonging to Valerie with any of those funds.

Valerie claimed and insisted the money was spent weekly for normal expenses, which was ridiculous. At the house auction I was informed she wanted to shake hands with me, but I did not even want to acknowledge her presence there. I now felt a deep hate for her, and I honestly wished her dead. She had had no respect for me or her son, ever!

I also had to share half of my superannuation fund with her. I claimed a lot of that money was the proceeds of my redundancy package all those years ago, but I was told that by law, Valerie was entitled to half of the total of my super account.

I moved to a rented apartment not far from our home and set up home there with my son. I bought all new furniture and kept our old furniture on the apartment's large balcony for the time being. Eventually, I gave this furniture away to different people in my family and to other acquaintances, as I did not want anything to do with it. I also gave all our photos and other memories to my sister to keep.

I could not believe at my age, when I could start enjoying the fruit of my hard work for many years, I had to start all over again.

I joined *RSVP*—Internet dating site - and *Table for Six*—another dining dating site. I got four dinner meetings through *Table for Six*, but each of the meetings was a waste of time. I had not made a list of my desired qualities in a partner yet, but the 12 ladies who turned up at the *Dinner for Six* appointments were definitely not suitable for me. Ten of them were late, so I had to discard them outright as I hate people being late; I consider it disrespectful. The other two possible candidates were dressed casually, and they were too rough for me. Obviously, I was not their type either, because they did not even address me once during the evening.

I kept busy with dates that the *RSVP* site provided though, as it was a lot easier for me to manage encounters one to one. Some of the women they referred to me were good company and fun, especially a Chinese businesswoman, who offered me at our first meeting her home, food, and her body, unreservedly.

However, I was far from happy. My family and some Assyrian friends tried to cheer me up, but despite some of my family and my friends' efforts to keep me entertained, inviting me to their homes and family events, I felt empty, broken, and often cried myself to sleep at night. Besides, I could perceive people were talking about me behind my back, as my story was surely making the gossip rounds in our small Assyrian community.

I consulted yet another clairvoyant who confirmed yet again what the other psyches had already told me. Valerie had been cheating on me basically from the beginning of our marriage. This last lady also suggested for me to check on Bobby, because possibly he might not even be my son! That truly rocked my boat!

She also said I would meet somebody who would make me happy. She would be my true soul mate and through her, I would experience real love, because she was being sent from God. And one day, she announced, I would at last become truly whole as a man. I could not believe her, but nevertheless, I took notes faithfully of her insights and recorded her predictions, so I would not miss or misinterpret anything from the session.

Reluctantly, I asked Bobby to be DNA tested considering what the clairvoyant had said to me. However, I assured him he would always be my son regardless of the results. Results came back stating Bobby was with 90% certainty my own son, for which I was indeed relieved and tremendously thankful to God.

At that stage, I was secretly still praying to God for my marriage to be saved and for Valerie to come back. However, the Almighty seemed to be completely deaf and would never answer my pleas; not even a phone call from her to enquire about her son.

I was never good at computers, but I kept busy at night checking the dating sites. I had made a list of the attributes I would religiously need in a lifestyle partner:

1. She should not be English—I had enough of hypocrisy.
2. She should not be Assyrian—I felt it might be too boring for both of us.
3. She should be 'punctual' … maybe if she was a little early, I would accept it but not if she was late, not even a few minutes.
4. She should be clean and keep her household in order.
5. She should be respectful—Respect was something I admired and fostered, and when I said RESPECT, I meant she should follow mainstream social, legal, financial, and ethical regulations to the T.
6. She should have lots of money, perhaps I should be able to get some back from what it was stolen by Valerie.
7. Maybe, just maybe, she should believe in God.

Suddenly I got a kiss from a lady from the RSVP website. Quickly, I checked her up on the internet. She did not have a photo, but her profile read easily and was straightforward. She had included a detailed list of what she would be expecting in a partner. She was too naïve for me…

However, the next night, I came back to read this lady's profile again and her list again and again and again. 'What a dope,' I thought again! 'She seems a bit raw for her age... as if anyone in these sites will tell the truth,' I thought.

I was curious though... Maybe I would send her a kiss back.

Gee, she rejected me outright because I was born in Lebanon, and she thinks I am a Muslim... How dare she... I could certainly teach her a thing or two.

I wrote back to her through the dating site explaining I was not a Muslim, but a proud Assyrian and I was indeed a Christian. I asked her for her email address and a few more details about herself.

Within a few minutes, she wrote back to me with her email address and much more than a few more details about herself. Her name was Carmela. She had been married twice and she had five adult children, who were her true treasure.

Nah! I left it at that! Her statement was enough to run for my life. Married twice, five children! No, God, this one would not do! Next...

I did not write back to Carmela, and she did not write back to me either, but I remained curious and approachable... What if Carmela was the one for me? There was something about this Carmela I could not get out of my mind.

After a week, I wrote back, asking her to have a coffee with me. She said she did not have coffee with strangers, and if I wanted to meet her, I would have to provide more information about myself and get to know each other more through emails. Awesome! I liked that! She had some nerve... Just like that, plainly but surely, it was the beginning of our friendship.

I did not know why but Carmela inspired me to trust again. I had not checked her against my complete list yet! However, I chose to pour out my heart to her, my marriage breakdown and my loneliness and she also confided in me. She said she was looking for companionship and she was lonely as well.

After a few weeks of exchanging emails, I asked her again to have a coffee with me, and this time she accepted. I had a long drive after work and I could not get to the coffee shop near her work until at least 6pm. Surprisingly, she accepted to meet me that late.

She appeared at 6pm on the dot! And she was certainly neither

English nor Assyrian! She was a bit shorter than me and still pretty in her 57th year. She was not shy, actually, she was quite chatty and, her phone did not stop ringing. Apparently, it was her daughter and one of her sons, phoning to check she was all right.

First impressions were favourable. She seemed smart, clean, attractive. Despite her past experiences, she seemed 'low maintenance' and independent enough. She also owned her apartment outright and drove a nice car, a newish Subaru if I checked it out correctly. She would do for a while... Maybe, I could get some money out of this one and get even... I would ask her to have dinner with me on Saturday, maybe.

Carmela had her mother with her over the weekend, therefore mum came over also and had dinner with us. I liked the lady and Carmela was revealing to me to be the exact lady I had first read in her profile. When I got home, I was really mortified to discover the jumper I wore to the outing had a moth hole and a large stain at the front... '*patchis, rataji, chispij, aniloc...*' What would these ladies think of me? I would have to be more careful and groomed next time...

We went out a few more times with Carmela's mother, who happened to be delightful. She laughed at all my jokes, even though her English was not that crash hot. She reminded me so much of my own mum...

At last, one Saturday, Carmela agreed to go just the two of us for a picnic to The Entrance up the coast; her mum could not come this time.

I picked her up at the main entrance to her apartment block and she was on time, well, a few minutes late, but I guess she must have been busy. She was well dressed in nice black pants and a silk pink blouse with a black blazer on top. She was wearing black high-heel well-polished shoes. I loved her perfume; it was Chanel No. 5, my favourite fragrance. She was wearing hardly any jewellery, just a small fine gold cross on a pendant.

It was a nice day and we spent it well together, talking and smiling. A good sign, I thought. I had put in my profile that I was looking for a permanent relationship just to attract the romantic ladies, but I found myself repeating it to Carmela during the afternoon. I wanted to kiss her hard, but I did not dare and at the end, I just gave her a light kiss under the blue skies and again when I left her at the door of her building that evening.

My Chinese lover kept on ringing me to go out with me, but I was enjoying my time with Carmela, and I was not a man that would ever play a double game, thus I tried to avoid her first and then I told her I was not interested in her anymore. The Chinese woman was furious, and she said we did not have any 'chemistry' between us anyway. Then she swore at me. However, she phoned me a few more times to see if I had changed my mind and, in the end, she stopped ringing me.

I was still hurt, but I found myself changing my mind and my prayers as I was starting to look at the possibility of getting to know Carmela more and more and see where this relationship would lead me.

I knew Carmela loved God and she attended church every Sunday. I asked her if I could join her the following Sunday. I was amazed and disappointed when she said I could not and gave me some silly excuse. However, she must have changed her mind because she then invited me to her church the following Sunday.

I had always enjoyed the traditional services at the Assyrian Church of the East and occasionally I had attended mass at the Catholic Church, although I could not say I had been a regular church attendant. I was also a bit cautious about some new churches' request for donations. I had indeed been bitten by my own church several times.

However, nothing had prepared me to witness what was going on in that church. To start with, there were no crosses or statues of Jesus, the Virgin Mary, or the Saints anywhere to be seen, as the church service was conducted in a public-school hall.

The priest, who everyone called Pastor Pete, was dressed as everyone else. He and his wife addressed me warmly and welcomed me at the door, along with other people who seemed to be there to greet the visitors. It was nice at last, to be introduced to some of Carmela's children like Cassandra, her only daughter and her youngest son, Champ.

We were ushered to our seats and the service started with everybody standing up and listening to the band playing loud contemporary gospel music, accompanied by the singers featuring Cassandra and her husband at the front. I was a bit flabbergasted. If I was correct, Champ was also drumming wildly. The noise was hurting my ears. I would need some ear plugs in the future if I were to come back.

We were allowed to sit down after the singing but not before everyone said hello to someone they did not come with. There were so many people to greet, it was getting to be a bit too much for me to cope with. Thankfully, this part only lasted a few minutes. Several people from the church read the news and announcements for the week and their prayer points. There was a short time dedicated to the tithes or donations, as I had anticipated, but I found no pressure to participate.

Most of the congregation members started to pray together in a loud voice and I heard some people speaking in a strange language. Somehow, I heard Carmela also whispering in another tongue. Then we had more of the singing, standing up and finally the pastor gave the church members a lecture about some contemporary points in the Bible and Christianity.

At the end of the service, we got the blessing from the pastor and an invitation to have coffee or tea and biscuits outside. All in all, just less than two hours had passed, and it felt like we had just started. This was a pleasant experience indeed compared with other boring Sunday services I had been involved with in the past.

I also noticed Carmela asked Jesus for everything she needed, even petty things like parking, and she appeared to get what she requested. For example, we were trying to get parking in Watson Bay to have late lunch on a very busy Sunday. I told Carmela we might have to go somewhere else, but she prayed and in front of us a spot became available. I was astounded, but I started to do the same with similar results.

I thought God must be busy with more significant world issues and other important matters, but Carmela said, 'He cares for all of us and that even the very hairs of our heads are numbered by Him.' I might have something to learn here, I thought!

I tried to tell Carmela to come to the clairvoyant with me again, but she refused, and she did not want anything to do with it. She said she could not say whether these people predicted the future correctly or not, but she said God's advice in the Bible was not make a pact with them, but rather to engage God's Holy Ghost for any advice, guidance, and comfort. I thought I surely needed to learn much more on this topic too.

I kept on going with Carmela to her church every Sunday and found most people there appeared to have a closer relationship with our Lord than what I thought it was ever possible. Somehow, when I was there, I felt a peace I had not experienced before, and I could say I was able to forget all my worries for a while.

There was a song that was repeated in almost every service and every time it was played and I sang it, I could not hold my tears back. This song was 'I surrender' by Hillsong.

It was not difficult for me to find it on the net under its name.

I felt so deeply touched by it that I wanted to make sure I also reproduced the lyrics in this text, hoping the song would bless the reader as much as this song had always blessed me:

Here I am
Down on my knees again
Surrendering all
Surrendering all

Find me here
Lord as You draw me near
Desperate for You
Desperate for You

I surrender

Drench my soul
As mercy and grace unfold
I hunger and thirst
I hunger and thirst

With arms stretched wide
I know You hear my cry
Speak to me now

Speak to me now

I surrender
I surrender
I want to know You more
I want to know You more

Like a rushing wind
Jesus breathe within
Lord have Your way
Lord have Your way in me

Like a mighty storm
Stir within my soul
Lord have Your way
Lord have Your way in me.

I apologise, but… did I mention that you could also listen to it on the website? I have a favourite YouTube site but there are more… Just Google it as "I surrender" by Hillsong and it will come up easily and you could listen to it by different singers!

Coming back to my story, when, at the end of the church service one Sunday the pastor asked if anyone wanted to give their life to Jesus, with tears in my eyes again, I was surprised my legs were rushing to the front to offer the rest of my life to our God Almighty!

I felt enveloped in the grace and love of God and the most serene peace fell on me. All my worries had lifted, and they were now placed at the foot of Jesus' cross! I felt secure, surrounded by His love, beyond any explanation.

I then understood what Carmela had told me from the beginning when we met, God was her absolute and first love and she would follow and praise Him all the days of her life.

I have also understood then why God did not answer my prayers to save my marriage. God could not have done it. He loved me too much for that! He could not have done it because He had something much better, so much better, so much better for me!

'I once was lost, but now I am found.
I was blind, but now I see...'

Chapter 12

SORTING PRIORITIES

'There are some things which cannot be learned quickly, and time, which is all we have, must be paid heavily for their acquiring. They are the very simplest things and because it takes a man's life to know them, the little that each man gets from life is very costly and the only heritage he has to leave.'
(Ernest Hemingway)

In times of change, learners inherit the earth, while the learned find themselves beautifully equipped to deal with a world that no longer exists.'
(Eric Hoffer)

Part 1 - Carmela Junior

This is the last recount of my life story Emanuel. I hope you can publish the book soon and I wish it becomes a bestseller... I will be looking forward to reading it altogether and if you need any photos, I can help you with them.

It has certainly been a long-time project from your part from when you started the collection of stories... Thirty-six years have gone by if I remember correctly.... Or was it longer?
Anyhow, good luck with it all! ...

My life was now complete. God had given me everything. I had a husband who loved me and spoiled me. He had a good job, and he was respected in his small circle of friends. My relationship with all my children was the envy of many of my friends. They were all independent and relatively happy and productive in their professional and private lives.

I had had some alarming medical issues but after a period of convalescing, my issues had settled, and I had come back to work during the week as a Head Teacher of the Languages in charge of about 14 teachers. On Saturdays I worked in a supervisory role of about 40 language teachers. I was also Chief Examiner at the Board of Studies organising and overseeing my language Higher School Certificate Examinations at different levels. My achievements were indeed too many to mention.

But this was not going to be my life for long. As we were approaching our retirements, Ari and I started thinking about travelling and enjoying the years left for us.

I had always dreamt of having a property in Spain, where I could go and spend some time every year, perhaps in Andalusia, near the Mediterranean Sea, where the climate was always balmy and where people with arthritis went and were able to move more freely. Besides, I thought a property there would be a good inheritance for my children.

I had seen the opportunity to purchase a small flat in the past, but after Spain entered the European Union, property prices had escalated to exorbitant amounts.

Then, out of the blue, we had the Global Financial Crisis and property prices in Spain, as in many parts of the world, tumbled dramatically. This was surely my opportunity!

I had some money available from my super fund, which I could use. Besides, I had also discovered that in the Spanish Coast, there was a very large number of people who spoke English, as they were escaping the unsettled climate of the United Kingdom. I was sure Ari would not have any problem adjusting to that environment.

Ari had his extended holidays due, and I could request long service leave from my schools. We planned to travel and research various areas in Spain with the prospect of perhaps purchasing a property.

Before we left, I wrote to several real estate agents enquiring about prices and other details like types of home, number of bedrooms, distance to the sea, shopping centres, public transport, and other facilities.

We travelled extensively around Spain and Ari fell in love with the country, its people, and its customs. The food was amazing; tasty, healthy, and cheap, the weather was terrific. Everywhere we went, the people accepted us as friends, as if we had always belonged there.

One of my old Spanish friends in Australia suggested we should check a small fishing village at the sea called San Juan in the Province of Alicante, where she was born. Following her advice, we booked a nice hotel to stay there for three weeks.

Whilst in San Juan de Alicante, we visited a few real estate agents, and one of them, a lovely man called Rafael showed us a delightful apartment very close to the sea, in fact about 70 metres from the main beach area.

Ari wanted to check exactly how many metres it was from the water, and I obliged. Ari recorded the area on his phone during the day and in the evening. He also recorded the chosen *piso* inside and outside to send them to our families.

When we discovered there was a Pentecostal Church just a few blocks from the *piso*, we went to check it out the following Sunday. The pastors and the congregation welcomed us warmly. We thought it was definitely a sign God approved of our plans, and we decided to go ahead with the purchase of the apartment.

I had already opened a Spanish bank account and, just in case, I had already arranged with my bank for the possibility to transfer a large amount of money.

Getting the right documents and lawyers and the financials for the transaction, proved relatively easy. The only regret was that our holidays had finished, and we could not stay to enjoy our new place longer.

But we had plans to come the next year and the year after and the year after... It would be easy to have this apartment as a base and travel around once we were already in Europe. Alicante had an international airport and from there we only had to jump in a taxi for a 30-minute ride to be in our *piso*. If we left some clothes in the apartment, we could even travel for the long trip with our carry-ons only!

In fact, during our winter in Sydney, which was the summer in Europe, we did travel extensively every year for the next six years and we were able to organise other trips to France, Portugal, England, Greece, Austria and even Assyria, along with various cruises along the Mediterranean Sea, the Baltics, France, and the Nile in Egypt. On the way back from Europe, we usually stopped in another warm place like Vietnam, Malaysia, or Thailand.

Then, Ari was asked to go to Kuala Lumpur in Malaysia for work for some time and I accepted to accompany him, as I had lots of long service leave. We stayed in the best hotel, but life was lonely for me until I discovered another Spanish speaking contractor's wife, Irma, from Ecuador was staying there as well.

Irma and I became instant friends. We were offered an Indian chauffeur from the company, Mr. Aabir, who took us everywhere that was of interest in Johor Bahru, including his 'Little India Shops'. The weather was scorching but there was good air conditioning at the hotel and everywhere else, including the luxury car our chauffeur was driving.

Mr. Aabir took us to the new modern shopping centres, which were tastefully adorned with Christmas Trees and seasonal decorations. I was surprised they were celebrating Christmas in Malaysia, as I knew Malaysia was a strict Muslim country. Even our hotel was decorated with a huge replica of the Three Kings.

During Spring, Summer, and part of Autumn, we remained in Sydney to enjoy our ever-growing family, to see our friends, to re-connect with our church and see my mother. Mother seemed to be living forever, and she was truly blessed as she remained healthy despite her very advanced years.

Quite soon, Ari and I had both more than reached our retirement age. Ari retired completely from work, but he was not happy at home when we were in Sydney. I often found him asleep when I returned from work. And he was usually grumpy and short tempered when things were not exactly in the order that he wished them to have or there was any change to our rather strict routine.

Ari would get upset for nothing with anybody who would not act as he expected, to the point he started to have difficulties sleeping at night. The following day he would invariably say the Holy Spirit had convicted him during the night, and he would usually ask for forgiveness.

I decided to retire completely from all my jobs to have more time at home with Ari, but life was boring in the flat for us. I tried to convince Ari we needed to change houses, but he insisted our duplexes were still unsuitable, just too large for the two of us.

On the advice of our accountant, we sold the duplexes at a good price, and at that time we were advised we could deposit a large amount of money into each of our respective super funds. These investments would allow us to live comfortably in retirement and keep on travelling for the rest of our active lives.

We also realized we had enough money left to purchase our own smaller cottage; therefore, we would be able to move out of my apartment into a more suburban setting. We started to investigate where this place could be.

Christopher wanted us to live up the coast, in Port Macquarie, where he was established as a Cardiologist. We went to visit him and inspected a few properties there. The houses were certainly cheaper and larger than what we could afford in Sydney. I would have gladly moved there, but Ari did not like the fact that we would not be able to see the other members of the family, as we got older, especially his son Bobby.

Cassandra wanted us to move in with her and her family. They talked about building a flat in their backyard to keep an eye on us if not now when we got older. Neither Ari nor I really fancied her idea!

Therefore, we concentrated our efforts in looking for a small house in Sydney. But the purchase of a decent freestanding smaller home closer to our families was out of our budget.

We started looking at villas and semi-detached houses, but the ones available in a nice suburb were old and we did not picture ourselves at our age living amongst building materials and paint for renovations.

Finally, we decided to explore Retirement Villages. Ari was not convinced this type of living would be ideal for us, after all, we were still in our 60s. But a house in a retirement village would be much cheaper and felt more sheltered and safer if we got sick or wanted to travel and leave the place securely locked up.

We looked everywhere for about two years. In the end, we chose a village in the Northern Beaches area of Sydney called *Paradise Country Club*.

We loved the village setting and the residents seemed to be so friendly at *Paradise Country Club,* but there were no larger villas available. We had to wait until one became available.

Just a few months before we had scheduled a trip to Europe, we were told a villa would become available soon at *Paradise Country Club* and the village manager invited us to inspect it. We loved it and we agreed to purchase it straight away. We included my mother in the deeds to make sure if she became old and unable to live by herself, we could bring her to live with us and look after her. Sadly, that was not to happen. I would have liked to look after her; but unfortunately, and as before, she preferred her friends more than my company.

My mother would come to visit for a few days if we picked her up, then she wanted to go home to her place where she said she felt the happiest amongst her gardens and her memories. She frequently stated she was looking forward to passing on to the other side. Therefore, she often said she felt more comfortable at home where she had already experienced God intimately and where she had had regular contacts with loved ones who had passed on. Besides, she had Maria and others to look after her, she told me outright.

At times, I thought my mother, being so old, was losing her mind, especially when she explained in detail some of her supernatural experiences at home, but other times, she seemed to be lucid and alert, with no memory loss or any other signs of dementia.

Before Ari and I left for Europe that year, we moved out some essential furniture and household items from my unit into the village garages. Ari was happy to organise everything. All items, even clothing, were systematically organised by box sizes, colours, and numbers. After managing ad hoc, the household and so many children in my life, I was amazed such a task could be done so efficiently.

We had also commissioned a builder to completely strip, renovate and modernise the apartment inside and have it ready for when we came back. We kept in contact with the builder to see how the major renovation was getting along, and it was easy, thanks to the advances in technology and communication with WhatsApp calls and messages, including photos of how our 'paradise' was being transformed.

By the time we were coming back, the project had been finished. We asked the builder to move inside the units our beds and boxes, methodically stored in the garage inside our new home. Miraculously the whole project ran so smoothly we had no doubt the Almighty had approved it fully from the start.

Our new home proved to be a winner. We basically were living in a new house. We renovated most of the furniture to match the village's French style and started to meet our new neighbours.

We loved living at the village, it was comfortable; I had a dream kitchen to experiment with cooking some Assyrian and my favourite Spanish dishes and our neighbours were approachable, friendly, and quite a few of them were of similar age to us.

We also had lots of activities offered at *Paradise Country Club,* an amazing library and group outings for the ladies and for couples, tennis and croquet courts, a fully equipped gym, and other conveniences which we did not access at the beginning. It was like living in an expensive resort! From time to time, we had to convince my mother to visit and stay with us and she also enjoyed some other village facilities, especially the hot spa and the modern heated swimming pool.

Despite all our blessings, my continuous presence in the house and our new opportunities at the Country Club, Ari continued to feel uneasy and grumpy and would jump at the opportunity of eating me alive if I did not agree with him on something.

I suspected he was bored.

Ari had had an argument with some of his close Assyrian friends because they had been late to a social meeting and with others because he thought they had not been quite fair sharing the cost of some meals or something silly like that.

I tried to calm him down. I assured him we were all different and certainly we were not all perfect and that perhaps we should be more tolerant with people.

I was astonished when he responded, 'I do not have to put up with differences. I do not have anything to talk about now I do not work,' and, 'It is too hard for me to follow their interactions, I am too old to force myself to fit in…I was not born to socialise.' '*patchis, rataji, chispij, aniloc*…' 'I have enough with you, and I love you,' he added.

Then, suddenly, we were hit with the Covid-19 pandemic, we were confined at home for long periods of time. We could not travel anywhere, let alone overseas.

Ari asked me if he could become in charge of the chores in the house, except the cooking, and I accepted. After all, his help would free me to be able to do other things, like reading, community interpreting and translations on the phone and writing to my friends, for example.

I was stunned at the transformation. Ari re-organized everything in the house. In the kitchen my pots and pans were now placed perfectly in the corresponding shelves, my cutlery stood laying perfectly straight in the correct drawers and my kitchen utensils soon had the same fate. All other cabinet contents had been put in colour-coded order along with my fridge that soon had everything in colour-coded containers exposed from high at the back to low at the front. The washing and ironing were likewise organised and done to perfection. I should have had him at home before to organise me when I was raising so many children…

We had had an efficient Korean cleaner, Kwan, who had come once a month to deep clean our unit. This arrangement included our windows, even when we were away in Spain; but now, Ari was vacuuming and dusting our place every day and he was also maintaining the garden, doing the shopping, and washing up the dishes after our meals.

Ari asked me if we could establish a set routine for our meals also. Therefore, we started having our meals at a certain time every day. Ari would set the table and after dinner he would collect the dirty dishes to wash them and wash them until he considered them to be clean enough for his standard. Nothing should smell of any food!

I suggested to Ari he might just enjoy joining a social group in the village, like billiards, cards or a new workshop group for men just being launched. But he did not look enthusiastic at these proposals.

I also noticed he could not concentrate for long at extensive reading, like a book for example. The same applied to long movies if there was not much action going on, especially when the scenes were long or there was a lot of dialogue in them.

All new household routines made Ari a bit happier. However, and despite all the never-ending house chores, I noticed Ari still seemed bored when he did not find anything to do, hence I introduced him to the puzzle, *Sudoku*, first in paper-form and then directly on his iPhone.

We sometimes both played the same *Sudoku* daily pattern to see which of the two of us could finish first. I was able to finish the game at the Intermediate Level, which I thought it was ok. But it was getting harder and harder to beat him. Not long after, I could not keep up with him anymore. He was playing at the highest level, competing with *Sudoku* champions all over the world and getting online trophies.

When I asked him to show me what he did to solve these difficult puzzles so fast, he said the formulas, *'patchis, rataji, chispij, aniloc...'* and, 'you need to remember the numbers in your head,' *'patchis, rataji, chispij, aniloc...'*

Wow! I could not possibly remember that many numbers in my head. I thought I was quite mathematically oriented, and I was told once I had a very high IQ at 145+. However, there was no way I could catch up with his thinking and reasoning... let alone his 'formulas'...

Ari's birthday was coming, and I bought him some double-sided jigsaw puzzles to solve in the 'challenging and demanding' range with 3,000 pieces each. They were all solved in a few hours.

I thought I had dealt with a lot of different disorders and other issues in children during my teachers' career. I had also had to deal with other detestable weird 'conditions' with my previous partners during my life.

I suddenly realized my dear, loving, third husband Ari was a real 'genius' and when I put two and two together, I realized he might surely have most of the symptoms associated with the Autism Spectrum Disorder I was sure though, Ari fortunately might feature as mild in the autism spectrum.

I double-checked the Asperger's websites and cross-referenced symptoms with Ari's issues, and I quickly found lots of matches:

- Problems making or maintaining friendships—yes or maybe
- Isolation or minimal interaction in social situations—yes or maybe
- Poor eye contact or the tendency to stare at others—yes or maybe
- Inability to recognize humour, irony, and sarcasm - yes or maybe
- Inappropriate behaviours or odd mannerisms- yes or maybe
- Problems expressing empathy, controlling emotions, or communicating feelings - yes or maybe
- Lack of common sense- No... I loved him too much to accept this
- Tendency to engage in one-sided conversations - Fascination with certain topics - yes or maybe
- Interpretation of information as literal - yes or maybe
- The preference for a strict schedule or routine—YES, YES AND YES!

And for high level functioning Asperger's adults:

- Might have a high IQ - YES
- The ability to focus on something intensely - YES
- A remarkable rote memory - YES
- A unique sense of humour - YES
- A high esteem for fairness and honesty- YES

I had been given *The Rosie Project* by Graeme Simsion to read at the Book Club. It was too much of a coincidence, or God! Was God trying to show me something?

'Oh God! What is to be done now?' I was not a doctor, but if not a mild touch of Asperger's, Ari was different to me, to everyone in our family, to everyone in his family, and certainly different to anyone I had had as a friend in the past.

Oh God! What was to be done? I was married, 'in sickness and in health'. I had promised before God to look after him until 'death do us part'. I had been married to him for 14 years. During these years, I got to understand Ari, despite our differences if not fully rather substantially.

This relationship was certainly not how I loved Amadeo, but it was another sort of love, care, respect, friendship, companionship. I had accepted his oddities. I had even already learnt how to compensate for his eccentricities.

We had no financial difficulties, and we were still looking forward to further travel once the new pandemic would be under control.

I had so many times spoilt him so much allowing to have his ways.

Ari had now become my friend, my partner, and my companion. And I did not think I could live without him…

I did not have any real close friends, apart from Ari, to be able to talk about my issues and feelings.

I would have liked to share my life with my mother, but I found it impossible to confide in her as I had now realized we never had that connection, besides and sadly, she then seemed to be living truly in another world.

Although I was not in the medical profession, I could see my mother was losing her mind and showing some freaky signs of dementia.

When I consulted with the doctors in our family, Chris, and Martin, and asked them about what we could do about it, they said *abuelita* was not senile, crazy, or confused at all. In fact, she was more mentally sound than any of us all. I decided to drop the subject at that point. Obviously, they did not know about her odd nocturnal visitors and our family's ever-dirty laundry disturbing her mind...

Chapter 13

FINAL WORDS

'Spread love everywhere you go. Let no one ever come to you without leaving happier.'
Mother Teresa

'Of life I do not want much,
I just want to know that I tried everything I wanted,
I had everything I could, I loved everything that was worth it;
And I lost hardly what was never mine.'
(Pablo Neruda)

Part 1 - La Macaca

'Arroz con leche,
me quiero casar
con una señorita de la capital
que sepa coser
que sepa bordar
que sepa abrir la puerta
para ir a pasear'[10]

You remember this song, Emanuel; when we used to play it together around and around in the circle with your brothers, your sister, and your cousins? Those were the days!! Were they real, Emanuel? I find it hard these days to distinguish between what is real or not real... Well, I am not young anymore, my dear friend.

I am ready for the Lord to take me anytime, but He wants me to keep going…

I have asked my Spanish speaking young friend and carer to make some sense of the last short scribbles I organised for you in English!

All the best for you in your endeavours my dear great grandson! I love you to the moon and back!

I always thought there was nothing more tragic than burying your own. The pain and the grief were truly heartbreaking. I put myself in 'Paquito's end queue many times as I wanted to depart from this place to greener pastures before the younger members of my own loving family, but God somehow had taken me off that line and into the world of the living so many times.

I still remember over 20 years ago, as if it was yesterday, when most of my family members were still alive and they celebrated my 90th birthday. This event has played in my mind like a broken record for so long now…

I remember Cassandra singing my favourite songs, *Besame mucho* and Juan Luis Guerra's hit, *Burbujas de amor* and her children running with the pink balloons all over the hall at the Marconi Club.

I also remember everyone was there, possibly together for the last time! Flor was there with her new partner Morris and her ever-growing family. Even Coops, Martin, and Lou's first son, who had just been born, came to join us in the celebration! Christopher had organised it all, I was told! Christopher by then had already amassed a small fortune and could certainly afford the extravagant afternoon!

I could not understand how Carmela could endure the shame of it all! Giuseppe, yes Giuseppe, her first husband had flown from Argentina with his old wife Margarita to be with us. He had already had a few heart attacks, and he was still the splitting image of his younger children Johny and Jack.

The wagging tongues had rumoured Johny and Jack were El Cuco's children, but after comparing them with Giuseppe at the party, the insult was forever rejected as false by the wagging tongues.

However, it was also rumoured Johny and Jack suffered the same condition as their father had suffered, they were never able to 'get hard' or make any woman happy in bed. This aberration could never be proven for certain, because Johny and Jack had married another set of twins and they were both producing a stream of twins of different sexes, all looking alike. God, there were so many kids at this party!

El Cuco was at the party too. He was reportedly having a good time, making friends, and laughing with Giuseppe and his wife all night. He had put considerable weight on, he was sporting a long greyish beard and could hardly walk unaided. It was rumoured he had been diagnosed with dementia and had come to the party dressed as a little boy, with red shorts, a football t-shirt, soccer boots and a Tyrolean hat. He was seen later in the night playing with the children and fighting fiercely for the pink balloons because he wanted to take some, or all of them, home.

My appalling daughter Carmela had recently married Ari or Aram in his native language. Ari was charming and generous. I had picked him for her especially and finally Carmela confessed to me she was, at last, happy with this new fellow.

Aram was such a gentleman, and he certainly knew how to belly dance to his heart's content. We saw him dancing all night with my friends, yes with all my dear, senile friends.

Rumours had it that Aram and Carmela had discovered God and their lives had been transformed by the power of His Ghost. I sincerely wished them well because after all my daughter Carmela deserved to be happy at last after such a disturbing life…

Aram's son was not conventional. Bobby was delightful and had personally organized all the fresh flower arrangement for my birthday party. But I thought nature made him too pretty for a boy and he looked too bubbly for me. *Oh, well*, I thought, everybody had a right to live in this world and if being 'a homo' was Bobby's destiny, so what? Nobody had the right to ever judge him or even criticize him!

The party was great! I was over the moon, because all my beloved friends were there having a good time, including our little group of Maria, Graciela and even Esther were there together again. Graciela had been driven there from the nursing home and she came with her new fling, who was at least 20 years younger than her. She was wearing her best clothes and jewellery. Esther had been given a special dispensation from paradise to be with us for the day. She looked ethereal in her new white dress with white forget-me-not flowers adorning the top of her head.

All my other living and soon to be not living friends were there as well. Christopher and Martin had to set up shifts to assist them in finishing the day without any incidents or anybody leaving for the hospital or suddenly passing to the other side without warning.

High tea was served with *sandwiches de miga* and *masitas* by white gloved waiters, exactly as in our parties in Buenos Aires. All crockery was of the best silver and the fresh flowers decoration arrangements at each table made with real fresh miniature pink roses personally made by Bobby were fully enchanting.

But that was 20 years ago, and in time the dynamics of the family had changed a lot. It is only the new generation who sometimes phones, texts or emails me with their gossip. My hearing aids do not always work, or the batteries run out and it is very difficult to keep up with our family dirty laundry. Or, to tell the truth, I am not interested in them anymore and besides, there are too many of them and I always get them all mixed up!

I am still in my old villa with my flowers and my memories. My new furniture never got old, so I still have a decent place to offer to my forever ethereal loved ones when they want to keep me company. I often cook *empanadas* on Saturdays, and they all come at night. We listen to music, and dance and sometimes we talk about our dirty laundry, past and present. We always have a lot of fun!

I forgave Paquito and Sara a long time ago, so they always arrive early and holding hands. My 110th birthday was approaching so I have invited them all: Giuseppe, el Cuco, my nephew Amadeo always hugging my daughter Carmela, Aram, Maria, Esther, Graciela and my other daughters Flor and her husband Morris and Edith with her husband Lolo. They will all come, and we will share a vermouth with soda and my *empanadas* as well and talk about the good all times and the new recent updates. And maybe, if we have time, we could also look at my old photos and see how we all looked all those years ago.

Everything is so different nowadays for me. Everybody is happy and there is no jealousy, hate or resentments amongst us.

Carmela used to come a bit earlier to help me make the *empanadas* for the night gatherings and sometimes she would stay with us but other times she would go away to visit and cheer up one of her still living children. She even confessed to me that sometimes, she visited her still living dear friend Gabriela in Argentina to catch up on the news over there and to keep practising her Spanish.

I guess it was sad for the 'still living' souls, the story on Johny and Jack's ending. Their names were always linked together in the family until their disappearance, also together during a holiday in the Amazon, Brazil when they were involved in a helicopter accident. Their bodies were never recovered, so they would be reminisced together forever. It was uplifting to know they had a generous life insurance, so all their numerous offspring were well provided for.

Champ and Joy are still in the world of the living, and they had so many children I have lost count. They are all extremely gifted and I believe they all also have a story to tell.

My daughter Carmela's children and grandchildren… they all kept Paquito's surname in his honour, which is now saved for posterity as he so much wanted it.

Champ's eldest child is especially clever. If I am correct, he has invented a device that takes you to space throughout time or something like that. He is on social media every day and I think his name is, if I remember correctly, Manuel. No, no, I think his name is Emanuel! Yes, my dear Emanuel! He is always pestering me to finish my life story, as he is keen to tell the world about us, our crazy family and our endeavours and failures in Australia.

But tonight, it is a special night, because it is my birthday again. I am not sure why I am having birthdays so often… Hopefully, this will be my last birthday in this planet! I have asked my Lord so many times to take me with Him, but somehow, I am still here! I sincerely wish I can depart very soon… Please God! Would you grant me that wish?

Look, I am truly sorry to have deviated from my story again, but I had so many birthdays I am not sure how old I am. Does it really matter?

Tonight, I have decorated my villa with lots of flowers from my garden. I have amaryllis and lilies, carnations and gardenias, birds of paradise and lots and lots of roses of different colours, including the red roses from Paquito's grave bush cutting that survived so many seasons. I also found baby's breath white flowers in the yard that I placed all over the flat.

I have cooked the *empanadas* again and I have the Vermouth ready. I have also cooked a huge paella just in case somebody 'new' comes to celebrate. Everybody loves my paella with the seafood it got delivered by my casual carer!

And yes, they are all coming. Praise God forever! I can feel them coming, yes, I feel them coming right now.

Welcome! Welcome! Welcome! Welcome! Have a seat! Yes, the plates are on the table! Have an *empanada*! What a surprise! Carmela and Amadeo just walked in cuddling, and you are both looking so young, slick, and in love!

Would you care for an empanada? Welcome! Yes, I also have your favourite chocolates! No, you should not have brought any presents! Just your ethereal presence is more than enough for me!

Yes, of course, I have some music! Paquito, how about *La Cumparsita* tango for us to dance! And Amadeo, I will find the Joan Baez *Forever Young* song and the Vivaldi *4 Seasons* for you! And Carmela, look, I have the Opera music you love so much… And I also have Despeinada by Palito Ortega for you Giuseppe and the Syrian Mix Dance music for you Aram to belly dance to your heart's content!

And what a surprise, I can see my own mum and dad and my dear siblings arriving too, along with Paquito's family and other friends throughout my life. I am sure I can accommodate them all. And if they do not all fit inside, surely, they can squeeze somewhere in my revamped garden in the back yard. What a starry night we have!

Gosh! Everyone looks so blessed and wonderful! What a party! God, you are so good! I am so grateful for tonight! I feel so much loved and accepted!

'Let's toast for La Macaca!'

'Let's celebrate her life.'

'Cheers!'

Thank you! Thank you, my dear! Thank you! Thank you, God, for this joy and blessing!

Tomorrow, I might be a bit lonely and miserable having to still live alone in my villa, but tonight I am so... and so... and so very happy!

---

[10] Rice Pudding
I want to get married
To a lady
Who knows how to dance.

Who knows how to sew,
Who knows how to iron,
Who knows how to open the door
To go out to play.

Epilogue

Emanuel

Let me introduce myself. My name is Emanuel, and I am as fair as I could be although my father is very dark because his ancestors were latinos.

When I was a child, they considered me a pest, because I used to get very bored and nothing in the school world motivated me. I always wanted to know more. Even in the naughty corner, I could not keep myself quiet for one minute, jumping, singing, and thinking about what to do next.

Whilst still very young, I built a working robot with some junk electronics I found in the storeroom. I used the robot to feed, burp, pacify and entertain my sister Pandora "the blondy" to allow my mum to put her feet up and have some rest.

By age 10, I had read all the books my dad had in his library. Some of them were weird I must say... Hmm... 'The use of modern magnets', 'How to fly a plane upside down', 'Forbidden Incest', 'The Power of the Holy Spirit' and others.

We went to Church every Sunday, and I loved that. My dad was chosen to be an elder and counsellor there at an early age... I, myself, had some spiritual experience with my sweet Lord already at that time.

In an effort to calm me down from my hyperactivity, my parents asked to join Mensa and I must admit that I had some fun with some of the puzzles they devised online for me personally.

The notion of writing my own book kept coming in my dreams. The idea was to write about my father's side of my family. They were amazing, but some of them were out of this world, well... yes... literally out of this world...

I suspected from the beginning they held many juicy and ghostly secrets, some involving spooky tales, from what I had heard. I must admit, I was not disappointed.

It was difficult to convince some family members at first: my great grandmother, 'La Macaca', then my grandmother, 'abuela Carmela' and her various husbands 'Giuseppe', 'El Cuco' and 'Ari'. Although I wanted to persuade some of my brainy cousins, I was not successful this time.

I am certain that these people told me their stories as truthfully as possible... and well... it is true I did manipulate some of the tales a bit to make it spicier.

I collected the last notes from my very old great grandma La Macaca a few months ago and I have tried hard to make some sense of it all!

I hope it is all not too messy for you!

To be sincere, I never really believed I would see the end of the project though I continued to be as thrilled and enthusiastic as at the beginning, whilst the stories kept coming.

My family was, is, and will be, a peculiar mob—you would have to agree—but I love them all and I would not want to belong to any other flock.

Personally, I grew up in a very secure family. My parents love each other and each of us individually. My dad became a successful entrepreneur first and he is now a world known pastor. I believe it is what he always wanted. He brought millions of people to our Lord Jesus all over the world and his ministry had often been compared to the great Billy Graham.

My mum was probably the engine behind my dad's success as she has always been with him, encouraging and supporting him all along. I have a multitude of brothers and sisters, some are my natural siblings, some are adopted, some are fostered. I was always too busy to find out where my parents managed to get so many kids from. However, we all share my father's surname, which is, I believe, my great grandfather's, Paquito's, as well. He would have been so very proud of his ever-growing dynasty!

You could never be bored in my house with adults and children coming and going and dumping their issues every day. My parents have abundantly provided us with all we needed along the way with financial, emotional, and spiritual support over the years. All my brothers and sisters have done well in this world and even those with special needs have been able to reach their potential and be valuable, functioning members of society.

My parents donated millions of dollars to the poor, charities and to the church. This was all thanks to the investments they held from a surreptitious treasure trove of cash, which they found hidden in an old house they purchased in some poor suburb of Sydney many years ago. What a blessing... I also believe my grandparents, Carmela and El Cuco, lived in the same old house with their children and El Cuco's mother Sara, at some point, but I cannot confirm this as accurate.

As for me, in general, I have been supported all along with a loving family and above all by God's splendid gift of human brains and my discovery dreams. I thought we were all the same in this world, but I got to realize God's gift to me was and still is far superior to anybody else's, for which I am forever humble and grateful.

My story now is simple: I had been able to study and discover at a very early age, the mystery of time and space and created an innovative relaxation device that could take people wherever and whenever they want to be, in their virtual space and it has made me one of the richest people in the world.

I am excited about my subsequent project, again, born after one of my dreams, which I understand now they come from my Creator.

I can share some of it for you here!

Whilst investigating a cure for the new world virus, my team have discovered, just by chance, an amazing amino-acid compound that might lead to 'the elixir of life'.

I have already sought first the authorization from the Almighty and my company has now also been given provisional approval from government authorities to go ahead and produce the elixir that would make humans live longer and fruitful lives. Perhaps, if God allows it, they might be able to live forever, that is, if they so desire.

I have been inspired by my Great Grandmother, La Macaca. I would love to preserve her life for even longer, maybe forever. She is now touching the 111-year mark, if one can trust her credentials...

She will be the ideal first candidate for my project as she still looks so youthful. It is really a miracle how energetic she still is at her age. Some gossip believes her mind is missing a few screws, which is understandable at her advanced age, although I do not think she is demented, as she is still very alert and resourceful. I am sure I will have her approval to use her; she never ever denies me anything...

The possibilities are endless!

If I am successful, I will be able to share my Great Grandma for history and medical projects; who knows for what else? She is certainly an example of a life well lived, of true love and of forgiveness. She is such a gem!

Finally, and coming back to this book, I have done a final check and I have been able to verify that whatever is in it are the true, amazing accounts of each of the character's life story. As I said before, I did have to slightly tweak bits to be able to make sense of it all.

I would have liked to continue my writing project, persuading my many uncles, aunts, cousins and siblings and their families to offer their stories, but I am giving my full time to my next major current project. Maybe I will be able to continue my editing activities later... Or even delegate them to another member of our family... Like my sister Pandora...

As for me, I have God's Word imprinted in my heart and I know I will succeed whenever He leads me. How can I possibly fail?

By for now, dear reader.

Cheers!

Emanuel

INDEX

Shawline Publishing Group Pty Ltd

www.shawlinepublishing.com.au